A Duke Always Has a Secret

REBECCA LEIGH

print ISBN: 978-1-66786-487-7

ebook ISBN: 978-1-66786-488-4

Chapter One

Brighton, England 1812

"Get out of bed, Catherine!" the Dowager Countess of Mulford shouted as she entered the bedchamber of her niece, Lady Catherine Gray.

Catherine put a pillow over her head and groaned softly. "Aunt Louisa, can this wait till later? I am so exhausted."

"No, this cannot wait till later," her aunt said as she jerked the covers away from her. "You have done it now, Catherine, and I will not be able to save you from the consequences."

That got her attention. Catherine slowly sat up in the bed squinting her eyes at the light coming through the draperies as she stretched her arms overhead, yawning sleepily. "What are you talking about, Aunt Louisa? It is much too early in the morning for dramatics."

"What did you think would happen, Catherine?" her aunt asked as she paced back and forth at the foot of her bed.

Catherine swung her feet to the floor and reached for her robe. "Please stop pacing Aunt Louisa, and tell me what is going on. Watching you is giving me a headache."

Her aunt stopped and faced her; a grave concerned look on her face. "The race, Catherine. That is what I am talking about. That is what everyone is talking about! How could you participate in anything so scandalous?"

Catherine honestly didn't know what all the fuss was about. "Louisa, you know I am an excellent horsewoman and I have raced many people and won. Why is the race between Lord Brookhaven and myself causing such a fuss?"

"Because Lord Brookhaven and his friends were foxed and the event drew a crowd. People were placing bets on you for god's sake, Catherine. And you rode astride! What the hell were you thinking? It has caused quite a stir. Your behavior is not fitting for a lady," her aunt fumed.

Catherine got up and walked over to her aunt. She placed a quick kiss on her cheek hoping to placate her. "I'm sorry, Aunt Louisa. I promise to act more ladylike in the future."

Her aunt shook her head, her lips set in a firm straight line. "It's too late for that, Catherine. Your brother has gotten word of your behavior. You have been summoned back to London. You will leave day after tomorrow and return to Hawksford House."

Catherine paused thoughtfully. "I wonder who told him. I bet it was Rockhurst, he was there. No, it wouldn't have been him. I can't imagine him running back to London to tattle. After the race he congratulated me and thanked me for the blunt he had won."

Her aunt threw her arms into the air. "Blunt, that is exactly what I am talking about. Ladies don't speak of such things. Did you ever think that your brother could have read about it in the scandal sheets?"

Catherine whirled around enthusiastically. "It was in the scandal sheets? And I was mentioned by name?"

Her aunt shook her head sadly.

"How exciting!" Catherine exclaimed as her smile widened across her face.

"Exciting?" Louisa repeated in disbelief.

"Yes, every time I read about Hawk's exploits in the scandal sheets, I always thought how exciting it would be to be mentioned one day myself," she replied with a bright smile.

"Might I remind you that your brother is a man, not to mention a duke. His being mentioned does not scar his reputation, you however will have a scandal attached to your name, and it will seriously hurt your chances for procuring a good marriage."

Catherine rolled her eyes as she sighed heavily. "That is ridiculous. Why is it different? He is celebrated for his exploits while I am being reprimanded for mine. And might I add, his climbing out of Lady Coventry's bedroom in the middle of a dinner party is much worse than my racing a horse astride."

"I am not going to argue with you over this Catherine. We live in a man's world and there is nothing you can do about it. I will urge you not to upset your brother any more than you already have."

Catherine seemed unperturbed. "I was planning on returning for the season anyway, Aunt Louisa. I have been looking forward to seeing Persephone again."

Her aunt sighed heavily and pinched the bridge of her nose as if praying for strength. "You are not understanding me, Catherine. Your brother is determined that you find a husband this season. He believes it is the only way to curtail your wild ways."

At this Catherine laughed. "A husband? I'm much too happy to want a husband not to mention I am only nineteen years old. I have plenty of time before I am considered on the shelf."

Louisa took her by the shoulders. "Catherine, Hawk has determined that if you continue on the path you are on, and do not use this season to seriously find a husband, he will find one for you."

Catherine for a moment was speechless. Her brother the wealthy and powerful Duke of Hawksford would not dare to force her into an unwanted marriage. "Persephone would never let him do that to me." Persephone her dearest childhood friend had married her brother several months ago and was now his duchess.

"Persephone will have no say, my dear. If Hawk is determined to see you wed, then wed you shall be. You have no one to blame but yourself. Ever since we got to Brighton, you have engaged in mischief. You have skirted the line between scandal and propriety and this time you have crossed it. Lord knows what trouble you will get into in London, but that will be your brother's worry."

Her aunt sighed heavily. "I love you Catherine, and I have tried to do my best for you since the death of your mother. I don't know what happened after the incident you and Persephone endured, but you have changed. I only want you to be happy dearest." She turned quickly wiping her eyes as she left Catherine alone in her bedroom to contemplate her words.

Once she was alone Catherine sat down to think. It had been almost six months since she and Persephone were ambushed and

Persephone kidnapped by Comte Domingo. He had a crazed obsession with Persephone and was furious that she had accepted her brother's proposal and rejected his. But the Comte was an evil man and enjoyed inflicting pain on the women with whom he came into contact. By the time Hawk and his friends, Lord Rockhurst and Michael Shelbourne the Duke of Leicester, found Persephone she had been beaten so badly that they all feared she might die. Her poor brother had been fraught with worry never leaving her bedside. Luckily, Persephone was stronger than any of them could imagine and did recover to the delight of everyone, especially her husband. Hawk, who by all accounts was one of the most notorious rakes in London, was now a loving and completely devoted husband to his wife. Catherine was so happy for the two of them.

She herself had sustained a few injuries at the hands of the Comte, but they did not compare to the injury her heart received when she overheard a conversation between her bother and the one man she had loved since she was thirteen years old, Michael Shelbourne, the now Duke of Leicester. She didn't even know how many times she wished she had not listened at the door and heard him state emphatically that he could never love her. Only to add more insult to injury by stating that he felt as if he was chased as a fox to hounds when she was around. She had been cautioned numerous times by both Persephone and her Aunt Louisa not to appear overly eager. But she had foolishly thought that because she loved him so much, he couldn't help but return her affections. She had been a fool and had sworn that very day that she would never be made a fool again by him or any other man.

After hearing Leicester's hurtful proclamation, she decided to join her aunt in Bath and then travel on to Brighton as most of the beau monde did when the London season came to a close. It had been a great time, and she had found herself the center of attention with several gentlemen seeking her affections. She had decided that it was her time to have some fun. So, she had determined that she would live life with a gusto and not worry about the consequences. Now that decision seemed to be coming back to haunt her. Her aunt was correct, she had skirted the line between what was proper and what was scandalous. While she would never want to bring any shame to her brother or her family, she did not see the harm in a little excitement and adventure.

Returning to London was probably for the best. She had been missing Persephone, and it would give her a chance to regroup. She wasn't overly worried about facing her brother. She was confident that if she could convince him that she had learned her lesson, he would forgive her. Persephone would champion her cause as well; she was sure of it.

The only drawback with returning to London was that she would eventually run into Leicester. He was one of Hawk's oldest friends and she knew there would be no avoiding him. Fortunately, she was not the same girl as before and was completely over her infatuation with the puffed-up overly conceited duke. She would not give him a second thought.

Hawksford House, London

"I heard that you have summoned your sister back to London, Hawk. When will she be arriving?" Lord Charles Newberg, Marquis of Rockhurst asked as he sat in the study of his friend, the Duke of Hawksford.

Hawk walked over to a decanter of brandy on the corner of his large mahogany desk. "She should be arriving today." He poured two glasses and walked over to hand one to his friend. "Someone has to take a firmer hand with her. She has been causing quite a stir in Brighton, and the race between her and Lord Brookhaven was the last straw. I can't allow her behavior to continue. This season she will find a husband, or I will find one for her."

Lord Rockhurst frowned at his friend's comment. "Surely you don't mean that, Hawk. I would hate to see Catherine in an unwanted marriage." He held the glass to his nose to breathe in the aroma of the liquor.

Rockhurst was faced with this same argument from his father. Anytime he and his father, the Duke of Avanley, were in the same room the conversation always centered around Rockhurst's refusal to marry a lady his father deemed worthy. So, hinting that Catherine might be in a similar situation didn't sit well with him.

Hawk sat down in the oversized chair beside him. "I don't want to force her into marriage, but if it means protecting the family name from scandal, I might be compelled to do something drastic." He took a sip of his drink and sat the glass down on the table beside his chair. "Catherine has always been headstrong and a little reckless, but her behavior the past few months has been beyond the pale."

"Perhaps Persephone will be a calming influence over her."

Hawk smiled at mention of his wife. "Yes, that is what I am hoping for, and Persephone is elated to have Catherine back in London. They have always been close."

Suddenly the door to the study opened and Persephone rushed in so excited that she forgot to knock. The men immediately jumped to their feet.

Hawk walked towards her to place a kiss on her cheek. "Good afternoon, my love."

Persephone smiled brightly as she remembered they were not alone. "My apologies, I did not mean to intrude."

Lord Rockhurst bowed deeply before giving the duchess a roguish grin. "Your company is never an intrusion, duchess."

She smiled sweetly. "Has Hawk told you that Catherine is returning to London? We are expecting her today."

"We were just speaking on the subject. I am sure you are happy to have her back at Hawksford House," he replied.

She moved closer to her husband and placed her hand in his. "We are both happy to have her with us again." She glanced up at Hawk and gave him a bright smile intended to melt all his anger towards his sister away.

Hawk sighed knowing it was going to be difficult if he had to fight his wife as well as his sister. It would be a fight he was certain to lose. He raised her hand to his lips. "Yes, my love."

She seemed mollified by his answer when Billings came to the door. "A carriage is arriving, your grace."

"Thank you, Billings," Hawk said as he made his way toward the door.

Persephone and Lord Rockhurst followed behind him. Persephone put a hand on Charles' sleeve to gain his attention. "Did you see the race, my lord?"

He leaned down and spoke softly so that only she could hear. "I did, your grace." He gave her a wink and smiled. "She rode splendidly. Brookhaven never stood a chance."

She grinned. "I wish I had been there. I am sure she looked magnificent. Were they really betting on her to win?"

"Yes, I won several hundred pounds myself."

She laughed out loud at his comment causing the duke to turn around and give them both a disapproving look. The three of them walked outside as the carriage bearing the Hawksford Coat of Arms came to a stop in front of the house.

Catherine leaned back against the cushions on the carriage. She could see Hawksford House from the window, and she had to admit it felt good to be home. She couldn't wait to see Persephone, but she was dreading the encounter she was sure to have with her brother. Hopefully, he would not rage at her too much. She was not in the mood for a lecture after all the traveling. As the carriage came to a stop and the door was opened by one of the footmen, she took a deep breath and put a smile on her face as she was assisted from the conveyance.

"Persephone!" she raced forward to hug her sister-in-law and dearest friend. "I have missed you so much. I can't wait to share all my adventures with you. Brighton was delightful, but it would have been a hundred times better if you had been there with me."

Persephone smiled and hugged her back. "I have missed you as well, and we are very glad to have you back home with us in London." She stepped back to allow Catherine a chance to greet her brother.

Catherine curtsied low then moved forward to kiss his cheek quickly. "It is good to see you, Hawk." She gave him a curious look. "For heaven's sake, don't look so sinister. You will frighten my lady's maid and give the impression that you are not quite as happy to see me as Persephone says you are."

Hawk narrowed his eyes at her flippant attitude but said, "I hope your journey was agreeable."

Catherine laughed softly. "How very formal of you dear brother, but yes it was most agreeable."

She turned and curtsied to Lord Rockhurst. "My lord, it is so good to see you again. I hope your visit to Brighton was as pleasurable as mine."

He bowed slightly toward her. "I do prefer London, but Brighton does prove to be quite exciting when the ton descends upon it."

Hawk took Persephone's arm and began walking back toward the house. "Let's not continue to stand around for the rest of London to gawk at as they pass by. Catherine, I desire an audience with you in my study. You have an hour. I will expect you to be prompt," he said using his superior ducal tone that normally caused people to stand at attention or jump to do his bidding.

Lord Rockhurst offered her his arm. "Allow me to escort you inside, my lady before I take my leave."

Catherine took his arm as they followed behind the duke and duchess. "You do not wish to stay for my scolding?"

He gave her a grin. "No, I get more than enough scolding from my own father. But I do wish you luck. I will see you again at dinner tonight. Leicester and I both have been invited."

At the mention of the Duke of Leicester, her steps faltered. She had tried to put him completely out of her mind since that fateful day. Coming to London, she knew she would see him eventually but had hoped to have some time before she had to face the odious man.

"Are you alright, Catherine?" Rockhurst asked as he looked at her curiously.

She recovered herself quickly. "Quite well, thank you. I was just thinking of all the fun the upcoming season holds for me."

He grinned. "Excellent, I was afraid my mention of Leicester had caused you distress."

She removed her hand from his arm. "Nonsense." She moved forward to where Persephone was waiting by the stairs leading up to the second and third floors. "I have gifts for you, Persephone. Come with me to my room and I will show you."

Hawk stood off to the side. "One hour, Catherine."

She waved off his comment. "Yes, yes, I heard you, dear brother."

Once she and Persephone were alone Catherine asked, "How nervous should I be? Is Hawk very incensed?"

Persephone sighed heavily. "I'm afraid when he read the scandal sheets, he became very angry. I tried to soothe him and remind him that most of what is written is not the truth, but of course he would not listen."

Catherine slumped down on the edge of the bed. "Is it true that he intends for me to find a husband this season?"

"He has mentioned it, but I am sure he would never force you into a marriage that you do not want." She moved to sit beside Catherine. "Are you truly over your obsession with Leicester? I know that you wrote to me that he had not even crossed your mind, but I was not certain."

Catherine patted her hand reassuringly. "Of course, I am. He was just a passing fancy, nothing more."

Persephone was not so certain. "I am glad to hear it, because he will be at dinner tonight."

"Please do not concern yourself, Persephone. I knew I would see him eventually. He no longer holds my affections," Catherine said as she moved from the bed to stand beside the window watching the stylish carriages of the beau monde drive by on the street below. "I was just a girl with silly romantic illusions, nothing more."

Persephone smiled pleased to hear the confidence in Catherine's voice. "Cook is making lamb tonight. I had her prepare all your favorites. We will even have sweet cakes, although I can't promise they will be as good as Mrs. Cooper's. I tried to get her to come to London with us, but she was adamant about remaining at Hawk's Hill."

Catherine turned away from the window. "Will we have other guests besides Lord Rockhurst and the repulsive duke?"

"I don't believe so. Most of the ton has not returned to London yet. The season will start in full swing next week. We will be hosting a ball here at Hawksford House in a few weeks. I am so nervous about being hostess. I will need your help of course. You know how vicious ladies of the beau monde can be, and it is my first ball to host as Duchess of Hawksford. I want Hawk to be proud of me."

Catherine came over and took her hand. "There is nothing you could do that would make Hawk any less proud of you. He is hopelessly in love with you." She secretly hoped that one day she would find the kind of love her brother and Persephone had but right now things were looking bleak. "I don't have much time before my interrogation with Hawk so let me show you the gifts I brought for you."

The meeting with her brother was not as bad as she had feared. He had at first firmly told her of his disappointment in her behavior, but she had taken Persephone's advice and allowed him to rage instead of arguing that her behavior was in no way nearly as bad as his had been at her age. She felt it best not to remind him that he was mentioned in the scandal sheets weekly before his marriage. So, she sat there looking contrite and concentrated on not rolling her eyes as he chastised her.

In the end, he reminded her that she was his sister, and he wanted what was best for her. And she truly believed that. He never mentioned forcing her into a marriage, but he did tell her that she should use this season to seriously consider her options for securing a husband.

After the gentlemen she had met in Brighton she was feeling as if her options were limited. None caught her fancy. They were either ignorant, pompous, drunkards, or unattractive. She had spent her girlhood days dreaming of a knight in shining armor riding in on a white horse to slay her dragons. The gentlemen she encountered, could barely ride the horse let alone slay any dragons.

She looked at herself in the mirror practicing her smile. It would have to be perfect tonight, as this would be the first time she saw Leicester since she left for Brighton and while her heart still hurt at his words, no one would ever know it. She wanted him to suffer for what he did to her. Perhaps she was being a bit vindictive, but Leicester needed to know just what he threw away. She was wearing one of her best dresses, one she had commissioned in Brighton. It was a pretty yellow that looked nice with her dark chestnut hair and brown eyes. The bodice was cut just low enough that the swells of her breasts were visible but not scandalously so. She put a diamond comb in her hair that had belonged to her mother. Satisfied with her appearance, she decided it was time to join the others downstairs and face her own dragon.

"How did your meeting go with Catherine this afternoon?" Michael Shelbourne, the Duke of Leicester asked as he sat drinking some of Hawk's best brandy while waiting on the ladies to come downstairs.

Hawk raised his eyebrows and cocked his head to the side. "I suppose it went well considering that I had planned on listening to a bunch of her theatrics and drama, but she seemed genuinely sorry for her misdeeds and promised to behave more ladylike in the future."

Leicester narrowed his eyes. "Catherine was repentant? I don't believe it."

"Well, believe it or not, she was quite mature about the whole situation, and I am confident she will give us no further trouble," Hawk replied mostly trying to convince himself than anyone else.

Rockhurst grinned over the rim of his glass. "Catherine certainly appeared more mature to me."

Leicester looked over at him curiously. "When did you see Catherine?"

"I saw her a few weeks ago in Brighton, and I was here this afternoon to welcome her home."

Leicester studied him for a moment before turning his attention back to Hawk. "I had business this morning, or I would have come as well."

"Do not fret over it, Michael. She did not even notice your absence," Rockhurst replied earning himself a fierce scowl. But before Leicester could reply they heard Persephone and Catherine coming down the stairs.

Leicester nearly let his glass slip from his hand when he saw Catherine. She looked positively beautiful. Her long brown hair was curled in loose ringlets, but she had not bothered to pin it up but rather had it gathered to the side so it flowed almost to her waist. Her cheeks were pink and her eyes radiant with laughter as she giggled at something Persephone had said before they reached the bottom step.

Hawk moved forward kissing Persephone lightly on the cheek. "Ladies, you both look lovely this evening."

"As long as my maid spent styling my hair, I would think you could come up with a word far superior than lovely, dear brother."

Rockhurst stealthily moved in. "I can think of any number of words that would surpass lovely, but none would come close to adequately describing your beauty, Catherine."

Catherine took a step forward and placed her hand on his arm. "You are quite the charmer, my lord."

"I would be honored to escort you into dinner, my lady," Rockhurst said as he raised her hand to his lips.

Leicester stood back and fumed as his friend captivated Catherine with his smooth words. "I trust your journey to London was pleasant, Catherine." She blinked a few times as if she had not heard him then glanced over quickly.

"Oh, I did not notice you standing there, your grace, but yes my journey was pleasant." She then immediately turned her attention back to Rockhurst leaving him stunned.

He fell behind the couples as they walked into the dining room. Catherine and Rockhurst were easily conversing about Brighton and the things that had gone on there between seasons while Persephone and Hawk listened intently. He watched her throughout the meal observing little things he had never taken notice of before. Like the way she ran her tongue lightly over her lips after a taste of champagne or the way her eyes sparkled when she laughed. He also took notice of her figure. Yes, Catherine had matured in more ways than one.

He frowned as Rockhurst leaned over and whispered something in her ear causing her cheeks to blush prettily. Was his friend seriously interested in Catherine?

Catherine felt Leicester's gaze on her the entire meal, but she did not dare glance in his direction. When dinner was over, they all adjourned to the drawing room for some port and madeira. She stayed close to Lord Rockhurst even though she knew Michael was watching her. During the meal, Rockhurst had leaned over to tell her that Leicester had not taken his eyes from her all evening.

"With the season not in full swing yet, I thought it might be a good time to go to the British Museum, Persephone," Catherine said. "Let's go tomorrow."

"That's a lovely idea, but unfortunately I have made arrangements to go over the ball preparations with Hawk's secretary and meet with the florist tomorrow," Persephone replied sounding rather disappointed.

"If you would permit, I would be happy to escort you to the museum tomorrow," Leicester offered as he moved to stand before her.

A year ago, Catherine would have been elated to have him offer to escort her anywhere, but now things were different. "Thank you for the offer, your grace. But perhaps another day would be best." She gracefully turned her attention back to the others.

Had she really refused him? He narrowed his eyes and just happened to look up to see Rockhurst grinning. This would not do. He didn't know what the hell Catherine was up to, but he would find out.

When the ladies excused themselves, Leicester looked at Hawk and asked, "Have I done something to offend your sister?"

"Not that I know of, why do you ask such a question?"

"Did you not notice that she could barely look at me? And when I offered to escort her to the museum, she refused me. That is not like Catherine."

Rockhurst laughed. "Perhaps you are losing your appeal. Did you not complain a few months ago that Catherine chased after you like a hound chasing the fox on the hunt? Well perhaps she has decided you are no longer worth the chase, and I assure you there are others who would eagerly take your place."

Leicester got to his feet. "Do you have intentions of courting her, Charles?"

Rockhurst leisurely walked toward the door. "A union with Catherine, the sister of a duke would be exactly what my father wants. He would be elated at the prospect. That in and of itself is a deterrent for me. Catherine is beautiful though and would tempt any man. I'm sure she will be the incomparable of the season." A footman came forward with his greatcoat. "Now, if you will excuse me gentlemen, I have an appointment with a very buxom actress. Enjoy the rest of your evening."

Leicester knew he could find solace in the arms of one of the lovely ladies of the demi monde, but tonight it held no appeal. Another time he would have asked Hawk to join him at the clubs, but he could tell his friend was anxious to join his wife upstairs. "Thank you for another excellent dinner, Hawk. I think I will go home early tonight."

Hawk walked with his friend to the door. "Don't take Catherine's behavior to heart. She is probably just tired from her travels. I'm sure she will be herself again tomorrow."

Leicester nodded then headed out the door to his waiting carriage. Before he climbed in, he looked toward the second floor where he knew Catherine's room to be. Rockhurst was right, he was getting exactly what he had wished. If that were true, then why did it feel so wrong and why was the thought of Catherine paying any other man attention driving him mad? He instructed the driver to take him home. He was not in the mood to be around anyone tonight. Hopefully tomorrow he would have come to his senses and Catherine would return to hers.

Chapter Two

Leicester had not slept well the night before so when he received word from his friend Thomas Harrison, who worked in the War Department, that he would like to speak with him in person at his earliest convenience, it had not improved his mood. Now he was impatiently sitting in his carriage as it was stopped in traffic. A cart full of vegetables had turned over in the street and they were in the process of getting it cleared away. He could hear the people arguing outside as the mess was being cleared for the carriages to continue down the congested street. He was growing more bored by the minute when he glanced out the window and saw her. He leaned forward to get a better look, but he could not be mistaken. He would recognize her anywhere. Catherine was walking down the sidewalk with her lady's maid. He observed her as she strolled through the people but didn't see anyone else with her. He continued watching her wondering as to what her destination might be. When she started up the steps to the British Museum, he flung open the carriage door and climbed out.

"James, find a place to park the carriage. I have decided to take a detour before going to the War Office." He crossed the street weaving through the parked carriages and the crowd of people that had gathered to watch the scene. He took the steps to the museum two at a time. When he walked inside, he looked around over the heads of the other patrons, and at first, he did not see her. Then finally standing off to the side wearing a pretty pink day dress with a matching bonnet he saw her speaking to her companion.

Catherine sighed heavily becoming exasperated with the conversation she was having with her lady's maid. "Really Mary, we are at the museum. Nothing untoward can happen. I know how you detest coming here, and I can assure you my brother will not be the least bit angry if you stay here on the bench and work on your knitting."

Her maid did not look convinced as she tilted her head to the side. "If you are certain, and you promise not to leave the museum without me."

At this Catherine giggled. "Do you honestly think I would leave you here, Mary? My goodness, what you must think of me. I promise I will not do anything to get either of us in trouble."

"There is no need for you to worry, madam. I can escort Lady Gray through the museum and then return her to you unharmed. I can also assure you that as the duke's friend, he will have no issue with me as her escort," Leicester said as he moved to stand beside Catherine.

Catherine was startled by the deep voice she knew all too well. "There really is no need. I am capable of maneuvering through the museum alone, your grace," she replied coolly.

He raised an eyebrow at her tone. "I'm sure you are, but it would ease the mind of your lady's maid."

Catherine narrowed her eyes then adjusted her gloves and brushed out her skirts with her hands before reluctantly agreeing to his escort. "Very well." She walked away not bothering to wait for him to catch up.

Leicester couldn't help but grin at her annoyance. She tried to outpace him, but he easily caught up with her. "I am surprised to see you here this morning. I thought you had decided that today would not be a good day to visit the museum, or at least that was what you had said last night."

She didn't bother to turn to look at him as she answered tersely. "I changed my mind. That is still permissible, I believe." She continued walking looking at the exhibits doing her best to ignore him.

"If you changed your mind, why did you not send word? I would have certainly offered to escort you."

She blew out a heavy breath, stopped, and turned to give him a frown. "You think I should have sent word asking you to escort me? That would have made me seem a bit desperate, don't you think? Besides, I enjoy seeing the exhibits. . . alone."

He did not miss her emphasis on the last word. He also took note of the sweet smile she bestowed on a young lord that walked by and nodded to her and a thought crossed his mind that he did not like. "Were you planning on some sort of liaison? Is someone to meet you here, Catherine?"

She continued walking as she spoke. "No, and might I add that if I did plan on meeting someone here, it is certainly none of your business as I am not your concern."

He took her arm to turn her to face him. She tried to ignore the warm sensation of his touch and the shivers that went through her and instead focused on her anger.

"What the devil has come over you, Catherine?"

She looked around the room noting that they had several people watching their exchange. She pasted a fake smile on her face and removed her arm from his grip. "I'm sure I don't know what you are talking about, your grace." She then leaned in closer and said more quietly so only he could hear. "You are causing a scene and regardless of what you might think of me, I did promise Hawk I would try to amend my reputation somewhat. The last thing either of us needs is to cause a spectacle that would have others gossiping about us." She let her smile fade and her eyes narrowed slightly. "We both know you would not like to be linked with me in a scandal. That could lead to ruin for both of us."

He could not remember the last time he had been so angry, but she was correct. They had garnered an audience. He nodded slightly and forced a slight smile. "Of course, my lady. Shall we continue?" His voice was tight.

He continued watching her as they made their way through the museum, but he did not trust himself to enter into conversation with her again, at least not in public. But he would damn well know what had her behaving like a shrew and he would find out soon.

Catherine continued moving through the exhibits trying to focus on the works on display, but it was no use, his presence seemed to fill her senses. She couldn't concentrate with him so near. She had read the same placard about the Elgin Marbles three times and still did not know what it said. But leaving so soon was out of the question. He might think she was uneasy around him, and that would never do. She must always keep the upper hand when dealing with him. So, she continued trying not to notice his presence beside her.

For his part, he did remain quiet the rest of the time and she did not attempt to draw him into conversation again. Eventually, she made her way back to the front to see her lady's maid quietly knitting while waiting for her in the same spot she had left her.

She turned toward Leicester and gave him a slight smile. "Thank you for your escort, your grace. My maid and I will be leaving now."

Leicester nodded politely, but he was still fuming. "It was my pleasure. Allow me to escort you to your carriage."

Catherine didn't bother to object knowing it would do her no good. She allowed him to take her arm and escort her outside to where Hawk's carriage was still waiting for her.

Leicester opened the door and assisted the maid into the carriage while keeping a firm hand on Catherine's arm. Once the maid was seated, he shut the door and knocked on the side of the carriage. "You may return to Hawksford House. Lady Catherine and I will follow behind in my carriage."

Catherine sputtered and tried to yank her arm out of his grasp. "Tsk, tsk, my dear. You are causing a scene, and we both know how you feel about that," he said as he smiled sweetly before leaning closer and whispering menacingly near her ear. "Now, you can either walk with me to my carriage, or I can throw you over my shoulder, either way, you are coming with me."

Catherine's mouth fell open before she hissed softly, "You wouldn't dare!"

He pulled her just a fraction closer to him and replied in a deep dangerous voice. "I would not advise you to try me."

"Very well," she hissed through clenched teeth.

Leicester led her down the street to where his carriage was waiting. She was tense beside him and did not speak. He helped her inside not surprised that she moved to the far end of the conveyance crossing her arms as her chest heaved with fury, but he was angry too.

Once he closed the door and the horses started moving again, he didn't waste any time. "Now that we have some privacy, you will tell me why you are acting this way towards me."

Catherine looked out the window ignoring him.

"Bloody hell, Catherine, you will answer me or I will instruct my driver to keep going until you do!"

She stiffened then turned to face him her eyes glinting with anger. "You should know, your grace."

"Well, I don't bloody well know so enlighten me," he answered back just as harshly.

"When is the last time you rode to hounds, your grace?" She saw confusion on his face and continued. "I feel for the fox always chased and run to the ground. Have you ever felt like that, your grace?" When he still did not seem to know what she was speaking of, she took a slow deep breath trying to control herself. Her hands were shaking. "I heard your conversation with my brother the day before I left for Brighton." Getting it out took more out of her than she realized. She closed her eyes and lowered her head for a brief moment as she tried to regain her composure. The last thing she wanted to do in front of him was to appear troubled by his actions or worse, cry.

Michael was silent as he sat there in disbelief for a minute or two. He had hurt her with his words, no wonder she was acting as if she hated him. "Catherine, I am sorry you heard me say something so insensitive about you. I am truly ashamed. If it makes you feel better, I was thoroughly foxed that afternoon and in no way meant what I said."

Catherine raised her head and he briefly saw a pained expression before it was quickly masked. "You meant every word, your grace. But you need not fear, I will no longer trouble you with my existence."

Michael narrowed his eyes in concern. "I never meant to hurt you, Catherine." He reached across the carriage and took her hand in his. He felt her fingers trembling and it bothered him that he had caused her such pain. When she tried to pull away, he held her tighter. "What can I do to make it up to you?"

In the closeness of the carriage, he noticed her long dark lashes and the perfection of her skin. He wanted to remove that silly bonnet so he could see her dark brown hair and run his fingers through the curls. How could he have not noticed her beauty sooner? The realization shocked him. He had never thought of Catherine in any aspect before other than Hawk's sister, but Catherine was a vision. He wanted to pull her onto his lap and kiss her perfectly pink lips. Of course, she was still incensed with him, and if he kissed her now, he was quite certain she would slap his face or worse. No, he would have to charm her and help make her forget the things he had said.

"There is nothing to do, your grace. I was a foolish girl with silly romantical fantasies that I wasted on you. I will not make the mistake again. But as you are Hawk's friend, I will try to be more civil in the future." She once again tried to remove her hand from his. He wrapped his other hand around it and began tracing the skin above her wrist with his fingers. She narrowed her eyes and looked at him warily.

"I will make it up to you, Catherine. I promise you that."

The carriage came to a stop in front of Hawksford House. When she tugged her hand away again, this time he released her. "I suggest we never speak of this again, your grace. We will keep our distance from each other but maintain civility for the sake of my brother, but we are finished with this."

His lips lifted at one corner in a sensuous smile. "I agree that we should forget my unfortunate misspoken words." At this she rolled her eyes and crossed her arms over her chest. "But we are not finished, Catherine, not by a long shot. And stop saying, your grace every time you address me. There was a time you called me by my given name. Why did you stop?"

"Calling you by your given name is not proper. I have been chastised for it before," Catherine replied feeling like something had gone wrong. She no longer felt in control.

He shrugged his shoulders. "We have known each other for years, and I don't give a damn what anyone thinks. Besides I have grown to like the way my name sounds coming from your lips."

Oh, something had definitely gone wrong. Catherine felt as if the air in the carriage was getting thinner and the space closing in around her. She had to get some fresh air quickly. Thankfully, a footman appeared and opened the carriage door. Michael descended first and then offered his hand to assist her. When he lightly squeezed her fingers before releasing her, she gave him a peculiar look before starting up the stairs to the house. He followed behind her and she quickened her pace. She needed to get away from Michael Shelbourne before her heart did something stupid, like fall in love with him again.

When Billings opened the door, Persephone came forward excitedly. "Oh Catherine, I'm so glad you are back. You will never guess who is here!" It was then that she noticed Leicester behind Catherine. "Michael, what a surprise, we were not expecting you."

He bowed his head slightly. "I am merely escorting Lady Catherine home."

Persephone gave Catherine a curious look before turning back to him. "Well, I am pleased you are here as well."

Catherine glanced at him before turning back to her sister-in-law. "What has you so excited, Persephone? Who is here?"

"Remember my cousin from Scotland who wrote to me last year and asked me to come visit her family there? Well, her son, Chieftain McDonough, is here in London for the season. He arrived a few days ago and decided to pay us a visit today. And guess what, in Scotland he is also known as the Duke of Sunbridge. Isn't that exciting? He is in the study with Hawk right now, but he will be staying for dinner tonight." She looked over at Leicester. "Of course, you are invited as well, Michael."

"I do have some business to see to this afternoon, but if I am not detained, I will certainly join you. Thank you for the invitation." He glanced over at Catherine who was frowning at him when the door to the study opened, and Hawk walked out joined by a man, he assumed was Chieftain McDonough.

"My goodness," Catherine said softly putting a hand over her heart causing Persephone to giggle and Michael to scowl. The man standing by her brother was unlike anyone she had seen before. He was at least three or four inches taller than Hawk with massive shoulders and a powerful body. He looked nothing like most of the gentlemen in London. He looked rugged and wild. His eyes were icy blue and his hair was dark blonde.

Persephone leaned closer to Catherine. "He is gorgeous, is he not? And he is here in London looking for a bride." She gave Catherine a wink Michael did not miss.

Leicester listened to the exchange between the ladies glaring as Catherine moved forward to curtsy low as the unwanted guest approached.

"Your grace, may I present my sister, Lady Catherine Gray," Hawk said solemnly as the man slowly raised Catherine's hand to his lips.

"I am pleased to meet ye, Lady Gray," he said still holding Catherine's hand in his own.

Catherine gave him a brilliant smile and lowered her lashes demurely. "I am pleased to meet you as well, Chieftain McDonough or should I call you, your grace."

Was the man ever going to release her hand and why the hell was he looking at her as if she were on a menu? Leicester stepped forward taking Catherine's elbow and moving her back to his side. "It is a pleasure to meet her grace's Scottish relatives." He said coolly as he offered his hand to the man.

Hawk introduced him, "This is my good friend Michael Shelbourne, Duke of Leicester. Michael, may I present Ian McDonough, Duke of Sunbridge."

"I am pleased to meet ye, your grace but please call me Ian." He turned to look back at Catherine. "If I had known such a bonny lass would be awaiting me in London I would have come sooner."

Catherine blushed prettily and lowered her lashes. "We happily welcome you to London. Would you like to take a walk in the garden? I could tell you some of the best places to visit while here in town."

"Aye, I would like that very much." He offered his arm to Catherine and Persephone eagerly fell in beside them.

Once the trio was out of sight Hawk looked over at Michael. "What the hell is the matter with you? Napoleon would have received a warmer greeting at St. James Palace."

"You should keep him away from Catherine," Michael replied petulantly.

Hawk crossed his arms over his chest. "Do you know something about the man that should make me worry for the safety of my wife and sister?"

Leicester walked a few steps away and then back to stand before his friend. "I don't know anything about him."

"Well, I do. I had previously inquired about the man and his family after his mother first wrote to Persephone. He is a wealthy and very respected man in Scotland. He has business holdings in Edinburgh and owns more than one estate and several acres of land in the Highlands as well as a house in Grosvenor Square. He is highly educated and his mother is English."

"And he is here in London shopping for a bride. You can't think to let Catherine marry such a man and move to the wilds of Scotland," Leicester said as he paced the floor again.

Hawk studied his friend carefully. "If Catherine was inclined to marry him, I would have no objections. Aren't you putting the cart before the horse, so to speak? They only met a few minutes ago. And if I am not mistaken, you have stated on more than one occasion that you wished Catherine would find a husband this season so she would stop harassing you."

Michael knew his friend spoke the truth. He had said exactly those words. But things were different now, Catherine was different. "I have an appointment that I must keep, but I will return for dinner."

Hawk nodded back at him without speaking as his friend turned to walk out the door. He did not understand what had Leicester behaving so oddly. He shook his head and decided to join his wife in the garden with their guest.

Michael climbed into his carriage after directing the driver to take him to the offices of the War Department. This morning had just gone from bad to worse. He thought about asking his friend Harrison to get information about this Scottish Chieftain, but there was no need. He knew Hawk would have already investigated the man thoroughly before allowing him anywhere near Persephone.

He thought back to the hurt and angry look on Catherine's face when she had thrown his words back at him. Never had he regretted something more in his life. He would have to convince her that he was truly sorry and had not meant what he had said and quickly before Ian McDonough got it in his mind to cart her off to Scotland.

Chapter Three

His mood had not improved by the time he entered his friend Thomas Harrison's office. "I received your note that you wished to speak to me, Thomas. I came as soon as I was able."

Mr. Harrison jumped from his seat. "Your grace, it's good to see you again, although I wish it was under better circumstances. Please have a seat."

Leicester took the seat he was offered. "Better circumstances? That doesn't sound as if it bodes well, Thomas."

His friend took a seat then folded his hands together on top of the desk. "I'm afraid it doesn't. This war with Napoleon is costing our country a great deal in both finances and lives. The one group that seems to be profiting from this bloody conflict are the smugglers that continue to bring bootlegged liquor and other items onto our shores."

Michael nodded in agreement. He had heard stories of the bands of men, little better than pirates, that braved the revenue cutter ships bringing contraband goods onto English shores for a profit. "I'm not sure what that has to do with me directly."

"As it so happens, we believe that there are a group of smugglers using a cove near your estate in Kent."

At this Leicester sat up and leaned forward. "That would be Harts Manor, it's not the family seat. My great grandfather acquired it in a card game years ago. It was one of my favorite places to visit when I was younger. The house itself is a few miles from the coast. Do you suspect someone in my household staff there?"

"No, of course not. We would however like to send an agent or two there to investigate and since it is on your lands, I wanted to seek your permission of course."

"Certainly, will your agents need to be housed at Harts Manor? If so, I will make arrangements," Leicester asked not sure how he felt about this development.

"My men will reside in the nearby village and will be undercover. I would not have them linked to your grace as it might be dangerous for you and those you care about. These smugglers are treacherous and if they get wind that we are close to shutting down their operation, there is no end to what they will do to keep the coin flowing. I simply wanted to warn you of the perils and ask you that if you do find yourself at Harts Manor and notice suspicious activity that you will contact my agents and not attempt to intervene on your own."

"Why not ask me to go there? I can be an extra set of eyes and you know I am an excellent shot," Leicester asked as he stood from his seat.

Thomas' lips turned up slightly at the corners. "I'm sure you are, and if you were a second or third son, I would be tempted to seek your help in the matter. But you are the heir to an old and powerful duchy. The crown would have my head if I knowingly put you in danger."

Leicester understood. Thomas was the third son to the Earl of Brantley so he knew all too well about being the disposable son. Instead of joining the church as was typically expected of a third son, he joined the foreign affairs office and dabbled in the world of intrigue and spies for the crown. With Napoleon threatening England's shores, he was certain Thomas had his hands full.

"If you need any further assistance from me, please let me know."

Thomas stood and shook his hand. "Thank you, your grace. And might I remind you to keep this completely between us."

"I give you my word."

"I couldn't ask for more than that, again thank you."

Leicester walked out of Thomas's office and to his waiting carriage. His head ached and he needed a drink. Not only did he have Catherine on his mind and the brawny highlander to contend with, but if that wasn't enough, now he had a group of smugglers on his estate to top it all off. When did his life become so complicated?

"Where will you be staying while in London, your grace?" Catherine asked as she sat with Persephone's extremely handsome Scottish cousin in the garden at Hawksford House having tea. She looked across at the attractive highlander thinking how odd he looked holding such a tiny teacup. He was a very large man and while he was dressed as fashionable as any London gentlemen, her imagination pictured him standing in front of his Scottish castle holding a broadsword wearing a kilt and tartan while facing off an invading army.

He smiled as if he knew where her thoughts had strayed. "I own a house on Grosvenor Square not too very far from here, Lady Catherine."

Persephone held out a plate of biscuits and sweet cakes. "I told him that he was more than welcome to stay here at Hawksford House, especially since he is new to London, but I'm sure he will be more comfortable at McDonough House."

"I would not want to be a burden to you, dear cousin," he replied taking two sweet cakes from the plate.

"You certainly wouldn't be that," Catherine added, earning a smile from the handsome Scot.

"If you will excuse me, I will go have cook bring us some more biscuits." Persephone gave Catherine a wink and then hurried back toward the house.

When they were alone Ian leaned forward propping one hand on his knee. "How long has the duke been wanting to court ye, lass?"

Catherine almost spilled her tea in her lap. "My goodness, how clumsy of me." She recovered herself. "The duke? Do you mean Leicester?"

"Aye, Leicester. I think he fancies you."

Catherine blushed and moved to set her teacup on the table in front of her. "You are mistaken. Leicester is a good friend of my brother and I have known him since I was a young girl, but that is as far as it goes."

"I think you might be the one who is mistaken, lass."

Catherine turned her head to the side genuinely curious as to what made him think something so far-fetched. "What would make you say that?"

"I saw the way he pulled you to his side when I was introduced. I ken how a man's mind works. He was marking you as his and making sure I knew it."

Catherine's laughter floated up from her throat. "That's ridiculous. You must take my word on this; I am the last woman Michael Shelbourne would wish to court or fall in love with."

He gave her a wink. "I can prove it to you, Lady Catherine. Might make this trip to London more entertaining."

Catherine did not like the sound of that. "Oh no, please. The last thing I want is for Leicester to think I am trying to make him jealous."

Just then Persephone decided to return with a plate of fresh biscuits and a sneaky smile on her lips. "These are fresh from the oven. You will have to try the lemon one. They will melt in your mouth."

McDonough reached over and took one of the cakes Persephone offered. "If you keep feeding me like this, cousin I'll have to find a tailor to add some fabric to my kilt."

Persephone laughed softly blushing at his comment. "I'm sure cook will be delighted to hear that. Do you like to ride, Ian?"

He nodded as he glanced over at Catherine giving her a wicked grin. "Aye, when I am at home in the Highlands, I ride every morning."

"Really, I am not much of a rider myself, but Catherine is excellent," Persephone said slyly as she glanced over at Catherine. "Hyde Park is not very far from here and Rotten Row is where you can go to have a good gallop."

He tilted his head slightly. "Perhaps Lady Catherine will be kind enough to go for a ride with me tomorrow morning."

Catherine looked over at Persephone who was smiling ear to ear and looking very proud of herself. "I would enjoy that very much.

Although Persephone may have exaggerated about my horsemanship skills."

He chuckled softly and his eyes danced with amusement. "I don't believe so. You look as if you would definitely be up for a good long ride."

Catherine blushed and lowered her head feeling as if his words had a secret meaning.

"Excellent, I am sorry I will be unable to go with the two of you as I already have plans for the morning," Persephone said causing Catherine to look over at her quickly. Was her friend playing matchmaker?

Ian McDonough stood from his seat and Catherine was reminded of how very tall and formidable he appeared. "If you ladies will excuse me, I do have some business to attend to this afternoon, but I will return for dinner." He bowed deeply and raised each of their hands to his lips.

"I will see you out," Persephone said taking the arm he offered as they walked from the garden leaving Catherine alone.

Ian McDonough was a handsome man, no doubt. Tall and broad with hair longer than what was fashionable. He looked fierce but at the same time a proper gentleman and those ice blue eyes of his promised trouble. She was sure most of the ladies would be swooning at his feet this season. It was obvious that Persephone was hoping the two of them would form some sort of attraction, and if she used her brain, she would encourage his affections. But damn it all, and damn Leicester for still plaguing her thoughts. She had spent her time in Brighton doing everything she could to purge him from her mind and soul. She flirted shamelessly with the gentlemen that danced attendance on her. She pushed the boundaries of propriety and skirted scandal, all in an attempt to convince herself that the duke's words had not broken her heart, that she was stronger than he gave her credit. She told herself that the feelings she had felt for him were just silly girlish fantasies. Now back in London and faced with seeing him again, she felt those old feelings that she had buried so deep inside start coming to the surface. But her determination would not allow it. She hated him and she would keep telling herself that every day. She knew in her mind it was what she should do, she just had to convince her heart.

Persephone interrupted her thoughts when she came back outside to sit with her. "Well?"

Catherine looked at her cautiously. "Well, what?"

"What do you think about him?" Persephone asked with a chuckle.

Catherine smiled. "He is very handsome and seems to be a very nice man, and I know you are pleased to finally meet some of your Scottish family."

Persephone looked disappointed. "That's it? All you can say is he is handsome and nice?"

Catherine laughed, amusement flickering in her eyes. "Persephone, we just met this afternoon. What else am I supposed to say? Were you expecting me to tell you to have St George's Cathedral booked for May and let's start planning my wedding trousseau?"

Persephone threw up her hands. "I don't know. Perhaps that you are sincerely interested and that you hope to form an attachment with him."

"My goodness, Persephone. Please don't have the banns read just yet. Even if I were sincerely interested, how do you know he would be interested in me?"

"You are the daughter and sister of a duke with a very impressive dowry. No one could have better familial connections without being royalty. You are exceptionally beautiful, smart, witty, and have a vivacious personality. Who would not be interested in you?" When she saw the shadow cross her friend's face, she instantly regretted her words. "Any man that isn't an unmitigated fool, that is."

Catherine reached over and patted her hand. "No worries, my dear. I am completely over Leicester. I learned my lesson and I am a stronger person for it. He is no longer a concern."

Her friend didn't look convinced. "I'm sorry he will be at dinner tonight."

Catherine stood and shrugged her shoulders nonchalantly. "He and Hawk are very close. There is no way to avoid him, and I would not have Hawk ruining his longest friendship due to my lack of self-control."

Persephone stood and linked arms with her as they began walking back toward the house. "I'm glad you feel that way. I know that you are strong, my dear. I just hope Leicester doesn't toy with your feelings. Tell me, how did he come to escort you home from the museum?"

"He just appeared out of nowhere and insisted on escorting me. We had words and I must confess I was less than cordial. My mother would have been ashamed of my behavior and sharp tongue."

Persephone laughed softly. "And how did Michael take your change in behavior?"

Catherine raised her eyebrow and tilted her head slightly. "He was not very appreciative of it either. In fact, upon leaving the museum, he bundled up Mary in Hawk's carriage and then told the driver that I would be riding with him before sending it on its way.

When I objected, he had the nerve to tell me that I would be coming with him even if he had to throw me over his shoulder."

Persephone gasped and put a hand to her mouth. "Surely he didn't mean it."

"From the look on his face, I was not brave enough to try him," Catherine replied. "Once in the carriage, he insisted I tell him why I was behaving so, and I told him about overhearing his conversation."

Persephone came to a stop. "And how did he respond to that revelation?"

"He apologized and said he had been foxed and certainly had not meant to hurt me." Catherine looked thoughtfully at Persephone. "It was odd really. His eyes seemed to be able to read how much I had been hurt by his statements. He took my hand and refused to release it for a time and promised to make it up to me, but really, I just need him to leave me be. I can't allow him to break my heart again. It took me a long time before I was able to hold my head high and not think of him daily. You would think he would be glad to see that I had moved on and no longer desired him. Truly, he would be the last man in London from which I would accept a proposal of marriage."

Persephone smiled as they continued walking. "I guess we will have to see how it all comes about. I do have a feeling that things are about to get very interesting."

Later that evening

Leicester waited at the foot of the stairway hoping to get a few minutes with Catherine before the Highlander arrived. He had been shown into the blue drawing room upon his arrival but decided that it would be best to be the first one she saw as she came downstairs.

When she didn't come down after waiting several minutes, and not being a patient man, he decided upon a better course of action. He took the stairs and turned left toward Catherine's room. He wouldn't dare enter, it was entirely improper, and he did not think Catherine would be very welcoming, not to mention he was certain that Hawk would not be too happy to find him in the bedchamber of his sister.

He waited around the corner for her to appear. After several minutes he started to pace until finally he heard the door open and she emerged. She was dressed in a lovely lavender gown of silk and was looking down at her silver slippers when she walked headlong into his arms.

She shrieked as a pair of strong arms enveloped her, but she knew instantly who held her. Even blindfolded she would recognize his touch, his smell. "What the devil?" She looked around quickly. "What are you doing here?"

He smiled and took a step back releasing her. "I was waiting downstairs for you but when you didn't come, I decided to seek you out."

Catherine nervously smoothed her skirts. "You shouldn't be here, as you well know. What was so important that you couldn't wait?"

"I wanted to talk to you before the others joined us."

Catherine sighed heavily and her eyes fluttered closed for a brief moment. "We really do not have much to say to each other."

"I disagree. There is very much that I want to say to you." He moved forward taking one of her hands in his. "You look beautiful tonight, Catherine."

Catherine suppressed a shiver at his touch and tried to pull her hand away. "Thank you, but there really is no need for flattery."

He moved closer still. "It's not baseless flattery, Catherine. You truly are beautiful."

A part of her longed to believe him, but a bigger part of her was cautious. "I should go downstairs. It would not do for us to be seen together."

He held her hand firmer as she moved to step away. "Will the Highlander still be joining us this evening?"

"McDonough, yes, I believe so. Why?"

His eyes narrowed slightly and his voice became just a touch deeper. "I don't like the way he looks at you, Catherine."

She laughed as she raised her eyebrows. "The way he looks at me? You are being ridiculous. Might I remind you once again that I am not your concern."

He moved closer allowing his finger to trace the side of her cheek. "That is something I intend to change."

Catherine squinted her eyes and looked at him curiously. "Have you been drinking, your grace? You must be foxed to make such a ludicrous statement. Now if you will excuse me." She moved past him toward the stairs.

"Damn it, Catherine. How long are you going to hold that against me? I was a fool. I apologized and I'm trying like hell to make amends."

She turned swiftly back toward him, her skirts swishing around her. "Is it forgiveness you seek? Fine, I forgive you. Your conscious is clear and you should sleep better knowing I no longer harbor any resentment toward you. Is that what you want?"

He took both her arms and pulled her closer into his chest. "Forgiveness is not the only thing I seek, Catherine."

She kept telling herself to breathe. He was so close. His eyes were dark with desire and seemed to hold her captive. The urge to lean in further and tilt her lips up toward his was growing stronger by the second. He put his finger under her chin and for a moment she thought he would kiss her. Her eyelids grew heavy and her lips parted slightly, but she was brought back to reality when she heard Persephone call her name down the hallway. *Thank heavens!* She quickly stepped away out of his reach pressing herself against the opposite wall. Her breathing was rapid, and she placed a hand over her chest to try and calm her rapidly beating heart.

"There is nothing else for me to give you, your grace other than my forgiveness. Please accept it and forget about me. Excuse me, I should go." She hurried down the steps trying to put as much distance between herself and Michael as possible. She hurried into the blue drawing room hoping to get a few moments of peace before the others joined her. She leaned against the wall closing her eyes and breathing deeply.

"You look as if you have a ghost chasing ye, Lady Catherine."

Her eyes flew open to see Ian McDonough standing before the fireplace. Her eyes widened at the picture he made and while she knew she was staring; it was impossible to look away as he was quite a sight to behold. He was wearing his traditional Scottish attire, a long green and blue plaid kilt that went to his knees. He had long wool socks and tall boots. His hair was tied back with a thin ribbon. His black evening coat looked like something her brother would wear with the exception of the large plaid draped across one shoulder held with a large brooch. He wore a leather sporran hanging from his waist and looked every bit the Scottish Chieftain he was.

"Your grace, I did not realize you had arrived."

He bowed at the waist. "I am early so I was shown in here to await everyone else."

Catherine regained her composure, straightened her shoulders, and put a dazzling smile on her face. "The others will be along shortly."

He moved forward to stand before her. "So, did you see a ghost, lass or is it something other than spirits pursuing you?"

As if on cue Leicester walked into the room. The Scotsman glanced at him briefly before turning to give her a knowing smile. "Aye, a ghost it was then."

Catherine was surprised at how astute McDonough's comparison was as Michael at times had seemed like a ghost to her, constantly haunting her thoughts and dreams. Now when she had finally convinced herself that she was no longer infatuated with him, he comes back into her life to resume his bewitching of her soul.

She returned his smile and reached over to place her hand on his sleeve. "Gentlemen, might I offer you some refreshment while we await the arrival of the duke and duchess."

"Aye, I never refuse refreshment especially if it is of the inebriating kind." He led her over to the settee and took the seat beside her.

Catherine nodded to the footmen in attendance to pour drinks. "Your grace, would you like something to drink as well?" She looked over at Michael to see him frowning fiercely in her direction and while she knew it would infuriate him further, she couldn't resist a small dig. "You do look as if you could use a drink, your grace."

He wanted to throttle her, to haul her out of the room over his shoulder, if need be, and shake her until she stopped behaving like a hoyden and then kiss her senseless. More than that, he was tired of the damn Scotsman interfering. He was about to say just that when a hand slapped him on the shoulder.

"Gentlemen, we are sorry to keep you waiting. My wife and I were detained and it took longer than expected," Hawk said as he escorted his wife into the room.

Catherine knew from the blush on Persephone's cheeks exactly what had detained them. "It's perfectly alright, Hawk. McDonough arrived early and I offered some refreshment before dinner is served."

Persephone moved forward to greet her cousin. He bowed over her hand before bringing it to his lips. "Oh my, you look marvelous, cousin! Doesn't he look magnificent, Catherine?"

"He certainly does," she replied deliberately making her voice practically purr the words before looking pointedly at Michael across the room. He was still shooting daggers in her direction.

"Ah, you ladies flatter me when it is I who should be extolling the beauty and grace the two of you exude," Ian said as he turned to look back at where Catherine was still seated.

Persephone blushed prettily before walking back to her husband's side. "Ian, would you mind escorting Catherine to dinner?"

"It would be my pleasure," he said offering Catherine his hand as she stood from where she sat on the settee.

Persephone walked over to Michael and looped her arm through his. "I certainly don't want to make you feel excluded, Michael."

He took a deep breath and smiled at the duchess. "I am honored, your grace."

As they moved toward the dining room, Persephone held Michael back a few steps. "They look lovely together, do they not?" She felt his arm stiffen beneath her touch.

"I cannot say I agree with that assessment, your grace. Are you by chance playing matchmaker between Lady Catherine and your cousin?" Michael asked.

Persephone smiled not at all trying to hide the fact. "I certainly am. I think he would be an excellent match for her, and I would like to ask you not to interfere."

Michael narrowed his eyes. "Interfere?"

"Yes, you confuse her. When you are around it makes it harder for her to see, think, and feel anything other than you. She has finally gotten to a point where she can move on and leave the past behind." She then gave him a serious look. "I will not have her hurt again, Michael."

He nodded knowing exactly to what she was referring.

Appeased Persephone smiled again and started to take a step forward, but this time, he stopped her. "I understand your feelings, Persephone, but don't mistake my understanding for acquiescence. I also do not want to see Catherine hurt again and believe me I am suffering a hell knowing that I caused her so much pain, but don't think for one minute that I will let that Highlander have her, duke or not." He looked at her for a few seconds before continuing to escort her into the dining room.

Catherine was seated on the left side of her brother with Persephone across from her and Ian on her other side. Michael sitting across the table was quiet throughout the meal, although he did keep staring at her. She focused her attention on their Scottish guest listening intently to his tales of life in the Highlands completely ignoring Leicester in the process.

When dinner was over Persephone stood. "Gentlemen, please take some time and enjoy your port. Lady Catherine and I will be in the blue drawing room when you are ready to join us." All three gentlemen rose from their seats as the ladies excused themselves.

"I have no stomach for port tonight. I believe I will join the ladies," Michael announced as he stood to follow them from the room.

Hawk gave his friend an odd look. "Are you alright, Michael? You were quiet throughout dinner and you look as if you aren't feeling well."

Michael shook his head then looked over at the Scotsman who was wearing a sly grin. He clenched his fists at his sides. He would love to knock that grin from his face, but as he was Persephone's cousin, he would have to refrain from doing so, not to mention the man was Hawk's guest. "I am perfectly well, thank you," he said before turning to the door to join the ladies.

His luck must be changing, for when he entered the blue room, he found Catherine there alone. She was staring out the window and did not hear his approach when he walked up behind her. "Catherine."

She turned to face him and he was struck again with how beautiful she was. He reached out intending to wrap an arm around her waist so he could pull her closer to him, but she backed away.

"I don't know what game you are trying to play, Michael, but I will not be a part of it."

He narrowed his eyes and stalked toward her causing her to back up against the wall. "I'm not playing a game, Catherine. But I think your Highlander might be."

She sucked in a breath in outrage. "Whatever do you mean, your grace?" He was so much taller than her and she found herself on her tiptoes and still couldn't meet him eye to eye.

"Stay away from him, Catherine," he replied in a deep stern voice.

She poked him in his chest. "You can't tell me what to do! I will see him whenever I wish and if he wants to kiss me, I will allow him that privilege too!" She was so angry she could feel her cheeks burning and her breath coming faster between her lips.

Michael struggled to keep his temper at bay. "Has the black-guard kissed you?"

"I have said this before, your grace. What I do and whom I choose to do it with, is none of your concern, and he is not a black-guard, he is a duke after all." She practically spit the words at him, but she was not prepared for his reaction.

He moved quickly and she sucked in a breath as he wrapped an arm around her waist pulling her into him. Then taking his free hand he turned her face to his and leaned closer so that his lips were just inches from hers.

"I'm only going to ask this one more time and I want the truth, Catherine. Has the Scotsman kissed you?" his voice was low and menacing.

She was breathing heavily and thought about lying to him, but because she would not want Michael to take out his wrath on Persephone's cousin for a lie she concocted, she hesitantly shook her head. "No, he has not kissed me."

She watched as a smile began to curl his lips upward at the corners, but before she could react further, he pressed his lips to hers. At first, the kiss was soft and tender but grew more passionate and possessive. He sucked her bottom lips between his teeth as his hand moved from her waist up her back to her neck. His other arm pulled her tighter against him. Catherine felt as if she couldn't breathe or move away. She clung to him as he deepened the kiss parting her lips so that his tongue could mingle with hers.

When he pulled away, he rested his forehead against hers as he cupped her face in his hands. "Everything about you is my concern, Catherine." He stepped away quickly when they heard Persephone returning to the room.

"You didn't want to stay for port, Michael?" Persephone asked before giving Catherine a concerned look after noticing her discomfiture.

"My tastes tonight were running toward something sweeter than port." He didn't take his eyes from Catherine. Her breathing had still not returned to normal and her lips were slightly swollen.

Persephone moved closer to her friend and sister-in-law. She wanted to ask her what had happened, but at that moment Hawk and Ian decided to join them. Michael moved to the opposite side of the room and remained quiet.

Ian walked over to where Persephone and Catherine were now sitting together. "Ladies, while I would love to stay longer, I have accepted an invitation to one of the clubs tonight." He took Catherine's hand in his and brought it to his lips. "I look forward to our ride tomorrow, Lady Catherine."

"I am looking forward to it as well, your grace," she replied in her best coquettish voice as she took a step toward him while she narrowed her eyes at Michael.

Ian made his way over to where Michael stood. "I enjoyed your company tonight, Leicester. I'm sure we will see each other again."

Michael nodded, but his expression remained grim. "I'm sure we will."

"Allow me to show you out, McDonough," Hawk said as he shook the Scotsman's hand.

Once they were alone Persephone whispered, "Obviously something went on between the two of you while I was away."

Catherine patted her hand. "Nothing happened that cannot be easily forgotten, Persephone." She glanced over to where Michael stood across the room. "I do think I will go upstairs and get some rest. Ian has promised me a long, hard, vigorous ride tomorrow, and I want to be well rested."

She heard Persephone gasp beside her and smiled when she saw Michael's hands clench into fists at his side. She smiled to herself as she left the room. Did he think that one kiss from him would make her forget everything and suddenly she would have the urge to worship at his feet? He obviously did not know her at all.

Chapter Four

Catherine walked downstairs happy to be wearing her new riding habit. She was very much looking forward to a ride in Hyde Park. Not so much to be with Ian McDonough as to just to feel the cool breeze on her face as she galloped down Rotten Row. Whenever she was at Hawk's Hill, the ducal seat of the Dukes of Hawksford, she would always enjoy a nice hard gallop and the freedom she felt as she rode. If her mother or even her brother had seen the jumps she had taken or the reckless way she had ridden at times, she probably would have been banned from ever riding again. Only Persephone knew of her feats and the near misses she had over the years when riding. She was considered an excellent horsewoman by most that knew her, but she longed for the freedom to ride as she wished.

Persephone and Hawk had not come down for breakfast yet so she sat alone enjoying the peace of the morning and her tea and biscuits. "Excuse me, Lady Catherine. This note arrived for you."

Catherine took the note from the butler's hand. "Thank you, Billings." She broke the seal and read.

Lady Catherine,

Unfortunately, I will be unable to join you this morning. Some urgent business has come to my attention, and I must see to it. Please forgive me. I do plan on taking you for that ride we talked about very soon.

Your Devoted Servant,

Ian McDonough

Chieftain of Clan McDonough

and Duke of Sunbridge

"Shall I have the grooms unsaddle your horse, my lady?" Billings asked waiting for her instructions.

Catherine folded the note and set it aside. "Certainly not, I shall ride alone."

"Alone, my lady? It isn't safe," the kind elderly man said nervously.

She gave him a small smile. "You are quite right of course, Billings. Please have a groom accompany me."

He bowed low. "As you wish, my lady."

"Drat it all," she said to herself as she finished off the last bite of her biscuit. She took another sip of her tea then picked up her riding gloves and headed outside.

Her horse was saddled and waiting and the groom that was to accompany her was almost finished saddling his mount. Catherine put on her riding gloves and made her way to her horse. She was accustomed to mounting herself and was surprised to feel strong hands surround her waist as she was lifted into the saddle.

"Riding alone? Is the Scotsman running late?" Michael asked with his hand still resting on her skirt.

"He was detained, unexpected business came up. He sent a note this morning. What are you doing here?" she replied tersely as she adjusted her reins in her hands.

He patted the neck of her mare and then turned to look at her. "I had some business this morning as well and while out I thought it a nice day for a ride."

Catherine eyed him suspiciously. "So, you decided that since you wanted to take a ride you would come by here first instead of heading directly to the park?"

"There is more than one way to get to Hyde Park, Catherine."

She rolled her eyes. "That still does not explain why you showed up here, although whatever your reason it certainly doesn't concern me. I hope you enjoy your ride." She nudged her horse forward, but he grabbed her reins.

"If you would like, I could ride with you as an escort." He saw her mind coming up with a reason to refuse so he said the one thing he knew would make her accept. "Unless you are afraid that is."

She stiffened. "Afraid? Of you?"

He slowly walked to the other side of her horse. "You know, afraid of your own self-control."

Her mouth fell open slightly. "My self-control?! After last night you talk to me about my self-control. Mount your horse, your grace. And pray try to keep up." She nudged her horse forward not waiting for him.

He gave her an elegant bow before returning to his horse. "As you wish, my lady."

He mounted smoothly then spurred his horse forward to catch up so he could ride alongside her. She was angry, he could tell by the hard set of her jaw and the rigidness of how she sat her horse. Her groom was following a short distance behind them.

"Do you really think a groom is necessary, Catherine?"

She turned her head sharply. "With your reputation, I should probably have an armed escort."

He laughed causing her to quickly look forward again. "Is my reputation so severe? I must say I have never given it much thought." She did not respond, so he tried a different tactic. "Hawk has told me of your fondness for reading the scandal sheets. But there are some of our adventures that thankfully were not printed for all of London to see. Did you know one time when your brother and Lord Rockhurst got so foxed at Vauxhall that Rockhurst managed to get on stage with the performers?"

He saw a smile forming on her face. "He was so good that he was offered a contract to travel with them."

She tried not to laugh but couldn't help letting a giggle escape. "I certainly didn't know about Rockhurst's love of performing."

He leaned over closer. "You should have been there. He was shockingly good."

"I'm surprised he has not tried to perform again," she said smiling.

"Well, he might have except he ripped the dress he was wearing and he couldn't find a modiste to repair it."

She stopped her horse and turned to face him. "A dress? He was wearing a dress?" She laughed so hard tears came to her eyes. "I would have loved to have seen that. I wonder why it was not written about. You would have to think it would have sold a lot of papers."

A deep rumble of laughter came from Michael's throat. "I believe the publisher received a visit that night and was urged most convincingly not to print anything about the incident."

She looked over at him with a bright smile. The first genuine smile he had seen on her face since she returned to London. Her eyes sparkled and he could not look away from her.

There were few people out this early in Hyde Park and only a handful on Rotten Row. "Do you care to race, your grace?" she asked still smiling.

"As long as there is a prize for the winner," he replied still unable to look away from her countenance.

She raised her eyebrows. "Since I will be the winner, I suppose I can agree to that. What is it that you want, your grace?"

He turned his head to the side slightly. "I can think of a dozen or more things I want from you, Catherine, but I will settle for a kiss."

She pulled her horse to a stop. "A kiss, I don't think so. I have a reputation to protect as well, your grace."

He gave her a wicked grin as he shrugged his shoulders. "I thought you were confident in your abilities. I guess I was mistaken."

"Alright, your grace. If you win you shall have your kiss. But are you not curious as to what I will ask for when I win?"

"As I have no intention of losing, it is of no consequence, but if you would like to share what you would ask for, please do so."

"Such arrogance, your grace. When I win, I will ask that you cease interfering in my life and that includes my suitors and you will no longer attempt to kiss me again." She smiled knowing she had him now.

He had not counted on that, but he could not refuse her. "Alright, I agree to your terms. But I will not give you a head start or show you any mercy."

She scoffed. "As if I would need it."

"So, we are agreed?" he asked as they neared Rotten Row.

"Agreed."

They pulled their horses to where they were even alongside each other. "I will allow you to give the countdown," Michael said as he readied himself.

Catherine nodded. "We will go on three and ride to the large oak at the end of the row."

Michael nodded in agreement.

Catherine grinned. She felt confident she would win and when she did, he would have to step back and leave her alone. "Ready? 1, 2, 3!" she yelled as she spurred her horse taking off at a fast pace. She leaned low over her horse's neck as she raced down the lane. This would be an easy victory! She sat up a little straighter as she neared the tree that they had agreed was the finish line. Just a little bit more and she, . . .

Suddenly Michael and his horse flew past her overtaking the tree quite a bit ahead of her. She slowed her horse to a trot. "Damn it," she said to herself.

Michael was trotting back to her. "I believe you owe me a prize."

Catherine frowned. She never did like to lose a race especially when the stakes were so high. "You have a new horse, I see."

Michael leaned over and patted the horse's neck. "Yes, I just bought him at Tattersalls a few weeks ago. I needed to add more racing blood to my stables."

"Well, he will certainly do that." She reached over and ran a hand along his horse's mane. "He is lovely." She looked over at him. "Can I ride him?"

"He is very high-spirited and I am not sure it would be safe." When he saw her smile begin to fade, he added quickly, "You are the only woman I would trust to ride him." He climbed down and moved over to assist her.

Catherine felt giddy. "Do you mean it? I promise to be safe." She allowed him to lift her to the ground.

Michael held her for a second longer in his arms than was necessary liking the way his hands spanned the circumference of her tiny waist. "Just be careful. He is young and can be a handful, at least that is what the grooms in my stables have been telling me. He bites too so stay away from his mouth."

She walked over to the horse and began rubbing his nose softly. "That's ridiculous isn't it, boy." She continued caressing the animal and Michael could see the beast relaxing under her touch. She leaned her forehead down to his and whispered something to him as her fingers continued their caresses.

He watched her and marveled at how lovely she looked and for a moment he thought could he seriously be jealous of a damn horse? "Would you like me to help you mount?"

She nodded her head and he easily lifted her into the saddle. Before he could move to mount Catherine's mare, she had already taken off on his stallion. She looked magnificent, leaning low over the horse's neck as she galloped. Her bonnet had come off and some of her hair had come loose from her coiffure. He mounted the mare and followed her. As he gained on her, he sucked in his breath as she took a jump over a fallen tree. It was a jump most men he knew would not dare attempt and Catherine sailed over it and landed as if it were nothing at all.

She rode back over to where he was waiting. "He is lovely, what's his name?"

"Bucephalus," he said still mesmerized by how exquisite she looked mounted on the black stallion.

She smiled as she rubbed the top of the horse's head. "Bucephalus, same as Alexander the Great's horse. A fine name for a magnificent animal." She looked up and their eyes locked. She felt as if she couldn't pull away from his gaze. He was so handsome it made her heart ache, but she could not let herself be fooled by him again. She sighed heavily as she forced herself to look away. "I should be going home. Thank you for allowing me to ride him." She climbed down before he could move over to assist her.

He watched as she petted the horse one more time and was surprised to see the animal lean into her touch. She looked sad and he felt the urge to do something to take her sadness away. "You can ride him whenever you wish, Catherine."

She perked up just for a minute before the mask she had been wearing since she returned to London descended once again upon her face. "I appreciate the offer, but I wouldn't want you to feel obligated to allow me access to your stables." She moved over to her mare and allowed him to assist her. "There is no need to escort me back, my groom will be sufficient."

He mounted his horse and pulled alongside her. "Do you really think I would allow you to return home alone? I'm more of a gentleman than that, no matter what you think of me."

For a moment she was ashamed of how nasty she had been to him since her return to London even if he did deserve every bit of her ire. They turned to start back to the house when she pulled up her horse and shielded her eyes to see two riders coming toward them. "It looks like we are about to have company."

Michael moved closer to her. "Bloody hell," he said under his breath. "It's the Scotsman and Rockhurst." His frown intensified when he saw her face light up brightly.

"Ah, Ian must have finished his business dealings earlier than expected and came to join us," Catherine said as she raised a hand to wave at the two men riding in their direction.

"Ian? You are calling him by his given name so soon?" Michael asked unable to hide the irritation in his voice.

Catherine glanced over at him. "He is Persephone's cousin so it is permissible."

Michael rolled his eyes and shook his head at her comment.

When the two men reached them, she was surprised at the fierce look upon McDonough's face.

"Good morning, Lady Catherine," he said tersely as he kept his eyes on Michael.

Catherine looked from one man to the other, both looked as if they wanted to shoot the other off their horse. "What has happened?"

Ian maneuvered his horse to go to her other side. "I received a note this morning asking that I meet Hawksford at his solicitor's office. I assumed it was about the business deal we discussed over port last night. So, I sent a note to you cancelling our ride this morning. Imagine my surprise when I arrive at the solicitor's office to discover that he has no idea why I should be there. So, I go to Hawksford House where I talked to your brother who assured me that he had sent no such note."

"It sounds as if someone may have been trying to get rid of him, doesn't it?" Rockhurst added to the conversation causing the tension to become even thicker between the two men.

Catherine gasped in surprise. "Who would do such a thing?"

Ian leveled his gaze at Michael. "I have my theories, of course, I can't prove anything. I do find it convenient, Leicester, that you happened to appear at Hawksford's house this morning just in time to escort Lady Catherine in my stead."

Michael moved his horse around to face the Scotsman. "What are you implying, Highlander?"

"I believe you know what I am implying."

Catherine looked over at Lord Rockhurst for help, but he seemed to be enjoying the exchange. If she didn't do something soon one of these idiots was going to challenge the other to a duel or just erupt in a bout of fisticuffs in the middle of the park. "Gentlemen, please. I know it may look bad, but I do know Leicester would never do something so underhanded. I'm sure there must be a simple explanation."

Both men held their tongues, but she could see the anger radiating from them both. She reached over and placed a hand over Michael's. "Thank you for riding with me this morning and of course allowing me to ride Bucephalus."

"It's my pleasure, Catherine."

She then turned and placed her hand on Ian's. "Since Leicester was good enough to ride with me this morning, perhaps you could escort me home."

The Scotsman smiled before giving Michael a triumphant grin. He had to clench his hands into fists to keep from leaping across his horse and pulling the Scot to the ground.

"Perhaps you are right, my dear. It must have been a mistake." He took her hand and raised it to his lips as he looked over at Michael. "I will be more than happy to escort you home and hopefully we will be able to have some uninterrupted time together."

Catherine glanced back over to where Michael sat stiffly on his horse. She knew he was using all of his restraint not to provoke a fight with Ian. It bothered her that their morning ended on such a bad note. She had actually enjoyed being with him. For the short time they had been in the park, she had forgotten her anger and simply enjoyed their time together.

She rode on with Ian by her side. "Why are you trying to provoke, Leicester?"

Ian looked over at her. "Because I find it amusing. I was just not expecting him to be clever enough to send me on a wild goose chase."

"You don't really believe he did that do you?" she asked in surprise.

His laughter was rich and deep. "Absolutely I do. A man does crazy things when he is pursuing a woman."

Catherine was getting irritated. "Nonsense."

He looked over at her. "Is there a reason why you spurn his attentions, Lady Catherine?"

She looked over at him quickly. "Perhaps I should ask you about your search for a bride this season, my lord. Persephone tells me that is the reason you are in London, to seek an English bride." His smile quickly turned to a frown.

"My mother believes I need an English bride as she is English herself. I am here to appease her but just between you and me, lass, I have no intention of finding a bride this season. But you are avoiding my question, my dear. What happened between you and Leicester? I sense there is something more between you."

Catherine didn't know if she should be upset by his questioning or relieved that she could finally unburden herself. "At one time as a young girl, I had a foolish attachment to Leicester. He spent quite a lot of time at Hawk's Hill as he is Hawk's oldest friend. I have known him since I was a girl." She blushed and looked away before continuing. "Needless to say, he did not return my affections. Last year when I came to London for my first season, I was certain that he might begin to take notice. I was wrong and the lesson I learned was harsh. I have since matured and realized that what I felt for him was nothing more than a silly girlish notion. Reality was much crueler."

Ian's eyes narrowed slightly as he watched her. "What did the scoundrel do that hurt you?"

Catherine gave him a sad smile. "I overheard an unfortunate conversation. Let's just say that Leicester made it very clear that he never will have feelings for me. He is polite because I am Hawk's sister, but that is where it stops."

"For a man that claims not to feel anything for you, he certainly went to a lot of trouble to keep me away, and do you not think he is being very attentive? I believe he is regretting his decision now."

"I believe he regrets his words as he did not mean for me to hear. But I'm not certain I will ever be able to forget them."

Ian rode closer to her. "I say we make him pay a little bit for the pain he caused you."

Catherine couldn't help but grin. "I think it is rather admirable of you to want to avenge my honor, your grace but I'm not sure it would be a wise idea to provoke him. What exactly do you have in mind?"

He reached over and pulled on her reins bringing her horse to a stop. "I am formally asking to pay my addresses to you, Lady Catherine."

Catherine felt the color leave her face. "You can't be serious."

He reached over and took her hand in his. "I am most serious, my lady. I will address your brother today if possible."

Catherine didn't know what to say, but she did have a feeling that her life was about to get much more complicated.

Chapter Five

Gentlemen Jackson Boxing Club, Bond Street

"One more round, Rockhurst," Michael said as he wiped the blood from his lip.

Lord Rockhurst leaned back against the ropes opposite his friend. "Why don't we call it a draw and go somewhere we can have a drink and maybe exert ourselves in a more pleasurable way with someone of the fairer sex."

Michael shook his head. "No, I need to release my frustrations in a more barbaric fashion today." He rubbed his sore knuckles and spit blood from his mouth.

Rockhurst moved toward him. "As you wish, if you desire me to beat the piss out of you, who am I to deny your request." His head jerked back as Michael landed a squarely aimed right hook. He stepped backward setting his feet. "What has you so feral this morning, Leicester? We have boxed before but never have I seen you this aggressive." He was ready when his friend struck out again. He bobbed left to avoid another hit, then struck out to catch Leicester on the chin sending him to the ground.

Michael jumped up quickly and landed a punch to Rockhurst's midsection, but Lord Rockhurst was famous for his boxing prowess and had never been defeated so it was not surprising when his friend landed three punches in a row in retaliation.

"We have been at this for over an hour, Leicester. Do I have to knock you bloody unconscious to get you to cease with this nonsense?"

Michael lowered his hands. "I suppose no amount of physical exercise is going to assuage my annoyance."

His friend slapped him on the back as they made their way from the ring. "Finally, you are seeing some reason. Let's clean up and go to White's for a drink."

"I'm in no mood for drink," Michael said as he bent over to retrieve a towel wincing at the pain in his midsection.

At this Rockhurst stopped. "Dear god man, are you unwell, or is it something more of the heart that causes you to look so glum?"

Michael narrowed his eyes. "What do you know of matters of the heart? You can't even stay with the same mistress for more than a month before you grow tired of them."

Rockhurst smiled knowing his friend was accurate in his assumption. "True, but still I can tell you are bothered by something. I thought it might be because McDonough has shown such interest in Catherine."

"Bloody Scotsman." He threw down the towel he had been using to wipe the sweat and blood from his face. "He doesn't strike me as a man that would gain Catherine's interest."

"From what I saw of the two of them yesterday, I'm not so certain."

Michael threw his head back to look at the ceiling and closed his eyes. "I wish you had knocked me unconscious so I didn't have to listen to you prattle about such rubbish."

Rockhurst laughed loudly. "My question to you, my friend is what are you going to do about it? It was a clever move on your part to send the note that took him on the wild goose chase this morning, but he is wise to your motives now and will not be so easily put off in the future."

Michael dropped down in a chair and buried his face in his hands. "I just need more time. Catherine still has not forgiven me for what I said about her in Hawk's study that evening, and until I can get her to do so I need McDonough to stay away from her."

"You should give her a gift."

"A gift?"

Rockhurst sat down in a chair beside him. "When a gentleman wishes to get back in the good graces of a lady, they give them a gift of significance that makes them forget all about the reason for their fury."

Michael looked at him thoughtfully. "As much as I hate to admit it, you may be right."

Rockhurst looked offended. "Of course, I am right. You just aren't thinking clearly. Last year when Lucy Davies got angry with you for your lack of attention to her what did you do to soothe her ire? You bought her a bracelet."

"Lucy is not a lady and does not even compare to Catherine in any way. What I did to Catherine will require more than a simple trinket," Michael replied as a servant came around with drinks for them.

Rockhurst raised his glass to him. "May you find the grand gesture that purges the resentment from Lady Catherine's heart."

Michael rolled his eyes at the toast but raised his glass, nonetheless.

Hawksford House, London
Residence of the Duke of Hawksford

"You have a visitor, Lady Catherine," Billings announced as he entered the drawing room where she sat with Persephone having tea.

"A visitor? Who is it, Billings?" Persephone asked as she sat down her cup.

"It is the Duke of Sunbridge, your grace."

Persephone glanced over at Catherine quickly and gave her a bright smile. "Ian McDonough has come to see you specifically, Catherine. How exciting?" She stood from her seat. "Please show him in, Billings."

Catherine smoothed her skirts and stood beside Persephone as Ian was shown into the room. He was carrying a large arrangement of pink roses and peonies. He gave her a wink that caused her to blush slightly.

"Ian, what a wonderful, unexpected surprise," Persephone said as he bowed to her.

"Aye, I hope it is a welcome surprise, Lady Gray."

Catherine looked over at Persephone hoping she would prove to be a very lack chaperone. "It is a very welcome surprise. The flowers are beautiful, your grace."

He walked over and put them on a table beside the door. "They are for you. I hope they please you, Lady Catherine."

Catherine smiled then turned her head as her sister-in-law cleared her throat rather loudly. "I do apologize, Ian but I must excuse myself for just a few moments. I will return quickly. Of course, the door will remain open for propriety's sake." As she walked toward the door, she gave Catherine's hand a small squeeze.

Once they were alone Ian moved closer. "That was easier than I expected. I was hoping to find some time alone with you but wasn't sure Persephone would permit it."

Catherine shook her head. "Yes, Persephone is proving to be a nonexistent chaperone and that could be very dangerous."

"A little danger can be quite stimulating. You look very beautiful today, mo leannan."

Catherine took a seat on the settee away from him. "Mo leannan? What does that mean?"

Ian crossed his arms over his chest as he grinned down at her. "It is Gaelic for my sweetheart."

Catherine blushed and studied him curiously. When he had suggested that he was going to pay his addresses to her, she had thought he was jesting. "That is lovely, but I am not certain it is appropriate."

Ian moved to sit beside her. "I find it most appropriate when a man is courting a lady." He reached for her hand. "The first ball of the season is tomorrow night. Would it be out of line to request your waltzes?"

Catherine lowered her lashes demurely. "I am not sure how things are done in Scotland, but you should dance no more than two dances with me. But yes, you may have my first waltz, your grace."

Ian nodded in understanding. "I ken what you are saying. Two dances and no more. Then we could perhaps take a stroll through the gardens."

Catherine gave him a warm smile. "You are up to something, your grace. Are you certain this isn't some mischievous way to cause more trouble with Leicester?"

He shrugged his shoulders. "I find that I thoroughly enjoy your company, and if it drives Leicester a little mad, then I will not deny that I derive some amusement from that."

Catherine turned her head to the side. "You are going to a lot of trouble to be a thorn in Leicester's side. I assure you that flowers and gifts are not necessary if that is your intention."

Ian frowned as he raised one eyebrow. "Now what kind of proper suitor would I be, lass if I didn't bring flowers and gifts." He saw her eyes narrow slightly. "Where is your sense of adventure, mo leannan? We do enjoy each other's company and it will definitely make the season more enjoyable."

She laughed softly. "I suppose you are correct."

His smile spread wider. "I'm glad we have that settled. Your brother was most agreeable when I stated my intentions."

Persephone quickly walked back into the room and seemed disappointed not to find them in a heated embrace. "My goodness, I see there was no reason to leave the door open. Ian, why don't you join Catherine on the settee? I will go over to my desk and write some letters or perhaps you would prefer a walk in the gardens."

Catherine stood quickly. "A walk in the gardens would be nice. Ian, would you escort me?"

He took her hand and placed it in the crook of his arm. "Aye, today is the perfect day for a walk in the gardens."

Persephone was pleased with this idea. "Perfect indeed. Of course, I can't leave you alone, but I will maintain a good distance to give you some privacy. The two of you go ahead and I will be right behind you."

Catherine shook her head sadly as Ian escorted her out of the drawing room. "She is going to be the worst chaperone, ever. I'm surprised she hasn't asked you to join me for tea in my bedchamber." She blushed when she realized what she had said out loud knowing it was highly inappropriate. "I apologize. My Aunt Louisa always worries that my mouth is going to get me in more trouble than I can get out of one day."

His laugh was bold and hearty. "Your unconventional manners are what is going to make spending time with you so enjoyable, mo leannan. Don't think you have to play the part of a proper English chit on my account. I prefer cheekiness to docility."

Later that same evening

Catherine sat in the window seat of her bedchamber looking out at the gardens and street below. Ian had only stayed for a short visit. Once they had walked through the garden and he had talked with Hawk for a bit, he had excused himself. It was good he had not extended his visit. She could already tell Persephone believed he was smitten with her.

She was surprised that Michael had not tried to visit her today. Perhaps her allowing Ian to escort her home from the park had angered him enough to give up his pursuit of her. She lay her head against the cool windowpane. It was lightly raining and she watched as droplets slid down the glass. It was well past midnight and although she had been in bed, sleep didn't seem to come. She walked back to the bed but saw something lying on the floor beside her bedside table. It was a note. She picked it up and read:

A gift awaits you in the stables.

It was not signed and although Hawk would be upset with her for going to the stables alone, especially at this time of night, she couldn't resist. There was too much mystery behind the note and sometimes mystery led to adventure, and she always had loved a good adventure.

So, she slipped on her slippers and put on her robe. It was cold and rainy outside so she grabbed a knitted blanket from the foot of the bed and wrapped it around her shoulders. The hallway was dimly lit, and she didn't see any servants about. There would be a footman stationed at the front door, but the back door leading to the stables would not be watched as closely.

She quietly made her way down the stairs and moved toward the back of the house. The rain had lightened up a little, and she pulled the blanket tighter around her as she hurried over the path to the stables. Once inside, she lit a lantern to light her way. She was sure a groom would be around somewhere, but at this late hour, he might be sleeping as well. She walked through the stables looking for this so-called gift that was awaiting her. At the end of the stables on the last stall to the right was a red ribbon. Cautiously she made her way over to the stall and held the lantern higher.

"Bucephalus? What are you doing here?" She opened the door to his stall and walked inside. The horse whinnied and nuzzled her outstretched hand.

"I was beginning to think that you would not come."

She jumped and turned around startled to hear Michael's smooth voice behind her. "My goodness, you startled me."

He opened the door and walked inside the stall to join her. "You do know that coming to the stables after midnight alone," he looked down at her attire, "wearing only your nightgown is extremely reckless."

She ran a hand over the horse's neck. "You knew I would come. I couldn't resist the mystery of the note. Did you really think I could have waited till morning to discover the gift I had waiting?"

His chuckle was deep and low. "No, I don't believe you could. That is why I stayed, to ensure your safety."

She laughed softly. "Who is going to keep me safe from you?"

He didn't reply, but his eyes took on a more predatory gleam. She moved to stand on the other side of Bucephalus to put some distance and a very large horse between them.

His smile made her pulse race. "Are you not curious about the gift?"

She eyed him cautiously over the back of the stallion. "I suppose so, that is the reason I risked my health coming out to the stable in the cold and rain." Bucephalus turned his head toward her and she softly rubbed his nose.

"Well do you like it?"

Catherine was confused. "Do I like what?"

Michael moved closer to her. "Your gift? Do you like him?"

Catherine's eyes grew wider. "Him?" She wasn't quite sure if he was talking about the horse or himself.

"Bucephalus is your gift. Ever since you rode him yesterday, he has been nothing but a nuisance in our stables. I believe he was pinning for you."

Catherine looked at the horse, his large black eyes staring back at her. "You can't be serious."

"I am most serious, Catherine. He is all yours."

Catherine breathed in slowly trying to control her excitement. "He is mine." When he nodded, she wrapped her arms around the horse's neck. "He is so beautiful; I promise to take extra good care of him." In her moment of excitement, she walked over to Michael, stood on her tiptoes, and pressed a quick kiss to his cheek.

Suddenly she stepped away and he saw a shadow cross her face. "I can't accept him."

He was stunned. "Why can't you accept him?"

She looked at the horse and then back to Michael. "It is much too grand of a gift. You know I can't accept a gift of this nature. People will assume there has been an agreement made between us."

"Let people assume what they will, Catherine. I want you to have him." He felt himself getting frustrated with her refusal until he saw a tear slide down her cheek. He moved quickly wrapping his arms around her and kissed the top of her head.

Catherine knew she should pull away, but there had always been something about Michael that made her want this. "I should go back inside before someone notices I am missing."

Michael released her but framed her face in his hands. "Bucephalus is yours, Catherine. I will talk to Hawk tomorrow and make the necessary arrangements. No one needs to know about him being a gift from me."

She perked up and looked up at him. "Do you think Hawk will allow me to keep him?"

He nodded as he looked into her eyes. "Yes, after I have discussed matters with him. He can tell people he purchased the horse from me and gifted him to you himself. No one would dare doubt his word or mine for that matter." He saw her smile grow.

"Thank you, Michael." She should have stepped away from his touch then, but she didn't. And when his lips slowly descended to hers, she didn't try to pull away. Something inside her longed for this. He kissed her long and slow as if he was trying to memorize every aspect of her lips. She leaned into him letting the blanket that was around her shoulders fall into the straw bedding on the stall floor. His arms wrapped tighter around her molding her body to his as his hands moved to cup her backside through her robe and gown.

He broke the kiss and whispered near her ear. "Am I forgiven, Catherine?" He began kissing the side of her neck.

She arched her head to the side so he could have better access. Her hair was loose down her back and he had intertwined his hand in it to hold her steady. "I forgive you, Michael, but I have not forgotten," she replied breathlessly.

His mouth took hers again more possessively this time. She sighed as his hand slid to her waist. When Bucephalus nudged her in the back, she abruptly pulled away. "I should go."

He picked up her blanket and wrapped it back around her shoulders. "Yes, it is late." He put a finger under her chin and lifted her face to his. "Do not come out to the stables alone at this time of the night again, Catherine."

She opened the door to the stall and stepped out but before walking away she turned to give him a defiant smile. "Do you really think you can stop me from doing what I want, your grace? If so, you should have learned differently by now." She then turned taking the lantern with her and quickly left the stables for the house.

Michael leaned back against the wall. He would have to thank Rockhurst, a grand gift had been exactly what he needed. He would speak with Hawk tomorrow morning and now that he had won her forgiveness, he could go about seeking a way to win her heart.

Chapter Six

Tonight, was the first ball of the season and Persephone had asked her to go to the modiste with her for the final fitting of her new ballgown. Catherine had gone to the stables after breakfast and given Bucephalus some pieces of an apple. She was beginning to feel guilty about accepting Ian's addresses especially after Michael had gifted her his horse. Perhaps she should revisit the idea with Ian before things went too far. As she was walking back inside the house, Persephone came forward all smiles.

"Where have you been, Catherine? We have been waiting for you."

Catherine looked at her inquisitively. "We? Is Hawk going with us?"

Persephone wrapped her arm through hers and walked with her toward the front of the house. "Heavens no, he has appointments this morning, but we do have an escort." She gave Catherine a wink. "An extremely handsome escort, I might add."

Catherine laughed. "Am I to guess or are you going to tell me who this mystery escort might be?"

"Ian stopped by this morning while you were in the stables and when I told him we were about to leave for Bond Street, he offered to be our escort for the morning." Persephone pulled her a little closer. "I think Ian has designs on you. He has come to the house two days in a row and to consent to be our escort to the modiste definitely says something about him."

"Yes, it says he is insane. It also says that he is new to London and doesn't know very many people yet."

Persephone playfully slapped her hand. "I think we may plan a trip to Scotland at the end of the season. I will speak to Hawk and see what he thinks of the idea. I hear it is beautiful and I'm sure Ian would agree for us to be his guests for a few days."

Catherine looked at her horrified. "Persephone, that would be an imposition. It would not be right to put him in that situation. Please stop playing matchmaker." She did not have time to argue her case further. When they approached the front door, Ian was waiting for them. He was extremely handsome. She was sure to be the envy of every unmarried lady of the ton this season.

"Ladies, you both look lovely this morning. I count myself lucky to be able to be in the presence of such beauty." He gave Catherine a sly grin.

"Persephone has informed me that you have agreed to be our escort this morning to the dressmakers. Is my sister-in-law using some sort of extortion against you or have you legitimately lost your mind? Because no man in his right frame of mind would agree to sit in a dress shop for hours while we ladies look over silks, ribbons, and lace."

He laughed heartily. "It was a form of extortion. Her grace promised that after we spend the morning surrounded by silks and lace, we could take a trip to Gunter's for ices. I have heard about the place since I have been to London, but this will be my first visit."

He held his arm out for Catherine and she looped her arm through his. "The ices are delightful, but I'm not sure you will think they are worth the effort."

"It is no effort to spend time with two of the most beautiful ladies in all of England I assure you."

Catherine heard Persephone sigh dreamily behind her. She hoped her friend would forgive her deception.

Leicester arrived at Hawksford House a few minutes after noon. He had met with his secretary earlier in the morning and had papers drawn up transferring ownership of Bucephalus to Hawk. Catherine had been correct; she could not accept a gift like that from him unless they were betrothed or married, but Hawk could gift him to her as his sister. The image of her standing in the stables wearing only a thin nightgown and robe had tormented him all night. Once he made his intentions known to Hawk, and the sooner he could get Catherine to stop entertaining that damn Scotsman, perhaps he would be able to get a decent night's sleep again.

He walked up the steps to the house and Billings opened the door for him. "I'm here to see Hawksford. Is he in his study?"

Billings took his greatcoat from him. "He is indeed, your grace. Shall I announce you?"

Michael shook his head. "If he is alone, I will announce myself. Is Lady Catherine about this morning?"

"No, your grace. The duchess and Lady Catherine have gone shopping with his grace, the Duke of Sunbridge."

Michael stopped briefly. "McDonough? Do you know when she will be back?"

"Her grace did not make me aware of her plans. Perhaps the duke knows more than I," Billings replied.

Michael nodded then turned to make his way to Hawk's study. He knocked lightly before opening the door. Hawk looked up from his desk where he had been writing in a ledger. "I thought I might be seeing you today. My head groom tells me we have a new horse in our stables. Would you care to explain that?"

Michael stepped forward. "At least offer me a drink before we begin the interrogation."

Hawk nodded toward the decanter of brandy on the table and Michael poured two glasses before moving to sit before Hawk at his desk. "The horse is a gift for Catherine."

Hawk turned his head to the side and regarded his friend carefully. "A gift for Catherine?"

Michael sipped his brandy. "Yes, she rode him in the park and I wanted to gift him to her as an apology for my hurtful words last year."

Hawk leaned back in his chair. "Of course, you know she can't accept."

"No, but you can. I had my secretary draw up papers this morning transferring ownership to you. As her brother you can freely give Bucephalus to her." Michael pulled the papers out from the pocket inside his coat and placed them on the desk before raising his glass in salute.

Hawk stood from his seat and walked to the window looking out over the gardens. "What are you doing, Michael?"

"I am trying to right a wrong."

His friend turned to face him. "And?"

"And to formally ask if I may pay my addresses to Catherine."

Hawk moved back to sit behind his desk but kept silent as he studied Michael. Finally, he took a deep steady breath before responding. "You are my oldest and closest friend and while I have no objections to you or what you could offer my sister, I would ask you to not approach Catherine at this time."

Michael put the glass down on the desk and leaned forward not quite believing what he had just heard. "You refuse me then?"

Hawk casually refilled both of their drinks. "It is not a refusal; I am asking you to step away and give her time."

Michael stood from his seat and began pacing before the desk. "Give the Scotsman time to win her, isn't that what you really mean, Hawk? Is he truly a better match for her than me?"

"Sit down for God's sake and listen to what I have to say." He handed Michael his glass as he sat back down.

"Catherine has been fascinated with you since she was thirteen years old maybe longer, and up until recently, you have made it abundantly clear that you had no interest in her. When she left for Brighton, I feared she would have a difficult time getting over the things you had said, but since she has arrived back in London she seems as if she has. If you show her attention now, she might become confused."

Michael narrowed his eyes. "So, I am to step aside while every other jackanape in the ton tries to woo her. Is that what you would have done if asked to stand aside for Persephone to accept the attentions of other men?"

He knew he had hit his mark. His friend had been dead set against love until Persephone walked into his life. Even after their marriage he had tried to deny that he loved her, that it was only desire he felt for her. But when Persephone was kidnapped by Comte Domingo and he was faced with losing her forever, Hawk finally realized how much he truly loved his wife.

"My relationship with Persephone is a little different. I intended and did marry her," Hawk replied still sitting behind his desk watching his friend through narrowed eyes.

"Do you think I have less than honorable intentions?"

"You know I don't think that. I am concerned that last year you were determined to be rid of her and now when she has finally come to terms with that fact, you seem to have changed your mind. She is my sister and I love her dearly, despite the fact that she drives me mad with her stubbornness and independent nature, I still do not want to see her hurt."

Michael drank the remainder of the brandy that was in his glass and stood from his seat. "I have heard what you had to say, now it's your turn to listen to me. I may have been the biggest arse in London when I said what I said about Catherine, but I have come to see how utterly foolish I have been. I don't know how it happened or why I did not realize it earlier, but I won't let McDonough have her, at least not before I have had a chance to show her that my feelings have changed. I know I have a lot to make up for, she is not going to forget what I said or forgive me easily. As your friend, I'm telling you that I will not step aside just as I know you would never have stepped aside in your pursuit of Persephone." He stood there defiantly not knowing if Hawk would support him or have him thrown out on his ear.

He saw his friend rise from his seat and hold out his hand. "I will not encourage her to accept either of you. It will be her decision."

Michael shook his hand. "I understand."

"Persephone isn't going to like this. She is hoping McDonough will ask for her hand, he is her cousin after all."

Michael frowned. "At least I don't have both of you against me. I assume you will be attending Pemberley's ball tonight."

Hawk's eyebrows arched slightly as he smiled. "Yes, I will be escorting Persephone and Catherine."

Michael nodded then turned to leave the room. As he opened the door, he could have sworn he heard Hawk mutter, 'Good luck' behind him. As Billings was helping him with his greatcoat, the front door opened and Persephone along with Catherine and Ian McDonough walked in from their shopping trip.

Persephone was the first to notice him. "Michael, have we missed your visit?"

He took her hand and brought it to his lips quickly. "I had some business to discuss with Hawk, but I'm sure we will see each other again at Pemberley's ball tonight." He looked toward Catherine standing beside the rather large Scotsman. "If I might have a brief word with you, Lady Catherine."

Catherine looked to Ian. "If you will excuse me for a moment." She moved to step toward Michael, but Ian grabbed her hand. She could see Michael's body tense instantly and wondered how much restraint he was using not to retaliate. Ian raised her hand to his lips letting them linger on her skin while keeping his eyes on Michael as he did so.

"I must be leaving anyway, but I will see you again this evening. Remember you promised the first waltz to me, mo leannan," Ian replied still holding her hand.

"I have not forgotten, I look forward to you teaching me more Gaelic and I will be happy to help you learn how to navigate through the ton."

"There is much I can teach you, Catherine." He said just loud enough that Michael could hear.

"We will see you tonight." She gave him a bright smile which he returned with a wink.

When she turned back to Michael, she was surprised to see what she thought was jealousy on his face. "Your grace, would you like to go into the blue drawing room." Persephone gave her a warning look. "We will keep the door open, Persephone." Her friend nodded.

Michael followed her into the salon. To her credit, she moved to a secluded area where they could not be seen from the door. "I had hoped to see you earlier this morning, but I didn't get my business finished in time before you left."

"Yes, Persephone had an appointment for the final fitting of her ballgown tonight and wanted me to go with her." She looked down at her hands before continuing. "Did Hawk ask you about Bucephalus?"

Michael could see the concern in her eyes. She was afraid that he was there to take back the horse he had gifted her. "He asked and I told him it was a gift for you."

She sighed and looked crestfallen. "He won't allow me to accept him from you, will he?"

Michael shook his head. "No, but he will allow me to gift the horse to him and he will, in turn, give him to you."

He saw her face brighten. "So, I can keep him?"

"Yes, he is all yours." He was surprised when Catherine moved forward and threw her arms around him. He smiled and held her close before she remembered herself and stepped away.

"Forgive me, I was overcome with joy. I forgot myself." She blushed and took another step backward.

Michael felt the loss, he liked the way she felt in his arms. "You don't need to ask for forgiveness, Catherine. I enjoy holding you in my arms. It is an action that I would like to see repeated often."

She furrowed her brow but didn't say anything.

He moved forward and took her hand in his. "Transferring ownership of the horse is not the only reason I am here. I came to let Hawk know that I intend to pay my addresses to you."

Catherine's eyes grew wide. "You mean to court me?"

"I mean to have you," he replied matter-of-factly.

"Spoken very much like an entitled duke used to always getting his way. What makes you so certain I am willing to accept your addresses? I suppose I do have a say in the matter or is this some arrangement you and my brother have made without consulting what I want? Is that the reason you gifted me Bucephalus? Was he some sort of bribe to try to make me forget everything that has happened?" she said putting her hands on her hips.

This was not exactly what he had been expecting and his senses urged him to tread lightly. "Of course, you have a say and I gifted Bucephalus to you because it made you happy not as some way to buy your affections. I understand that McDonough has also made his intentions clear and I'm sure throughout the season others will try to win your favor as well. I'm merely saying that I will be the one who is triumphant."

His arrogance was astounding. "I guess we shall see won't we, your grace? You did say that McDonough had made his intentions known." She moved closer to him standing on her tiptoes so she wouldn't have to look up at him as much. "And while in Brighton, there were several men who said they would approach my brother come the season. Do you plan on thwarting all of them?" She laughed knowing what she was about to say might push him too far. "Perhaps I will not even get married, I might decide that I would have more freedom as a mistress than a bride."

He gripped both of her arms tightly. "Enough, Catherine! Perhaps I am not good with expressing my feelings without a trace of superiority. I am a duke after all. But by god I will not let you demean yourself just to get back at me." He leaned in closer still holding her tightly. "Yes, there will be men who seek to have you, but make no mistake I will be the one who takes you for his wife and the only man to take you to his bed." He noticed her breathing intensify. "If you would put aside your anger and search your heart, you would know it to be true." He stepped away and released her raking a hand through his hair. "My apologies, I didn't come here to fight. I was hoping to make you happy. I'll be taking my leave."

He turned to go and Catherine made her way over to the settee and sat there with her head in her hands in silence.

He stopped at the door but didn't turn around. "He called you mo leannan, what does it mean?"

She took a breath and hoped her voice would not belay her feelings. "It's Gaelic for my sweetheart."

"Over my dead body!" he said as he walked from the room.

"Are you alright, Catherine? I couldn't help but hear some of what was said. If you would like I could speak to Hawk about Michael," Persephone rushed over to her.

Catherine rolled her head back and blew a frustrated breath out. "No, Michael didn't do anything wrong, I baited him and pushed him to that reaction."

"But whatever for, Catherine?"

She got up and walked toward the window. "I don't know. You of all people know how much I loved him. He apologized for what he said, and I accepted his apology but another part of me doesn't want to make it too easy for him either." She turned back toward Persephone. "I am stubborn like my brother."

Persephone walked over to her and hugged her. "He certainly deserves to have to work a bit harder to earn your affections. But of course, you do have Ian to consider. A fine match he would be and certainly a man that could stand toe to toe against Michael."

Catherine nodded her head and gave her friend a small smile. "Of course, one never knows what their future holds, my dear."

"No indeed, I never in a million years would have thought that I would marry Hawk and look how blissfully happy we are now." She stood and linked her arm through Catherine's. "We have a long night ahead of us, my dear. The first ball of the season. We should both go upstairs and get some rest before getting ready."

Catherine nodded then headed up the stairs to her room. She was feeling wretched for how she had treated Michael and wouldn't doubt it if he didn't bother speaking to her again. Her temper and mouth had gotten her into trouble before. But what did he expect? Was she to fall at his feet thanking him for choosing her to be his bride?

After the remarks he made last year, he should have known better. And now Hawk and Persephone both believed Ian was interested in her for his bride as well. She was weaving herself into a web she was afraid she would be unable to escape.

The first ball of the season was everything she expected it to be. Everyone of importance was there. Young debutantes that were just out for the first time nervously moved through the crowd closely watched by their guardians. Other ladies glittered in their jewels and brightly-colored ball gowns while the well-dressed gentlemen watched from the sides of the room. She nodded in greeting to some of the gentlemen she had met in Brighton. When she had told Michael that several gentlemen had approached her in Brighton about seeking permission from her brother to pay addresses to her, it had not entirely been a falsehood. She did fail to mention that none of the gentlemen had gained her interest. She found herself scanning the ballroom looking for him. After their exchange this afternoon, she wondered if he would attend.

"Good evening, Lady Catherine, you look positively delicious."

Catherine turned around and laughed. "Lord Rockhurst, you do have a wicked way with words. No wonder you are considered the most notorious rake of them all."

He swept her an exaggerated bow. "At your service, my dear." He offered her his arm and together they strolled along the edge of the ballroom. "Might I ask the name of the lucky gentleman that you were searching for so diligently, my lady?"

She looked up and gave him a warm smile. "And what may I ask gave you the impression I was looking for anyone, my lord?"

He put his hand over hers as they continued to stroll around the room. "My dear, I have been an astute observer of the fairer sex for a good many years now. I can tell when a lady is searching out her lover."

She was so taken back by his words that she dropped her fan and nearly choked on her tongue. She coughed loudly drawing eyes toward them. "My goodness, a lover, my lord?"

"Hmm, well I can think of no other reason why a lady would scan the ballroom so intently. Also, Leicester has been visiting Jackson's on a daily basis trying to release his frustrations out on me."

She stopped and turned to him. "What has Michael going to Jacksons to let you beat him senseless have to do with me?"

A grin played at the corners of his mouth. "You my dear, are leading him on a merry chase and it is causing him great distress. He doesn't know what to do with himself." He leaned closer and said softly so only she could hear. "And I think he deserves everything he is getting. But mind my words, Catherine even the hounds grow tired of chasing the fox after a time." He raised her hand to his lips as Hawk and Persephone came toward them.

"Do I have to remind you that my sister is off limits, Rockhurst?" Hawk said teasing as he shook hands with his friend.

"Being seen with the most beautiful lady in attendance bolsters my reputation. Although married ladies are more to my liking. Would you honor me with this dance, your grace?" he asked giving Persephone a wink.

Hawk laughed, "You most definitely will stay away from my wife."

Persephone playfully slapped at her husband's hand. "Don't be so overprotective, darling. I would love to dance, my lord."

Hawk reached over and kissed her cheek. "Watch him, my love, his hands have been known to wander."

Rockhurst feigned insult but offered Persephone his hand as he led her to the dance floor. Hawk watched them go and Catherine could see the love he had for his wife shining in his eyes. He then turned his smile to her. "And what about you, Catherine? Has no gentleman offered to dance with you yet?"

Catherine moved closer to her brother. "Since I have been with Lord Rockhurst and now I am standing with you, I am not sure anyone is brave enough to approach me," she replied with laughing eyes.

"I believe I am brave enough, mo leannan."

She recognized the Scottish brogue without even turning to see who was speaking. "Your grace, how good it is to see you again," she replied sweetly.

Hawk held out a hand to him. "I see you survived shopping with my wife and sister today. After that ordeal I think you deserve a dance."

Ian smiled leisurely at Catherine. "I believe the next dance is to be a waltz."

Catherine placed her hand in his and allowed him to lead her closer to the dance floor. "You look lovely, Catherine. The most beautiful lady in attendance I dare say. I was surprised not to see a flock of gentlemen circling about you. I did notice however that they are watching you. Have you seen Leicester this evening?"

Catherine shook her head disappointment showing on her face. "I am afraid we had words again today, and I am not sure he will be here tonight."

The strains of the waltz began and he took her into his arms. "He won't give up that easily. If my guess is correct, he is here somewhere probably watching you."

Catherine took a moment to scan the room, but she didn't see him. "Perhaps but have you noticed that we have quite a few other people watching us."

"Aye, it's not every day they see a Highlander in a kilt dancing across an English ballroom. They are already telling all sorts of stories about me. My favorite being that I am here to kidnap an English heiress to cart back to the wilds of the Highlands or that when I arrived in town, I was dressed like a barbarian carrying a claymore in one hand and a dirk in the other."

Catherine laughed out loud causing everyone around them to look in their direction. "How ridiculous people can be. I hope you were not too offended. Not everyone in the ton is so nonsensical. Imagine, thinking you would kidnap a bride."

He continued to swing her around the room. "It's not all that ridiculous. A hundred years ago, I might would have done just that. It wasn't that uncommon to steal a bride during a raid on a rival clan."

Her brows furrowed with interest. "How very fascinating. No wonder the other ladies look as if they are afraid of you."

His brows arched mischievously. "If I did try to take you, I'm sure Leicester wouldn't let me get very far."

Her smile faded. "I'm not so certain of that. He visited Hawk today and informed him that he would be paying his addresses to me."

"And you don't want him to?"

Catherine looked up and furrowed her brow. "I don't know to be honest. I shouldn't after what has happened." She then put a smile back on her face. "But enough about my troubles, you should know that Hawk and Persephone are planning a trip to Scotland at the end of the season. I believe they are expecting you to offer for me."

Ian pulled her just a bit closer. "I would be happy to entertain you at McDonough Castle and who knows, perhaps I might find myself offering for you in the future."

Catherine laughed softly. "I wouldn't say that too loudly, your grace, but as long as we are to spend time in each other's company perhaps I should help you navigate through the ladies of the ton. Do you see the lady in the red dress beside the refreshment table? She keeps looking in our direction."

He spun her around so he could see the lady over her shoulder. "Yes, the one with unnaturally red hair."

Catherine giggled. "Yes, that's the one, Lady Tenneson. She has a daughter that she has been trying to marry off the past three seasons. Last year she tried to trap Captain Stevens in a position where he would have to marry her. Luckily the good Captain managed to escape before her mother could burst into the room. It is said they are desperate for funds. From the way she is eyeing you, I think you should definitely watch your back."

Ian quirked his eyebrows questioningly and smiled. "Is the daughter so unseemly?"

"You can ascertain that for yourself. If I see her, I will point her out."

The music came to an end and Ian led her to the side of the ballroom. "Until the next waltz?"

Catherine nodded. "Yes, but no more. Remember only two dances and I am not certain both dances should be waltzes."

He bowed to her as another man walked over to claim her for the next dance. Catherine allowed the young lord to lead her away. She scanned the room again looking for any indication that Michael was in attendance.

"Are you going to continue lurking about in the shadows all night brooding?" Rockhurst asked as he moved into the darkened alcove where his friend was leaning against the wall.

Michael continued to watch the dance floor as Catherine once again was claimed for another dance. "Why are you here? I thought you detested these kinds of things."

Rockhurst slipped a flask of brandy from beneath his jacket. "It's the first ball of the season, a chance to look over the new crop of debs as well as which newly married or widowed ladies might wish to seek a dalliance with a rogue like myself." He offered the flask to his friend. "Why are you so melancholy and sulky? It's not a good look for a man of your station."

Michael took the flask and turned it up. "I'm not in the mood to socialize."

"With anyone or just Catherine?"

"Bloody hell, Rockhurst go away."

His friend chuckled. "As you wish, Leicester but a piece of advice before I go. Lurking in the shadows will not endear you to the lady. You should turn the tables on her. She seems to be enjoying the company of McDonough, perhaps you should show her that you are enjoying yourself as well."

Michael stood away from the wall. "Are you suggesting that I should make her jealous?"

Rockhurst replaced his flask securely under his jacket. "I'm suggesting you stop with the despondent miserable duke act; it's not appealing. You have a reputation for roguishness, start using it to your advantage."

Michael watched as Rockhurst walked away. He was right of course, so he straightened his cravat and materialized out of the shadows into the crowd and straight toward one of the beautiful young unmarried ladies of the ton, Lady Annette Beasley.

Chapter Seven

Catherine noticed Michael the minute he emerged from the shadows into the crowd. He was tall and stood over most of the
people in attendance. He was quite the picture of masculinity as
he moved through the throng of people. His black evening attire in
stark contrast with his white shirt and cravat gave him a menacing
appearance. Men quickly moved out of his way and the women,
while not wanting to appear attracted to such a scoundrel, admired
him through their lowered lashes and began fanning their blushing
cheeks more vigorously. She had wondered if he would be too upset
with her to attend tonight but from the roguish look on his face, he
was not upset at all. He made his way through the crowd toward
Annette Beasley. Annette was the daughter of an earl. Her family was
well connected and her dowry sufficient. She was also very pretty and
only a year younger than Catherine. She watched as Annette smiled
and blushed at something Michael said and when he took her hand
in his to lead her toward where the others were dancing, she thought
the girl might faint.

"I never would have thought Leicester interested in Annette Beasley. She is incredibly immature even if she is beautiful," young Lord Harrington said as he escorted her off the dance floor.

"Do you mind getting me a drink, my lord? I think I will sit out the next dance if you don't mind."

The young lord grinned ear to ear obviously thrilled to be asked to complete such a task. "Of course, my lady. I will return shortly."

Catherine watched Michael as he twirled Lady Annette through a quadrille. Lady Annette was beaming with pride at being chosen to dance with such a distinguished gentleman, a duke, nonetheless. Catherine was certain Lady Annette's mother was somewhere already planning on her daughter becoming a duchess.

"Enjoying yourself, Catherine?"

She jumped at Ian's voice behind her. "Yes, I suppose although I am growing bored and would love to retire early."

"Nae lass, you can't do that. I ken Leicester has upset you but leaving now is out of the question." He held out his hand. "Shall we venture onto the terrace?"

Catherine looked at him as if he had lost his mind. "Onto the terrace? We can't do that; it is much too dangerous and entirely improper."

"That it is, but I happen to know something that Leicester doesn't, your brother and the duchess are on the terrace and we would be joining them."

Catherine looked toward the refreshment table where young Harrington was still in line. "I sent Lord Harrington to get me a drink, it would be terribly rude to disappear."

Ian took her arm. "We will make an excuse later. Now when we walk toward the open doors leading onto the terrace, I will lean down and whisper something in your ear, when I do, try to blush and look up at me with those beautiful eyes of yours. I will do the rest."

Catherine looked toward the dance floor and saw Annette flutter her eyelashes at Michael. "Alright, if you say so."

Ian led her past the dancers making certain he took the way she would be most visible to Leicester. As they approached the terrace doors, Ian did lean down and said, "Now lass, look up at me."

She did as he requested and he wrapped an arm about her waist pulling her to his side and lifting her off her feet before depositing her out of sight onto the terrace.

"Catherine, why aren't you dancing?" Persephone asked when she turned to see her sister-in-law and cousin walking toward them.

"I needed a breath of fresh air and since Ian had seen the two of you on the terrace, he suggested we join you," Catherine said as she moved to stand beside the railing overlooking the gardens below.

Hawk had an arm around his wife. "Persephone wasn't feeling well so we were thinking about leaving early."

Persephone leaned her head against her husband's shoulder. "Don't be ridiculous, we can't ask Catherine to leave the ball early."

Catherine gave her friend a concerned look and smiled sweetly. "I was just telling Ian that I was growing bored with the ball so if you wish to retire early, I would welcome it."

Hawk looked over at Ian. "I believe the ladies have spoken. If you would escort them to the front, I will go ahead and have my carriage brought around."

"I will walk them through the garden to avoid the crowd and the insufferable heat of the ballroom," Ian said as he offered his arm to Persephone.

Catherine walked on the other side of her friend as they made their way down the staircase to the gardens below. There was a path that would lead them to the front so they could avoid being seen leaving early. She was glad to be going home. After seeing Michael with Annette, she didn't think she had the stomach to go back inside to face anyone. After the way she had behaved with him this morning she shouldn't be surprised, but those old feelings were coming to the surface and her heart, a heart she thought fully healed, was beginning to feel the familiar pangs again.

Michael watched as Catherine walked past him on the arm of the Scotsman. She never even glanced in his direction. He continued his dance with Lady Beasley, but when the bloody Scot whispered something that made Catherine's cheeks flame and then wrapped an arm around her waist before lifting her out the terrace doors, it was all he could do not to leave Annette on the dance floor. When the music ended, he bowed tersely to her and escorted her back to her mother. Without another word he hurried toward the terrace.

A hand reached out and grabbed his arm. "Easy, Leicester. You can't go rushing out there like a calvary charge."

Michael was incensed, he clenched his teeth in rage. "Let go of me, Rockhurst. I'm going to kill the bastard if he has put his hands on her."

Rockhurst glanced around the room noticing that they were garnering a bit more attention than either of them liked. "Walk with me."

Michael pulled his arm free. "No, damnation he could be doing anything to her by now!"

At that moment a young Lord Harrington came forward. "Excuse me, your graces but have either of you seen Lady Gray? She sent me to seek her refreshment but has since disappeared."

Rockhurst rolled his eyes as Michael very nearly growled at the young lordling. "My god, Harrington if you value your safety, you will get the hell away from us."

The young lord nearly dropped the glass of lemonade as he fled to the other side of the ballroom.

Michael headed out the terrace doors with Rockhurst on his heels. "Where the hell has he taken her?"

"For Christ's sake man, calm down. She isn't here."

Michael rounded on him furiously. "Where is she?"

"I saw her and Persephone leaving with Hawk in his carriage. I do not have an idea as to where McDonough is, however."

Michael raked his hand through his hair as he paced the balcony. "What the hell is she doing to me? Food has no taste, I haven't had a decent night's sleep since she arrived in London, I find myself wanting to thrash anyone that tries to speak to me. Brandy, lots of it, and having you beat the hell out of me a few times a week is the only way I get any relief from thinking about her." He sighed heavily and looked at his friend. "I've never had a woman do this to me."

Rockhurst chuckled, "Lady Catherine isn't just any woman."

Michael narrowed his eyes. "No, she isn't, but it's time she comes to terms with her fate."

Rockhurst called out as his friend turned to leave. "I'll see you at Jackson's in the morning. I have a feeling this conversation isn't going to go as you expect."

Catherine did not go up to her room right away. Instead, she had gone to the library. It was the only place she could be alone and not be disturbed. Persephone and Hawk had retired to their chambers and the house was fairly quiet. She moved to an oversized chair that was positioned close to the fire and curled up in it. She watched the flames dance in the hearth feeling the warmth of the fire seep into her bones. She should be excited about the beginning of the season. Last year had been her first season, and she had been beyond excited to go to the balls and parties. But she had always thought to catch the eye of Michael and perhaps she did try too hard to do so. Now, she was tormented by him. Part of her wanted to cut off his ballocks while the other part of her wanted to crawl into his bed and damn the consequences. How was she to enjoy herself in London while he paraded about before her dancing with other women and heaven knows what else? She closed her eyes not wanting to think about where he went after the balls and parties. She had spent many years reading about Leicester and her brother's adventures in the scandal sheets. So, she had an idea of what he would be up to once the dancing stopped.

She couldn't stay downstairs all night so she reluctantly left the warmth of the fire to go to her bedchamber. Her room would be warm and the fires lit, but she had asked her maid not to wait up for her. She didn't feel like listening to all of Sarah's questions about the ball and if she had danced with anyone of importance. The hallways were dark as she made her way down the corridor to her bedchamber. She opened the door expecting to find the fire in the hearth needing to be stoked but to her surprise it was still burning brightly. She closed the door and moved closer to it. The room was dark except for one candle burning beside the bed and the glow from the flames. As she moved further into the room, she couldn't shed the feeling that she wasn't alone or that she was being watched. She made her way to the chair by the fire and slowly leaned down to retrieve the knife she had strapped to her thigh. When the knife was free, she spun around quickly ready to defend herself against whoever was in her room.

"Christ, Catherine! Since when did you start carrying a blade?" Michael asked as he materialized from the corner beside her bed.

She didn't lower her arm but replied, "Since when did you start sneaking into a lady's bedchamber? No, don't answer that. I'm sure you have had plenty of experience."

He smiled as he came forward. "Are you going to gut me or will you lower the blade?"

Her brow furrowed. "I haven't decided yet. Why are you in my room?"

"You made sure to ignore me at the ball tonight, and I needed to see you without the interference of that blasted Scotsman." He kept walking forward determined to get his hands on her, blade or no blade.

Catherine tossed her blade onto the side table. "If you don't leave my room, I'm going to scream. Everyone will be in here in seconds, including Hawk."

Michael stopped and held out his arms. "By all means, go ahead." He moved back toward the bed and propped himself up on the pillows.

Catherine watched him in amazement. "What are you doing? You know what will happen if you are caught in here."

He crossed his arms behind his head. "I do and as far as I am concerned it will just speed up the inevitable."

She narrowed her eyes. "Where is my knife?"

He chuckled and moved off the bed stealthily moving towards her. "Where is your lady's maid?"

"I told her not to wait up for me, a mistake I will not make in the future."

She was in arm's reach of him now. "Turn around."

"Pardon me?"

He put his hands on her shoulder and spun her around. "How did you think to get out of your gown tonight?"

She moved to turn back to face him. "I can manage on my own, thank you. Surely you don't think that I am going to permit you to undress me."

He spun her back around. "I just mean to help with your buttons, nothing more unless you wish it."

"This is ridiculous. You really should leave. How did you manage to get up to my room in the first place?"

"Darling, I know this house almost as well as my own. Your brother and I used to hide in the secret passages as young lads and as older boys we used them to sneak around for more nefarious purposes. It was terribly easy and as most of Hawk's servants know me if I had been seen, any excuse I gave would have been accepted."

She stepped away as he moved his fingers lightly over the back of her neck. "How was your dance with Annette Beasley?" She regretted the words as soon as they left her lips. The last thing she wanted him to know is that he had made her jealous.

He moved closer causing her to back up closer to the fire. "I could ask you about your dances with McDonough or your time spent with him on the terrace."

She saw his expression change at the mention of Ian and her heart soared just a wee bit. He had been jealous. "He is an excellent dancer and an even better, . . ." she paused for effect, "well we won't talk about the terrace."

She did not know a person could move so swiftly. Before she could even suck in a breath, he wrapped his arm about her waist and pulled her into his arms. "If I had thought McDonough had put his hands on you or kissed you, darling, I would not be here right now. I would be finding him and making certain it did not happen again." Before she could react, his lips descended upon hers in a searing possessive kiss.

Catherine's eyes drifted closed as Michael devoured her. His kiss was demanding. It felt as if he was claiming her. She felt her knees growing weak and leaned into him for support. When he lifted his lips from hers, she tried to catch her breath. His thumb moved slowly over her swollen bottom lip before he leaned down to take her more gently this time as if he was memorizing the feel of her lips beneath his, tasting her, savoring her. She couldn't help herself; she slowly placed her hands against his chest letting her fingers splay wider to feel more of him.

Michael wanted to touch her; he had never wanted anything so bad in his life. He moved quickly lifting her so she straddled his hips and moved toward the bed. He sat her on the edge of the bed not taking his lips from hers. Her hands moved from his chest to his back. His mouth moved from her lips to her neck slowly kissing and nibbling the sensitive skin below her ear. His tongue flicked over her earlobe and he heard her breathing increase.

Catherine knew she should put a stop to this, but she had longed for this for so long. What would it hurt to enjoy his kiss and touch for a few minutes longer? "Take off your coat," she whispered.

He pulled away to look at her and smiled at the intoxicated look on her face. "As you wish, my dear." He pulled back and quickly shed his jacket throwing it on the floor. He leaned back toward her. "I am yours to command, my lady."

Catherine liked this. "And your shirt."

He whipped the shirt over his head and she sucked in her breath. She had never seen a man without his shirt this close before. He was very muscular and she wanted to touch him. She tentatively reached out with one hand and flattened it against his chest. His skin was so warm. She let her hand slide slowly down his chest to this taut abdomen. When she got to the waistband of his trousers, he reached out and grabbed her hand and raised it to his lips sucking in the tip of each of her fingers into his mouth. Catherine watched him mesmerized as his lips and tongue touched her. His eyes never left hers and she felt immobile, frozen. He leaned closer and took her lips again. She put both hands on his chest letting her fingers move over his skin. Suddenly he pulled her to her feet and turned her around.

Catherine shivered as he kissed the back of her neck. She let her eyes drift closed as his fingers popped the buttons free of her dress. He turned her back to face him and slowly put his hand on her shoulders pushing the sleeves down her arms and the bodice of her dress to her waist. His hands slid back up her arms and her skin prickled with his touch.

"It's only fair that since you touched me, I should get to touch you as well." He moved his fingers to the ribbon of her chemise. He hesitated to give her time to tell him to go to the devil if she wished, but when she just looked up at him eagerly waiting for his touch, he gently pulled the ribbon free. He felt his hands tremble when he reached inside her chemise to cup her breast. By God, she made him feel like a boy seeing a naked lady for the first time. Her breasts were firm and filled his hands. Her breathing became more ragged as he let his fingers flick over her nipples. "I want to see you, Catherine."

Her eyes opened and met his. She didn't say anything but reached up and slowly moved the straps of her chemise down her arms. He had never seen anything so seductive. She was exposed to him from the waist up. He slowly slid a finger from her collarbone to circle her breasts causing her nipples to tighten.

"Bloody hell, Catherine. You are the most beautiful woman I have seen." He kissed her again pulling her into his chest. He felt ravenous for her. He wanted to kiss every part of her body. His hand moved over her breasts to her flat stomach. She was just as voracious, her hands moved over his back and she was now returning his kisses matching his passion. He leaned her backwards onto the bed letting his mouth move from her lips to her breasts as his hands gathered her skirts to her thighs.

Catherine arched her back as he sucked her breast into his mouth. How much longer should she let this continue? She felt his hand move up her leg to her knee where he slowly traced circles behind the sensitive skin there. It may make her a wanton but she needed this, she needed him to touch her and she needed to touch him. She leaned forward and pressed her lips to his chest. When she heard his sharp intake of breath, she flicked her tongue out to taste him. His response was immediate. He pinned her back against the bed. "I don't know how much more of this I can take, Catherine. You are tempting me too much."

She smiled liking the power she seemed to have over him. "If you feel like you can't handle anymore, we can always stop," she replied teasing him.

He grinned at her cheeky comment as he let his hand roam further up her thigh. When his fingers reached out and touched her sensitive mound, she sucked her breath sharply between her teeth. He let his fingers rub slowly over her nub causing her hips to arch and buck against him. He was so hard his cock felt as if it were trying to burst free from the restraint of his breeches. He ached for her. He slowly pressed a finger inside her. She was warm and so very wet. He kissed her stifling the noises she was making as they grew louder. She became more frenzied as he pressed further inside her.

Catherine felt pressure building inside her as if something were about to explode from her. She moved against his hand in a rhythm matching his own. "Michael," she called his name out in a breathy whisper.

"Shh, love."

The build-up inside her grew and when it burst forth from her, she felt as if a million stars had exploded at once. She cried out and Michael quickly covered her mouth with his own praying no one heard her. When he felt her body stop trembling and collapse beneath him, he raised up on his elbows to look into her eyes. He kissed the tip of her nose. There was a sheen of sweat on her forehead and her cheeks were rosy. Her lips were swollen from his kisses and she looked completely satiated. He closed his eyes trying to will himself to move away from her. His cock was swollen and hard. He wanted nothing more than to bury himself deep inside her, but he would not take her tonight.

He moved to her side and pulled her into his arms. "I should be leaving, love."

Catherine could not seem to get her breathing under control. She had never felt anything like that before. She flicked her tongue over her lips, but her mind could not form the words yet.

Michael held her closer and pressed kisses to her forehead and cheeks. When she drifted off to sleep, he pulled back the covers on the bed, removed her dress the rest of the way leaving her in her chemise and covered her up with the coverlet. He stood looking down at her for a few minutes. She was incredibly lovely and she was his. There was no way he would allow any other man to have her now. He would begin making arrangements, the sooner the better, after tasting her tonight he wanted her more than anything, and the sooner he got her in his bed the better. He put his shirt back on and grabbed his jacket from where he had tossed it on the floor and made his way down the hall to the secret passage that led out to the garden. His carriage would be waiting for him down the street. Tomorrow he would return and he and Catherine would talk about the future and how soon they could be married. He smiled very pleased at the prospect.

Chapter Eight

The next morning Catherine was more confused than ever. She wished she could talk to Persephone about things, but now that her best friend was married, there were some things she was reluctant to speak with her about. Last night should have never happened. When she discovered Michael in her room, she should have demanded that he leave at once. She didn't know what it was about the man but once he touched her, she had been lost. Now she was going to have a devil of a time not thinking about what had happened between them in her bedchamber every time she saw him. It was just going to make things more difficult.

She dressed in one of her prettiest day dresses. She was to attend a garden party this afternoon with Persephone. Perhaps it would give her a chance to speak with her friend and ask for advice without revealing too much. She grabbed her parasol and headed down the stairs to where Persephone was waiting for her.

"Good afternoon, my dear. I am so glad that you are here to attend this dreaded party with me. Being a duchess, I must attend a number of these functions when I would much rather be elsewhere,"

Persephone said as she gathered her shawl from the back of the settee where it had been resting. "Lady Weatherby's party will be quite dull I am afraid. She is a lover of poetry and loves to recite her own works, which I have heard are really rather terrible," Persephone said as she wrinkled her nose in distaste.

"Perhaps we will not have to endure it for long. We can always make up excuses and take a long ride in the park," Catherine said as she followed her sister-in-law outside.

"We had the same thoughts. I had Billings tell the grooms to bring up the barouche. It is a bright sunny day and not a cloud in the sky. Besides I feel some fresh air would do me some good especially since I have not been feeling so well lately."

Catherine caught up with her. "Persephone, have you consulted a doctor? I know Hawk is worried."

"He has been overly attentive lately, but I am certain it is nothing. Just a little more tired than usual." She patted her hand reassuringly. "Come, let's go listen to bad poetry and salacious gossip."

Catherine laughed. "I always love some salacious gossip as long as I am not the subject."

Lady Weatherby's Garden Party

The party was everything Catherine had expected. Ladies from many of the great families of the ton were in attendance. Lady Weatherby had chairs and tables set up in the garden. Tea and sweet treats, biscuits, and pastries were abundant. Persephone and Catherine had chosen to sit closer to the back of the garden. Lady Weatherby had everyone gathered near so she could begin her treacherous recitation of her poetry.

"My goodness, you would think she would get better at this with time, but I think she is getting worse with every year," Persephone whispered into Catherine's ear.

Catherine giggled into her handkerchief. "Oh, I don't know, I rather liked the one where she compared the color of her lover's eyes to the putrid scum of a stagnant pond."

Persephone spit out her tea and covered her laughter with a cough. "Stop. I just can't."

Catherine leaned closer. "Did you see poor Lady Chesterfield? She nearly fainted when Lady Weatherby announced that she had half a dozen more poems to recite and that she had one she had put to music."

Persephone shook her head sadly. "I will have to excuse myself if she bursts into song. In fact, I think I will go to the lady's retiring room now." She sat her teacup down and stood from her seat.

"Coward," Catherine said as her friend moved past her. She looked around her noticing most everyone there looked as if they were struggling to stay awake or fighting the urge to break out in laughter. Of all the garden parties to attend, why did Persephone pick this one?

"I don't know how you ladies can endure such torture on a regular basis," a strong deep voice she recognized said from behind her.

She quickly looked over her shoulder to see Michael grimacing as Lady Weatherby's voice notched an octave higher. "What the devil are you doing here? I would not have thought garden parties were exactly your cup of tea?" She turned back around quickly just as applause broke out at the conclusion of the latest rhyme.

"I'm here, darling because you are here," he said just as he caressed the back of her neck lightly with his fingers.

Catherine swatted his hand away. "Stop that! Someone might see you," she whispered back to him. "And don't refer to me in such familiar terms. We wouldn't want people making assumptions that aren't true."

Michael leaned forward blowing a breath across the back of her neck causing her to shiver in response. "I don't give a damn what people think and if you will remember, we are on familiar terms, very familiar in fact."

Catherine looked over her shoulder. "We should not mention that incident again nor should we be foolish enough to repeat it."

He didn't respond and Catherine turned her attention back to the horrible prose being recited. When Lady Weatherby finished her last poem and the crowd stood and applauded not for the elegance of her words, but because the torture was finally over, she turned to see if Michael had stayed. The seat behind her was empty and she couldn't help but feel annoyance at his absence. She slowly moved around the other ladies hoping to find Persephone. She thought it would be good manners to compliment her hostess so she made her way over to Lady Weatherby but was swiftly intercepted by none other than Lady Annette Beasley.

"How nice to see you here, Lady Catherine. I wasn't aware you were fond of poetry."

Catherine pasted a false smile on her face. "I'm sure there is much about me you do not know, Lady Beasley."

Lady Beasley narrowed her eyes in disapproval. "Hmm, did you happen to see the Duke of Leicester?"

Catherine cocked her head to the side. "I did happen to notice that he was in attendance. Why do you ask?"

Lady Beasley placed her hand on her arm and leaned closer as if she were drawing Catherine in to tell her some sort of secret. "At the ball last night, I asked him if he would like to attend with me." Her smile widened. "And he came today. My mother says it is quite the conquest if I can finally get Leicester to the altar. In fact, I have scarcely seen him pay much attention to any other lady."

Catherine didn't know if she should laugh at the ridiculous notion of Annette Beasley with Michael, or if she should set the record straight and tell the ambitious woman that if she wished to be a duchess, she should look elsewhere.

"Yes, it would indeed be a victory worth celebrating if you could pull that off, Lady Annette. But Leicester has given no indication that he is looking for a bride." Catherine smiled and tried to walk away, but Annette grabbed her arm.

"I know that you wanted him for yourself, Lady Catherine. Everyone knows that you have set your cap for him for years. I just hope you can be gracious about losing him to another when the time comes." She released Catherine's arm, "Afterall, you are a very lovely girl and I'm sure you will find someone to take his place in your heart. I have heard that the Scottish Duke of Sunbridge has shown you a particular interest."

Catherine felt her temper rising and if not for Persephone and the scandal it would cause, she would tell Annette Beasley to go to the devil. Instead, she took a deep steadying breath and held her head high. "Pray do not concern yourself with my welfare, Annette. Now if you will excuse me, I need to find my sister-in-law and I believe Leicester might be headed your way."

Lady Annette quickly turned to see Leicester walking toward them. She put a hand to her hair and dipped into a deep curtsy at his approach. Catherine rolled her eyes and gave Michael a smirk.

"Good day to you both. I wish the two of you a lifetime of happiness." She giggled at the confused look on Michael's face as she sailed past him to join Persephone under the shade of an oak talking to Lady Chesterfield.

Michael stared after Catherine as she moved away and would have followed had Lady Annette not placed her hand on his arm.

"I am so glad that you were able to join me here today, your grace," Lady Annette said as she batted her eyelashes and looked up at him with a sickeningly sweet countenance on her face.

He was beginning to put things together. Lady Annette had asked him about attending the event last night at the ball, and while he must have told her something to make her think he would attend; he was here only because he found out from the staff at Hawksford House that Catherine was in attendance.

"It is good to see you again, Lady Beasley. I do hope you are enjoying the party," he said trying to make polite conversation without encouraging the lady further.

Lady Beasley hooked her arm through his and smiled. "It was dreadfully boring until your arrival, your grace. Shall we walk to say hello to my mother, she will be overjoyed that you have chosen to join us today."

Michael felt a trap closing in on him. He had avoided unmarried ladies and their ambitious mother's attempts to drag him to the altar since he inherited his title. Now because of Catherine, he found himself in a most unpleasant situation. He would need to extricate himself quickly.

"While I would love to say hello to Countess Milton, I do see some other people I must urgently speak with, if you will excuse me, my lady."

Sadly, Lady Annette was not so easily deterred. "It will not take very long and then we can visit with your other friends. Come along, your grace." She pulled on his arm and he was loath to follow unless he wanted to attract attention, but as soon as possible he would extract himself from Lady Beasley before her trap closed any tighter.

Catherine sat down on a bench farther away from the party just wanting to find some peace and quiet. Persephone, despite her doubts, had fallen into her role of Duchess of Hawksford with ease and was still visiting with the other ladies. In the short time she had been Hawk's wife, she had earned the respect and admiration of the ladies of the beau monde, not an easy feat for anyone, especially a lady not instructed her whole life to fill the role.

Catherine was quite the opposite of Persephone. She didn't really care two figs what the other ladies of the ton thought of her, and she did not bother to hide her feelings about it. She had always been the one wanting adventure. As young girls, she and Persephone had hidden in caves and pretended to fight dragons or gangs of villains. Her mother had tried to instill lady-like virtues in her like painting, embroidery, and the love of music. But she had much preferred to ride her horse recklessly across the meadows, jumping streams, and climbing trees to sitting in the parlor talking of mundane things like the weather or the latest parties.

She had been envious of her brother and his friends. They had the freedom she would never be allowed to have, and it irritated her that there was a separate set of rules for men. Her brother along with Leicester and Lord Rockhurst were frequently mentioned in the scandal sheets, their exploits applauded by others in the ton. They were referred to as the devils, depraved, or her favorite nickname for the trio, the Debauched Dukes of Mayfair and yet their reputations had not taken a hit because of their indiscretions. She and Persephone had eagerly read about their scandalous pursuits imagining what it would be like to have that kind of freedom.

Now that she was near twenty years of age, it was expected of her to marry and bear her husband heirs to further his lineage. Persephone had once shared her love of freedom but now seemed more than happy being Hawk's wife. At one time Catherine would have been thrilled to be the Duchess of Leicester, now she was not so certain that was the path meant for her.

"You are in deep thought, my dear."

She looked over her left shoulder to see Michael walking slowly toward her. She couldn't help but smile. "How did you get away from Lady Beasley and her mother?"

He sat on the bench beside her. "It wasn't easy I assure you. It would have been less difficult had you not abandoned me."

She couldn't help but laugh. "I had already been warned off."

His eyes narrowed. "Warned off?"

"Yes, Lady Beasley reminded me that while I might have had my cap set for you at one time there would be other men and I need not worry. She said she had heard that Ian McDonough was showing a particular interest in me and hoped I would be gracious about losing you." She looked over at him and said teasingly. "She will make a lovely duchess, Michael."

He reached for her hand. "Lady Beasley will never be the Duchess of Leicester. I already have a lady in mind to fill that position." He raised her hand to his lips.

For a moment Catherine was moved by his touch, the feel of his lips on her skin, and images of the night before briefly moved through her mind. Then she remembered herself and quickly got to her feet. "I should go. It wouldn't be good to be seen together so far from the others."

He held her hand firmly when she started to walk away. "No, we need to talk, Catherine."

"There is nothing to say, your grace. I assure you that I expect nothing."

He got to his feet quickly readying himself for another argument when an unwelcomed voice called out to them.

"Ah, there you are, mo leannan. My cousin said you had walked in this direction," Ian McDonough said as he walked forward glancing first at Catherine then at Michael.

"Ian, I didn't know you would be coming to Lady Weatherby's party. I'm sorry to say that you missed the poetry," she said cheerily as he came closer.

Michael possessively moved closer to her side. "That endearment is much too familiar and highly inaccurate. I suggest you return to the party; Lady Catherine and I need a few moments."

Ian narrowed his eyes at Leicester before turning to look at Catherine. "I have been instructed to escort you back to the duchess. She is ready to depart, but if you need a few minutes I can wait for you."

"I would not like to keep Persephone waiting."

Michael moved to intercept her when a shrill voice called out to him. "Your grace, we have been looking everywhere for you." Lady Annette along with her mother joined them.

Catherine could feel the fury radiating from Michael as Lady Beasley and her daughter pushed between them. "We really must be leaving. Lady Beasley and Lady Annette, I hope you have a wonderful afternoon. Leicester, it was good to see you again." She curtsied briefly before linking arms with Ian.

Michael shrugged off Lady Annette's arm and caught up with her taking her other arm to stop her from walking away. "We are not finished with this conversation, Catherine."

"I'm afraid we have to be, Michael." She gave him a sad smile as he dropped his hand and allowed her to walk away.

As Catherine was escorted away to where Persephone was waiting, Ian leaned closer and said softly, "I didn't realize you had such a cruel streak, lass."

Catherine turned to look at him and chuckled softly, "A cruel streak? I'm not sure I know what you mean."

"Leaving poor Leicester with Lady Annette and her mother was cruel. What if he doesn't manage to escape?"

Catherine glanced quickly over her shoulder to where Michael still stood watching her. "Leicester is more than proficient at avoiding the marriage trap. He has honed his skills for years. Lady Annette and her mother are no match for him I assure you."

As he watched the woman he wanted and desired above all others, walk away on the arm of another man he found himself in a most foul temper.

"Poor girl, always chasing after a man, making a spectacle of herself. I'm sure she causes her brother no end of worry," Lady Annette said as she came to stand beside him.

He rounded on Lady Annette and just the look of unmitigated fury on his face made her take a step back and reach for her mother. "I would suggest you mind your tongue, my lady."

Lady Annette caught a sob, but her mother was quick to soothe her. "Pardon her, your grace, she has forgotten what close friends you are with Lady Catherine's brother. Of course, being the gentlemen that you are renowned to be it is only right that you defend his sister."

Michael looked at the older lady as if she had lost her mind then turned on his heels and moved away quickly. Every time he got a few minutes with Catherine so he could discuss their future someone shows up to get in the way. At this rate he would have to kidnap her and take her to Gretna Green.

He left the party without thanking his hostess and made his way across Mayfair to Bond Street. If Rockhurst wasn't at Jackson's he would most certainly be at White's or Boodles. Right now, he wasn't sure if he needed to hit someone or just get foxed beyond thinking. Catherine was driving him crazy. Perhaps making her his wife was not the wisest decision, but the thought of any other man possessing her was more than he could stand. No, Lady Catherine Gray would be his duchess one way or another.

Chapter Nine

"Is there nothing else to do other than go to the shops on Bond Street? At least in Brighton there were other pursuits such as racing or picnics by the sea. London is dreadfully dull during the day," Catherine said as she pouted while having breakfast with Hawk and Persephone.

Her brother glanced at her over the paper he was reading. "I thought you would be happy to spend more of my money on dresses and ballgowns."

Catherine spread some jam on her biscuit. "Don't get me wrong. I do love all the finery and fripperies ladies require. There just has to be something more ladies can do beyond all the garden parties and balls. Perhaps we can go to Vauxhall one evening or the theater."

Persephone smiled. "We will endeavor to do just that, my dear. I'm sorry I have been under the weather lately. Since I am feeling much better, we should do something more exciting. The ball here at Hawksford House is in four days and after it is over, I promise we can focus on more exciting endeavors."

Hawk reached over and took his wife's hand bringing it to his lips for a soft kiss. "I'm glad you are feeling better, my love. I was beginning to worry."

Persephone looked lovingly at her husband, and Catherine immediately felt as if she were intruding. "Will you be joining me today, Persephone?"

Her sister-in-law blushed and looked away from her husband. "No, I think I will stay here this afternoon with Hawk. As I said, I am feeling much better and since the ball will be keeping me so busy in the upcoming days, I think I will spend a good portion of the morning with him."

Catherine smiled knowing it was time for her to take her leave. "I will take Sarah with me. Do you mind if I take the carriage?"

"Take whichever carriage you like, Catherine."

She stood from her chair leaving the dining room closing the doors behind her to give them the privacy they desired. She hoped one day she would find a love like that, one worthy of a fairy tale.

Duke of Leicester's London Residence

"Excuse me, your grace, but a Lord Thomas Harrison is here to see you. Shall I show him in?"

Michael rose from where he sat behind his large mahogany desk in his study. "Yes, show him in, Finn."

Thomas Harrison walked in, hat in hand, looking very grim. "I'm sorry for the disruption, your grace, but a matter of utmost importance has come to my attention."

Michael held out his hand indicating for his friend to take a seat as he walked to a decanter of whiskey on the other side of the room.

"It's no disruption, Thomas and from the look on your face it must not be good news either."

Thomas reached forward and took the glass of brandy Michael offered him. "I'm afraid the smuggling operation that is taking place near your estate in Kent has taken a more serious turn. The men I had sent there to keep an eye on things and gather information have been called away to other business, but that is not what concerns me. There is also reason for me to believe the man involved might also be gathering information and sharing it with the French."

Michael leaned back against the edge of the desk. "My God! So, not only is there a gang of smugglers near my estate, but now they could also be spies for the French. This definitely makes it more dangerous. You must tell me everything you know, Harrison. Is it only the one man you suspect and if not, how many are involved?"

Thomas took another sip of his brandy. "Yes, things have gotten more dangerous. A smuggler is ruthless, but if the man is also a spy it tells me he is also intelligent and that can be a deadly combination. From the information that my men gathered before they were reassigned, I am fairly certain there is one man who is the leader so to speak. He most certainly has others working for him, it would be virtually impossible to smuggle a significant amount of merchandise by ones 'self. I of course will be sending more agents to take their place as soon as they are available and hopefully, we can gather enough information to determine exactly who is running the operation and what they are doing exactly. Unfortunately, as the war with Napoleon continues to heat up, our agents are dealing with other pressing matters."

Michael nodded his head in understanding. "Is there anything I can do to help? You must know how this concerns me, especially since all this treachery is occurring on one of my estates."

Thomas inhaled deeply and sat his glass on the table beside him. "I was hoping you would offer. Until we get a new agent firmly implanted, I was wondering if you had any servants that you trusted impeccably to maybe keep their ears open and report any goings on to you."

Michael pondered this suggestion thoughtfully. "I'm not sure I am willing to put any of my servants at risk for something I could do myself."

"I am not asking them to actively investigate the smugglers or engage them in anyway. But if they go into the village and hear of anything that might be important to this mission to report it back to you. You certainly would want to make sure they had limited knowledge of what we are discussing. The less they know the better." He stood and began pacing the room. "It would just be a temporary situation. Our agents will handle the matter as soon as they arrive."

"But you cannot guarantee when that will be."

Thomas stopped and shook his head in resignation. "No, I can't."

Michael moved back around to his desk and retook his seat. "The majority of the servants at Harts Manor are older and would not be of much use. However, I do have a man who oversees my stables there. He was a soldier a few years ago until injured. He has been at Harts Manor for the past six years and his father oversees the stables at Leicester Hall. I'm fairly certain he could be trusted to keep his ears open to anything suspicious."

"Will you send word to him?"

Michael shook his head. "No, I will leave first thing in the morning and speak with him in person. I am not exactly certain how to explain everything to him without giving too much information, but I feel as if a note would not be wise especially if it fell into the wrong hands."

Harrison looked relieved. "Your country owes you a debt of gratitude, your grace. Will it take you long to reach Harts Manor?"

"If I travel by horseback, I should be able to make it to Harts Manor and back to London in three possibly four days' time."

Thomas stood and offered his hand. "Thank you, Leicester. I assure you I will mention your help to my superiors when all this unpleasantness is behind us." Michael shook his hand and walked with him to the door.

"Take care, your grace."

Michael nodded as Finn showed Thomas to the front door. He walked back into his study closing the door behind him. This was inconvenient. He would be away from London for at least four days. That's four days he would not be able to keep an eye on Catherine and the damn Scotsman. He poured himself another glass of brandy. It was just four days, how much trouble could she get into in four days? He drained the remaining liquid in his glass and began writing a note. Perhaps he could have Rockhurst keep McDonough busy and away from Catherine until his return. And once he returned from Kent, he and Catherine would have some things to settle between them.

Bond Street, Madame Lafforgue's Dress shop

"This gown was definitely made just for you, my lady. There isn't another lady in London who could make this confection more delectable," the young seamstress said as she continued pinning the hem of the beautiful cream-colored silk gown.

"The lace is lovely and I love the cut of the neckline. Madame Lafforgue always amazes me with her creations," Catherine said as she admired the beadwork on the bodice. This dress was off the shoulder and showed a generous portion of her bosom. "I hope the color does not make me look washed out."

"No, my lady. With your dark brown hair and brown eyes, the dress compliments your complexion."

"What do you think, Sarah?" she asked her lady's maid that was sitting across the room reading a book.

She looked up pressing her glasses up from her nose and yawned. "It is very revealing, my lady."

Catherine rolled her eyes. "You are such a prude, Sarah. Why don't you go ahead and return to the carriage and let them know I will be ready to leave shortly. You can take a nap while you wait."

"Are you sure?" her lady's maid asked closing her book.

Catherine laughed. "Please, if you keep yawning, I will fall asleep on my feet." Her lady's maid hesitated but finally made her way out to the carriage.

The seamstress pinched in the sides of the gown. "I will need to take in the sides a little bit as well, my lady. I can pin them up quickly but I must hurry. I have a second job that I need to get to before it gets too late."

Catherine watched the younger girl work. "You work here all day and then have to go somewhere else to work all night?"

The girl shook her head with a few pins still in her mouth. "It doesn't take me all night and I make more working for Mr. Kingston than I do for Madame Lafforgue."

Catherine eyed her questioningly. "Oh, it's nothing like that, my lady. Mr. Kingston is the owner of a gaming hell, and I go there every evening before the gentlemen arrive and clean his personal rooms and serve his meals. He always makes sure I am gone before the nobs arrive and the gaming begins."

This had Catherine intrigued. "A gaming hell? I've never seen the inside of one before."

The girl looked at her startled. "I should think not, my lady."

Catherine took her hand and asked excitedly. "What is it like? What's the name of it?"

The girl looked nervous. "I'm not sure I should be speaking to you about something so inappropriate. Madame Lafforgue would be angry with me."

"I will not say anything to her, trust me."

The girl looked around to make sure no one was within hearing of her conversation with Catherine. "It's called, *The Devil's Lair*, it's the most famous hell in all of London. Mr. Kingston runs a clean establishment too, and it is frequented by the richest men in the ton everyone from titled nobility to the prince himself."

"I've heard of it. My brother and his friends used to frequent there before he married of course. What is it like inside?"

The seamstress smiled. "I'm always gone before the gentlemen arrive. I've only seen the empty rooms, but they are lavishly decorated with paintings on the walls, velvet curtains, and rich thick carpets on the floors. And so much gilt on the walls and ceilings that when the light hits it just right you have to squint your eyes. It is what I imagine a palace would look like."

Catherine clasped her hands in front of her. "I would love to see it." Then an idea occurred to her. "Do you think I might go with you this evening just to take a peek inside?"

The girl dropped the pincushion she was holding. "Oh no, my lady. Mr. Kingston would sack me for sure, and if your family found out I would be run out of London with no way to take care of myself. It just can't be done."

Catherine sighed heavily and sulked. "I just wanted to see the inside. You know as well as I do, that I will never get the chance to do so. I could go with you and take a quick peek then be back here before my maid ever noticed I was missing. I will go tell her that I have decided to try on a few more dresses and go over some patterns. She will be content to stay in the carriage and read her book."

The seamstress did not look convinced. "I'm sorry, but Mr. Kingston will not like it. I simply can't take such a chance."

Catherine took a minute to think of how she could get around this predicament. "How often do you see Mr. Kingston when you clean his rooms?"

The seamstress shrugged her shoulders. "Very seldom and only in passing. He has his valet pay me once a week, but now that you mention it, he is never around while I am cleaning."

Catherine's face brightened. "See, it is possible. I promise I will not get you into any trouble. If found out, I will tell your employer that I forced you to bring me there."

The seamstress frowned. "I have to leave here in a few minutes to get there on time. If you are going with me, you should go inform your coachman and maid to wait for you."

Catherine nearly jumped for joy. "Thank you, . . ." she hesitated, "What is your name by the way?"

"Serena, my lady."

"Help me get out of this dress without impaling me with pins, and I will quickly get dressed so we can leave."

"Yes, my lady. Are you sure you will not reconsider?"

"Absolutely not. I was just saying this morning how bored I was with the season. This is exactly the kind of distraction I needed." She reached out and squeezed the girls' hands. "Thank you, Serena."

Catherine quickly dressed and then went out to the carriage to tell her coachman and Sarah that she would be much longer than intended. When she returned Serena was waiting for her.

"It is not a very far walk from here. It is on the other end of Bond Street. It may be a gaming hell, but Mr. Kingston runs a fine establishment."

Catherine grinned at the younger girl. "I have read a lot about it and have probably passed by a few times and just not realized what it was."

The girl nodded as they left out the back door. "It doesn't have a sign out front, but it seems everyone knows where it is. We will be safe going there as long as you get back to your carriage before dark. It wouldn't be safe to stay till the nobs arrived, my lady. Someone might recognize you."

"Yes, you are correct. I will not linger. I certainly wouldn't want anyone to discover me there. Thank you again for taking me, Serena. I owe you a debt of gratitude."

The girl turned to look at her. "I just don't want you to get me sacked, my lady."

Catherine remained quiet as they continued their journey until they came to a white stone building. The front portico had two large columns on either side and a dark blue door with brass lanterns beside it. Two large windows were on either side of the portico, but heavy burgundy curtains hid the inside of the building from view.

"This is it, my lady."

Catherine continued to admire the building's facade. "It certainly doesn't look like any place with the name of *The Devil's Lair*."

"The name is deceiving, is it not, my lady? I'm not allowed to enter through the front. We should go around back. Mr. Kingston's man will let us inside."

Catherine followed the girl through the alley around to the back of the building. "What will you tell them if they ask about me?"

Serena stopped and looked nervous as if that thought had not crossed her mind. "I will say you are a relative visiting from out of town. Pull your cloak closer so they can't see the finery of your dress and keep your head bowed. And for heaven's sake, don't speak. Your cultured voice will give us away for certain."

Catherine pulled her cloak tight around her and pulled the hood over her head. She hoped this worked. For the first time, she was now thinking that perhaps this was not the wisest idea. Hopefully she could take a quick look around and be back at the dress shop before Sarah finished her next chapter.

Serena knocked on the door and an overly large brawny man dressed in fine livery answered. "Good day to ye. I'm here to clean Mr. Kingston's rooms." She made to move around him, but he put out a hand as large as a dinner plate and stopped her.

He nodded toward Catherine and she shivered a little hoping he didn't question the girl. "Who is this with ye?"

"She is a distant cousin visiting from out of town. She is coming to help me clean today," Serena said wringing her hands in her apron.

At first Catherine was sure this would never work and she was about to be turned away, but suddenly the mountain of a man stepped aside and allowed them entrance. "Try to keep your voices down. Master Kingston is busy going over his accounts and will not like being disturbed."

Serena nodded her understanding and moved past the man into a large lavishly decorated sitting room. Catherine lowered her hood and looked around in amazement of the finery before her. "My goodness, I feel as if I am in a palace." She ran her hand over the furniture. Furniture that was fit to be in any of the grand homes and estates across England. Paintings hung along the walls and while she wasn't extremely knowledgeable about art, she did recognize that the pieces were expensive and she was certain they were originals.

"This is Mr. Kingston's sitting room. His bedroom is just through that door," Serena said as she began dusting.

Catherine walked towards the door. "Is it just as lovely as this room?"

"It is the largest bed I have ever seen, my lady. I swear four or five people could sleep in it comfortably," she said then blushed brightly.

"Do you think he is in it?"

Serena looked up from her work. "No, he stays out of these rooms while I clean. Besides, his man said he was going over his accounts and that would be in his office upstairs."

Catherine moved toward the door and turned the brass doorknob. The room was larger than the ducal bedchambers at Hawksford and Serena was correct about the bed. It was the largest she had ever seen either. Why a person could get lost moving around on it.

She moved about the room admiring the masculine furnishings then gasp as she looked up to see a large fresco painted on the ceiling and blushed at the sight of naked ladies being chased by ardent admirers, their appendages in plain view for all to see.

"My goodness," she whispered under her breath as she studied the provocative artwork.

"It is rather interesting, isn't it?"

Catherine spun around at the sound of a deep masculine voice. There standing at the doorway was an elegantly clad gentleman with the brawny footman behind him holding Serena by the arm.

"It was painted by an Italian artist. He had a vision and I allowed him the perfect canvas with which to create it," he said as he stepped further into the room.

Catherine took a step backward. "I apologize for the intrusion."

"Ahh, a cultured lady of quality." He turned to look at his man. "You were right of course, Jackson. She is a lady." He moved closer to her, and Catherine held her ground. "Did you come to steal from me, my lady or was it something more nefarious that brings you here?"

Catherine raised her chin a notch higher. "I did not come here to steal, Mr. Kingston, and I insist that your man release my friend immediately."

He nodded to the man who let go of Serena's arm. "I have done as you commanded, my lady. Now, I believe it is time that you tell me who you are and why you are here."

Catherine wondered if she should use her real name, but perhaps at a time like this it would be beneficial to be linked with her brother. "I am Lady Catherine Gray. I came here today on an impulsive whim which Serena should receive no punishment for at all."

The man before her lifted an eyebrow. "Would you be Ethan Gray, the Duke of Hawksford's sister?"

She nodded hoping her admission was a good thing. "I would and if it pleases you, Mr. Kingston, I should be leaving."

"Not quite yet, my lady." He held his hand out indicating a table with two chairs around it. "Please join me. I promise you will come to no mistreatment. Your brother is an old acquaintance of mine. I would never see any harm befall you."

Catherine eyed him warily. "I think I should be going."

He inclined his head slightly. "Please, indulge me."

Catherine wasn't certain, but she had an idea. "I will join you for tea if you promise that Serena will suffer no repercussions for bringing me here."

"Ah, a lady that knows how to bargain. I accept your terms, my dear," he offered her his arm, and Catherine placed her hand on it as he led her out of the bedroom and back into the sitting room. "If it will make you feel safer and protect your virtue, Serena may stay as well and act as a chaperone."

Catherine nodded toward the young girl. "Thank you, that will be acceptable."

"Excellent! Jackson, see that refreshments are brought in for us." The burly footman bowed at the waist and left the room to do as he was instructed.

He held a chair out for her. "Please have a seat, my lady."

Catherine did so and watched as he walked over to a bottle of wine and poured two glasses. "It's French and extremely hard to come by these days." He handed the glass to Catherine. "Now, why is the sister of a duke sneaking around *The Devil's Lair?*"

Catherine sipped her wine. "It is a rather silly excuse I am afraid." He sat in a chair across from her, his smile a bit disarming. "I came here because I wanted to see the inside of a gaming hell."

He eyed her over the rim of his glass. "Pardon, did I hear you correctly?"

Catherine rolled her eyes and hoped he was not about to mock her naivety. "Yes, I know it was ill-advised, but I wanted to see what the inside looked like. I have read about gaming hells in the scandal sheets and had never dreamed I would ever be inside the most famous hell in London. Serena was doing the final fitting of my ballgown, and she began mentioning her second job. I asked her about it and when I found out that she worked here, I begged her to allow me to accompany her, for when would I ever get the opportunity again?"

He leaned forward to better study her reaction. "You do realize how dangerous this plan of yours was, don't you?"

She sat down her glass. "Yes, I am beginning to realize how stupid I was for suggesting it. Unfortunately, I am known for making rash unwise decisions. Please accept my apologies and I will leave you to your business." When she started to rise from her seat, his deep baritone voice stopped her.

"It would be a shame to come all this way and not see everything you came to see, my lady. I would be happy to show you around the establishment, if you so choose. But of course, if you would like to leave, as would be the wisest decision, I will see that you are escorted back to wherever you need to go."

Catherine had stood from her seat but hesitated at his offer. "Can I have your word that no harm will come to me if I stay for a few more minutes?"

"My dear, your brother would have my head if I let any harm come to you. He is a friend of mine, and I will protect you as if you were my own sister." He gave her a wink. "You do know I named the place after your brother and his friends."

Catherine smiled. "I had heard that, yes. I would love a quick tour of your establishment, Mr. Kingston. But I can't stay very long and Serena must accompany us."

"As you wish. I will show you the gaming rooms while we await our refreshment."

Duke of Leicester's Residence

"So, you will not share with me the details of why you have to leave town so abruptly but want me to entertain McDonough to keep him away from the lovely Lady Catherine?" Rockhurst said as he reclined leisurely in the large, overstuffed chair in Michael's study.

Michael sat across from him at his desk casually rolling his finger around his glass. "It's important, Charles."

His friend gave him a wicked grin. "I would rather keep the company of the lady while you are gone. I have more skills when dealing with the opposite sex."

Michael smirked at Charles' comment. "That's why I am asking you to keep an eye on the Scotsman and not Catherine. Just keep him occupied so his every waking minute is not spent with her."

Rockhurst nodded. "As you wish, I suppose I could take him under my wing and show him the more delightful and appealing side of London."

Michael smiled but his reply held no humor. "I don't care if you take him to White's or the docks just so long as he stays away from Catherine."

Just as the words left his mouth, the door to his study burst open, and Persephone ran inside with his butler hot on her heels. Both men jumped from their seats and Michael quickly moved from behind his desk to meet her taking both of her hands in his. Her face was pale and her hands trembling.

"My God, Persephone, what's happened?" He nodded to his butler to leave them.

Persephone swallowed and took a deep breath. "You have to help me."

Both he and Charles were concerned now. "Of course, what is it?"

"It's Catherine."

Michael felt a cold chill go through him and his chest tightened with anxiety. "What about Catherine? Is she hurt?"

Persephone shook her head. "No, it's nothing that dreadful. It's all my fault. I should have known this morning when she started talking about wanting to find something to do other than shop for dresses that she was getting bored."

Michael gripped her shoulders and shook her a little. "Persephone! Where is Catherine?"

He saw her eyes mist with tears. "She is at *The Devil's Lair*."

"Bloody hell!" Rockhurst hissed between his teeth.

Persephone closed her eyes and willed herself to calm down. "She had her lady's maid wait for her in the carriage while she was inside the modiste shop. After waiting for more than an hour, Sarah became nervous and went inside, but Catherine wasn't there. She interrogated the seamstresses and discovered that she had gone with one of the girls to the gaming hell. Apparently, the girl works there cleaning the owner's personal rooms, and Catherine convinced her to allow her to accompany her there."

Michael released her and turned away not wanting Persephone to see the anger on his face. "Damn it."

Persephone reached out and grabbed his arm. "Please, I have to get her back before Hawk returns and finds out what she has done. He was livid with the incident in Brighton, and if he finds out about this, I'm not sure if I can talk him out of a most severe consequence."

Michael spun around quickly letting his anger boil to the surface. "She needs a severe consequence!" He saw Persephone take a step back and clasp her hands in front of her chest. "Where is Hawk?" he asked in a calmer voice.

"He went to the House of Lords this afternoon."

"Charles, escort Persephone back to Hawksford House."

Persephone shook her head. "That will not be necessary, my coach is waiting for me." She looked up at him with pleading eyes. "Are you going to find her?"

He reached out and squeezed her hand. "Yes, I will find her and endeavor to get her back home before Hawk returns. But when I get my hands on her she may wish Hawk had found her first and sent her to the convent he has been threatening her with for years."

Persephone nodded in understanding. "I know she is wrong and should have never gone to such a place. I really don't know what could have possessed her to do such a thing. Do you think she has met with some harm in a place like that?"

"I'm sure she is fine, Persephone. You should not worry. The only harm Catherine is going to receive will be from me when I find her. Now go home, have some tea, and try not to worry. Let me handle this."

She gave him a weak smile. "I know you care for her, Michael that's why I came to you."

Rockhurst took her hand and placed it on his arm. "Allow me to escort you back to your carriage, Persephone."

Michael was angry. How could she put her life and reputation in jeopardy like this? The only thing that was keeping him from going mad with worry was that he knew the owner of *The Devil's Lair* very well, and he was not a man to take advantage of a lady. He walked out into the hallway. "Have my carriage brought around immediately, Finn."

"Yes, your grace."

He walked over and grabbed his greatcoat from a footman.

"Would you like me to go with you?" Rockhurst asked as he approached.

Michael shook his head. "No, it is better if I do this alone."

His friend gave him a grave look. "Don't do anything you will regret, Michael. Catherine is young and foolish but also a stubborn headstrong woman."

"She is the one that is going to have regrets."

Chapter Ten

"I must say, Mr. Kingston, your establishment is nothing like I expected it to be," Catherine said as he escorted from the gaming rooms back to his private sitting room.

He smiled at her. "It is much livelier in the evenings when all the patrons arrive. Of course, this is not the place for a lady like yourself."

He held a chair out for her and she took a seat at the small table where his servants had placed some tea and food. "I know but at least my curiosity is appeased." She placed her hands in her lap and gave him a mischievous grin. "Now, tell me how well you know my brother?"

He sat across from her. "I know him quite well, as do I know his friends the Duke of Leicester and Lord Rockhurst. They used to frequent here often. Their antics and reputations were the inspiration for the name, The Devil's Lair."

She took a sip of tea. "Yes, you mentioned that earlier. While I stayed with my Aunt Louisa, I often read about my brother's conduct in the scandal sheets. That was where I first heard of a gaming hell."

He watched her curiously. "You are unique, my lady. I have never met anyone quite like you from the glittering bells of London. Most ladies would swoon if they ever crossed my threshold and here we are having tea as if we were sitting in the parlor of St James Palace. You do know that if you were discovered here, your reputation would be ruined."

She looked down, her long dark lashes framing her brown eyes. "I do know that, and I should probably be heading back to my carriage before my maid discovers my absence. I have already been gone much longer than I intended." She gave him a bright smile. "Thank you so much for your hospitality."

He reached for her hand to bring it to his lips. "It has been a pleasure, my lady. And while I fear we may never meet again, please know that you will be welcome back anytime you wish." He gave her a wink. "Even though I do not advise it."

She smiled and pulled her hand from his but was startled when the door flung open. Mr. Kingston pulled a pistol from beneath his coat with a speed that surprised her and pushed her behind him. She sucked in her breath when she saw who stood in the doorway.

"Michael?!" she said wondering how he knew she was here.

He walked further into the room eyeing the man before him. "Kingston."

Mr. Kingston put away his pistol. "Leicester, it is good to see you, it's been a while." He turned to look back at her. "I suppose you are here to collect, Lady Gray."

"I am." Michael was barely able to keep his voice controlled.

Kingston stood to the side and Catherine had the impulse to follow and hide behind him. Michael looked mad enough to kill. He was practically shaking with rage. "How did you know I was here?"

He glared at her then turned back to Kingston. "I assume she is unharmed."

She saw Kingston straighten his shoulders and his features harden. "Do you really think you had to ask me that?"

Michael relaxed a bit. "I apologize. Of course, you know that no one must ever find out she has been here."

"Of course. Does her brother know where she has been?"

Michael shook his head. "He didn't when I left to come find her, but I am not certain if he is aware now."

"If he is aware, you will make certain he knows she suffered no harm while here."

"I will."

Mr. Kingston turned and bowed to her. "Lady Gray, it was a pleasure."

She nervously looked from him to Michael and back to him again. "Thank you again for indulging my fascination. But I can find my way home."

"I am afraid his grace has other ideas, my lady." He turned and walked away leaving her alone with Michael.

She casually picked up her cloak and wrapped it around her shoulders. "How did you know I was here?"

He stalked toward her and she took a step backward. The anger on his face actually frightened her. She knew he would never hurt her physically, but the intensity she saw in his eyes made her wary. He reached out and grabbed her arm without saying a word and began hauling her toward the door.

She pulled back against him. "I can find my own way home, your grace."

He stopped and turned to glare at her again, but never said a word. She thought it best to avoid a fight with him when he was in this mood. She allowed him to lead her out the back door to his waiting carriage in the alley. He opened the door and practically shoved her inside.

"Really! There is no need for this, Michael. I suppose my maid has already returned to Hawksford, otherwise, you would not have been sent to collect me."

She looked across the carriage at him. He sat there stoically staring at her with those dark heated eyes. His arms were crossed over his chest.

Catherine rolled her eyes and sighed heavily. "I suppose we are to continue in silence for the remainder of the trip to Hawksford House." He still never answered. "Fine, I admit it was wrong of me to sneak away from the dress shop. I will not do it again."

Her words were met with silence. "Alright, if you want silence, you shall have it." She crossed her arms across her chest to match his posture, but she couldn't stare into his face. If she was honest with herself, she would admit that seeing him like this made her more than a little anxious.

They continued to Hawksford House neither one saying a word. When the carriage pulled up to the front of the house a footman came forward and opened the door. Michael climbed out first then reached in and roughly pulled her from the carriage. She jerked her arm from his grasp and marched up the stairs through the front door. She didn't look back but could feel his presence behind her.

When the front door closed, he said harshly, "Go to your room, Catherine."

She rounded on him. "You do not have the right to tell me what to do! You didn't say a word the entire way here and now you wish to bark orders at me as if I were a child." She saw Persephone come out of the front sitting room watching the confrontation between them.

Michael took two steps forward so that their noses were almost touching. "Go. To. Your. Room."

She leaned forward defiantly. "No."

Before she had time to react, he reached out and seized her, throwing her over his shoulder like a sack of flour, and began marching up the stairs. She shrieked and slapped at his back as he bounced her roughly. His response was to sharply smack her bottom.

She sucked in her breath. "How dare you!"

He continued on to her room with Persephone following close behind them. Once he opened the door, he walked over and dropped her on the bed none too gently. "You have no right to treat me this way!" she shouted at him.

"If you continue to behave like this, I will do more than that!"

Catherine moved from the bed to stand before him, her anger matching his own. "I do not want you meddling in my affairs. What I do and how I behave is no concern of yours," her voice raising with her anger.

Persephone moved forward and said sharply. "Be quiet, Catherine."

Catherine was shocked into silence by her friend's remark.

"I sent Michael to find you after Sarah returned home in a panic because you had disappeared from the modiste's shop. I was frantic with worry and thank God Hawk has not returned from the House of Lords yet. Do you realize the foolishness of your actions?"

Catherine moved toward her. "Oh Persephone, I am sorry. I honestly didn't mean to cause anyone this much trouble. When the seamstress told me she worked there, I just saw an opportunity to see what it was like. It was an adventure. You remember how we used to sit around and wonder what it was like in those places. When I saw the chance to see for myself, I couldn't resist. My only regret is that you were not with me. I never meant to stay gone as long as I did. I suppose time got away from me."

Persephone's tone softened. "Catherine, I know you never meant to cause trouble, but this incident could have ruined you. What if someone finds out? I'm worried about you, dear."

Catherine sighed and tried her best to look contrite. "I promise not to do anything so foolish again."

Michael looked at her wondering if she was truly sincere or if it was just a ploy to keep Persephone from being angry with her. "I have to leave London for a few days. You are to stay in this house until I return."

Catherine glared at him as if she had not heard him correctly. "You can't keep me prisoner here, your grace. This is not your domain, nor am I under your control."

He moved closer. "You will stay in this house until I return, or I will inform Hawk of everything that has happened here today."

"You wouldn't dare," Catherine hissed before looking back to Persephone. "Are you conspiring with him too?"

"I think it is best, Catherine. When Michael returns, he can escort you and I will feel better knowing he is keeping you safe."

"It's all been decided then, hasn't it? I guess I have no choice, but make no mistake, your grace, I will not forget this or forgive you." Her eyes narrowed with animosity.

Persephone looked worried. "Michael has your best interest in mind, Catherine."

Catherine eyed her friend warily. "Why is he the one to escort me around London? What of Ian? Is he no longer considered capable of keeping a lady safe?" She saw Persephone look down nervously. She looked back to Michael who while he looked a bit calmer was still angry and tense. "Is there something you two are keeping from me?"

Persephone sighed. "I'm going back downstairs. Hawk will be home soon and I don't want him to know anything about this." She turned and left the room closing the door behind her.

Catherine walked over to the fireplace and removed her cloak. "Are you going to avoid my questions too? I feel as if there is something you aren't telling me." When he made no move to explain she said, "You should be leaving as well. I don't need a jailor."

"I will be in Kent for a few days, but I should be back for Persephone's ball." He walked towards her. He was still angry, but he would not leave her like this.

"Do make haste then." She turned her back to him hoping he would just leave.

He reached out and took her arm and spun her around to face him. When she tried to pull away, he tugged her closer. "I know you are furious right now, I can feel it in the tension of your body, but your anger doesn't compare to how horrified I felt when I heard you had disappeared and then to find out you were in a gaming hell. It was a fear I never want to experience again. Anything could have happened to you."

She was not in the mood for a lecture. "As you can see, nothing happened to me. I was perfectly safe."

He turned her chin so he could see her face. "Do you know the horrors that could befall a lady alone in London? I do, and the thought of someone hurting you ate away at me. When I opened that door and saw you sipping tea with Kingston, I felt a rush of relief that was replaced with a fury I have scarcely felt before. So many people love you and care for you, Catherine and you disregard their feelings." He saw regret in her eyes. "Persephone came to me in tears. She was so afraid for your safety as well as what would happen to you if Hawk found out."

He saw her eyes begin to mist. "I would never hurt, Persephone. She has been my best friend for years."

"But now she is married to your brother, and your actions are causing her to keep secrets from him. How do you think she is feeling knowing he would be angry at her for helping you and sheltering you against any consequences?"

She looked down not wanting him to see the tears gathering in her eyes. She had not thought of the consequences to her or anyone else. "I said I was sorry, just leave me alone." she said weakly.

He raised her chin again and kissed the tear away as it slid down her cheek then kissed her other cheek. "I can't do that." He softly kissed her lips. "When I return from Kent, I will speak to Hawk and we will be married."

Catherine felt the blood leaving her face and her knees grew weak. "Married? What on earth are you talking about?"

He tightened his hold on her waist. "I'm tired of the games, Catherine. You were meant to be mine. I will have you for my wife. The jealousy I feel every time I see you dancing in the arms of another man or knowing that Ian McDonough would love nothing better than to take you away from me is unacceptable. And when Persephone burst into my home in tears because you had gone missing, I knew I would wait no longer."

She narrowed her eyes. "So, this is the decision that has been made as if I have no say in the matter."

He leaned closer so that his lips were inches from hers. "When I found you at the Devil's Lair, I knew then the only way I could make certain you were safe was to have you in my home and in my bed. I will not wait any longer, Catherine."

Her eyes narrowed. "What makes you think I would be willing to accept your proposal because you know as well as I that Hawk would never force me into any marriage?"

Catherine tried to pull away, but one strong arm wrapped around her waist anchoring her to him while his other hand caught in her hair to hold her head steady as his mouth descended upon hers. At first, she wanted to fight against him, but inevitably she felt herself melt into him and her arms wrapped around his neck holding him to her. He tasted sweet, and she couldn't get enough of him. His lips left her mouth to move down her neck. She sighed as his hand left her hair to slide down her back and then around to cup her breast through her dress. How did he manage to do this to her? He could make her melt into a puddle with just a few kisses. She felt her hands clutching the lapels of his coat and pulling him closer to her. He quickly pulled the bodice of her dress down to expose her breasts and dipped his head down to suckle her. He lifted her off the floor and she moaned loudly as he moved to give his attention to her other breast. Her head fell backward wanting more but was suddenly set back onto her feet. He quickly moved her bodice back into place to cover her breasts. When he pulled away, she was ashamed that his touch could so easily weaken her resolve. There was something about him that she couldn't deny.

"That is how I know you will not refuse my offer," he smirked arrogantly.

She narrowed her eyes. "You are the most conceited, arrogant, odious man I have ever known. Get out of my room!"

"That may very well be, my dear, but you will be my wife regardless."

She clenched her hands into fists wanting very much to punch him right in the nose. "Don't bet on it, your grace. I would fight you all the way to the bedchamber."

He gave her a wicked grin. "Sounds invigorating. I look forward to it, darling. Now, will you agree to remain at Hawksford till my return?"

She stepped away from him. "I will make you no promises, your grace." She saw him raise an eyebrow and for some reason, she wasn't confident that he wouldn't carry through with his threat to tell Hawk about her visit to the Devil's Lair. "I will, however, remain at Hawksford for Persephone's sake."

He smiled and nodded not surprised in the least by her defiance. Her spirit and fire were just one of the many things he found so attractive and he looked forward to seeing if that fire would carry over into their lovemaking. The thought of having her spitting fire in his bed was almost more than he could stand. The sooner he got this business finished for Thomas Harrison and could return to London the sooner he could find out.

The next morning, Catherine slept later than usual. It had been one of those nights where she tossed and turned. Michael's highhanded superior attitude had infuriated her. She still could not get over the fact that he demanded she remain a prisoner in her brother's house until he returned. If it had not been for Persephone and the stricken look in her eyes, she would have told Michael Shelbourne, Duke of Leicester to go to the devil, but Persephone meant the world to her and the fact that her friend was upset with her did not sit well. She had skipped breakfast but staying in her room all day was not appealing. So, she finished dressing and made her way down the stairs hoping to find Persephone so she could make things right between them. When she was near the bottom of the stairs she saw Dr. Buchanan, Hawk's personal physician, being helped into his coat by one of the footmen. She rushed forward anxiously wanting to know what brought the family's physician to the house this morning.

"Dr. Buchanan, how good it is to see you. What brings you out today?"

The older man gave her a smile. "Lady Catherine, my how you have grown. I don't believe I have seen you since that night you fell out of the tree when you were trying to sneak out your bedroom window during one of your mother's parties. I believe you were twelve years old at the time."

Catherine laughed. "Yes, I remember. You said I was very lucky not to have broken my neck. Once my father found out I would survive, it wasn't my neck that ached afterward I assure you." She smiled at the memory. "I'm sure you have other reasons for being here."

He patted her shoulder much as he had done when she was a little girl. "I was summoned by the duchess. I'm sure she will be down directly and you may speak with her." He put his hat on his head and quickly made his way out the huge front doors.

Catherine bit her bottom lip and began pacing the floor in front of the stairs. Persephone had been feeling unwell for the past few weeks but had assured her that it was nothing serious. She must have taken a turn for the worse for her to summon the physician. And where was Hawk? He should be here with her right now. She continued pacing until she saw Persephone coming down the stairs. When her friend reached the bottom step, the anxiety she had been feeling tumbled out.

"Oh, Persephone why didn't you tell me you were unwell? I would have stayed with you. Please tell me it is nothing serious."

Her friend chuckled. "My goodness, stop making such a fuss. The servants are beginning to stare, and you will have all sorts of rumors flying about the house before I can even share my news." She took her hand. "Come with me to the drawing room where we can have a bit of privacy."

Catherine followed her friend and closed the doors behind them. When they were alone, she nervously clasped her hands in front of her. "I'm so sorry, Persephone. You have been ill and I have been behaving like a spoiled child. I feel terrible causing you so much worry yesterday all while you are so very sick." She pinched the bridge of her nose with her two fingers. "I am such a horrible friend."

"Catherine please. Let me explain."

Persephone sat on the settee and patted the seat behind her. "I'm not sick, Catherine. I'm going to have a baby."

Catherine felt her mouth fall open. "A baby?" she practically squeaked. "Oh Persephone! I'm so happy for you. I'm going to be an aunt." She reached over and gave her friend a tight hug. "That's why you have been so tired?"

"Yes, and why I have been sick every day for the past two weeks."

"Does Hawk know?"

Persephone shook her head. "No, he doesn't know yet and I would appreciate it if you did not say anything to anyone yet. It is still very early and I want to make certain everything is alright before others find out." She smiled sweetly as she lightly touched her belly. "Of course, I will tell Hawk today when he comes home."

Catherine laughed. "He will be so happy and terribly over-protective. I wouldn't be surprised if he didn't lock you away till the baby comes."

Persephone laughed. "Yes, I will have to convince him that will not be necessary." She reached over and touched Catherine's hand. "How are you? After yesterday I wasn't sure."

Catherine sighed heavily. "I feel rather foolish for causing so much trouble." She gave her friend a cheeky grin. "You should have seen it though, Persephone. Never in my wildest dreams would I have ever thought to be inside *The Devil's Lair*. It was everything I thought it would be. Deep red velvet curtains, plush carpets, gilt on everything, and the gaming rooms had huge crystal chandeliers." She grinned. "And there was a terribly risqué mural on the ceiling depicting unclothed ladies being chased around by their naked admirers. It was so wonderfully indecent. I wish you could see it."

Persephone shook her head slightly. "My goodness! I wasn't talking about that, Catherine. How are things with Michael?"

Catherine's smile slipped from her face as she heaved a heavy sigh. "Do we have to talk about him?"

Persephone raised an eyebrow. "I think we need to."

Catherine got up from the settee and walked to the window. "I don't know what to think, Persephone. When I left for Brighton that day, I swore to myself that I would forget all about him, and I tried. When I came back to London, I knew it would be difficult to see him again. Do you know what he had the audacity to tell me?"

"No."

Catherine turned back around to face her. "He told me, that when he returns to London, we will be married. Can you believe him? As if I would accept a marriage proposal from him."

Persephone laughed. "That's wonderful."

"Wonderful? It's terrible. I have no intentions of marrying him."

"You don't?"

Catherine moved back to the settee. "Absolutely not."

"Have you fallen in love with someone else, Ian McDonough perhaps?"

Catherine shook her head. "I hate to tell you this, but Ian has no intentions of seeking a bride this season. He was only paying addresses to me in order to irritate and aggravate Michael. He derives some pleasure from that I suppose. Ian is very easy to talk to and we do enjoy each other's company, but I am not interested in being his wife. I'm afraid Scotland would not suit me." She looked over to see the shocked look on her friend's face. "I'm sorry we deceived you."

"I guess it's for the best." Persephone smiled brightly. "I'm not certain I would want you living so far away. If you were in Scotland, we would scarcely see each other. But what about Michael? When he returns, he will expect an answer."

"An answer? He was so sure of himself; he didn't even ask me. He simply announced his dictate and assumed I would be pleased. Honestly, I don't know what to do. It is everything I have always wanted, but I'm almost afraid to believe it's real. He wounded me so badly last year, and I don't want to ever feel that way again. I'm not sure my heart can trust him not to hurt me."

"I'm sure he would never hurt you again, Catherine. He seems quite smitten." They heard the front door open and Hawk's voice asking about Persephone's whereabouts. "If you don't mind, dear I would like some time with Hawk alone."

Catherine nodded. "I understand." She leaned over and gave her friend a kiss on the cheek. "I'm so happy for you. I know that when you first married you were nervous about being a duchess and afraid you wouldn't be able to fill the role adequately, but I want you to know there has never been a better Duchess of Hawksford." She began walking towards the doors just as they swung open and Hawk came inside. He gave her a quick smile but moved toward his wife and kissed her on the cheek. Catherine shut the doors behind her leaving them the privacy they needed. She was so happy for her brother and Persephone. Could she one day find that same kind of love and happiness? And if so, would it be as the Duchess of Leicester?

Chapter Eleven

Hawksford House was all abuzz with activity and preparations for the night's ball. Servants were busy moving around here and there carrying out their assignments. Persephone was diligently overseeing the arrangements of flowers and candles in the ballroom. Catherine had been helping her most of the morning and trying to keep Hawk from hovering about her. Ever since Persephone told him that she was with child, he had been impossible. He had instructed the servants that she was not to lift or carry anything and suggested that they cancel the ball altogether. Persephone wouldn't hear of it and suggested that he leave and go to his club so she could get everything ready. It was the first time she would be hosting a ball as the Duchess of Hawksford, and she was feeling the pressure.

Catherine came to stand beside her sister-in-law as she arranged some flowers on a side table. "Everything looks beautiful, Persephone, but you look dead on your feet. Why don't you go upstairs and rest? I can help with everything that is left to do down here."

Persephone breathed deeply. "Do you think everything will go well, Catherine? You know how nervous I am about tonight. If this ball isn't a success everyone will think I am a failure and that Hawk should have married someone more suited to be his duchess."

Catherine laughed. "Goodness Persephone, you worry too much. Hawk doesn't care what anyone thinks. You are his duchess, and if someone doesn't like it, they can go to the devil."

Persephone gave her a small smile. "I just want everything to be perfect."

"And it will be. Now go upstairs and get some rest. You will need to look rested if you are going to be the perfect hostess tonight. Most everything is ready and if something comes up unexpected, I can handle it."

"You are right of course." She gave her friend a hug. "I am tired and it will be a long night. Has your ballgown been delivered yet?"

"No, but I expect it anytime now." She turned her friend toward the ballroom doors. "Go and rest."

Persephone nodded and headed out of the ballroom. Catherine shook her head and turned back to where the servants were making some final adjustments. The chandeliers had all been polished as well as the mirrors and silver. Flowers seemed to be everywhere and tonight once the candles were all lit, the ballroom would look magical. She remembered hiding from her governess as a young girl so she could sneak down the stairs and peek over the railings at all the excitement when her mother would host a ball. At that time all the gentlemen wore the white powdered wigs and she remembered thinking how silly they all looked. Thank heavens that style had come and gone except for the footmen and servants.

"I hope you plan on saving me a dance, mo leannan."

Catherine spun around quickly and her smile widened as she saw Ian McDonough walking toward her. "Ian, I haven't seen you in a few days. I was beginning to think that you had left London and returned to Scotland."

He laughed as he reached her before taking both of her hands and raising each one to his lips. "I have been spending a great deal of time with Lord Rockhurst. He has introduced me to several of his clubs and even Gentlemen Jackson's."

Catherine arched her eyebrows. "At Jackson's? Did you beat him?"

He grimaced as he rubbed his jaw. "While I happen to consider myself good at fighting; did quite a bit of it in the Highlands, I'm ashamed to admit that Rockhurst seems to have mastered the art."

Catherine chuckled. "Don't feel bad. He has never been beaten. Even Jackson himself refuses to spar with him. Hawk and Michael have an ongoing bet as to which of them will finally be victorious against him." She moved to the side as another large arrangement of flowers was brought into the ballroom. "So, you have been with Rockhurst the past few days?"

He grinned and pulled her off to the side. "I think Rockhurst was assigned with keeping me away from you while Leicester was out of town."

Catherine stopped to stare at him. "What makes you say that?"

He shrugged his shoulders. "Last night at Whites, Rockhurst was deep in his cups and said as much."

Catherine crossed her arms over her chest. "Did he happen to say where Michael disappeared to the past few days?"

"If he knows, he isn't saying. It's all very secretive."

Catherine frowned as her thoughts disturbed her. "Yes, it is."

He put a finger under her chin and lifted her face to his. "Is it true that you went to *The Devil's Lair?*"

Catherine felt herself blush and turned away. "Unfortunately, yes. It was an impulsive decision I regret." Wide-eyed she turned back to him quickly. "Oh, please don't tell me it is all over London."

"No, Rockhurst mentioned it to me, and you know I would never repeat it. But I doubt very much that you regret it, lass."

She sighed in relief. "Thank goodness. Hawk doesn't know. He would be furious with me."

"And Leicester?"

She rolled her eyes. "He was beyond furious, and Persephone was so upset with me. I think that is what bothers me most of all. I can't stand for her to think bad of me." She looked up at him. "But it was magnificent inside. I have never seen so much gilt and Mr. Kingston was very much the gentleman. He gave me a personal tour of the gaming rooms. I would not admit this to anyone but you, I wish it would be possible to go back when it was full of people. I think it would be so much fun."

He laughed. "While I am certain you would be most successful at gaming, I'm sure your family would not approve. If your brother and my cousin would not see me drawn and quartered, I would escort you there at night and allow you to play some of the games simply because I know it would get under Leicester's skin."

Catherine giggled then turned serious. "I can't believe Michael had Rockhurst keep you away from me. He just keeps meddling in my life."

"Men tend to do that with the women they love."

She looked at him as if he lost his mind. "Love has nothing to do with it."

He chuckled again causing her to look at him strangely. "Is my cousin about?"

"Persephone is upstairs resting."

He nodded then bowed at the waist. "I will take my leave then but will see you later tonight at the ball, mo leannan."

Catherine watched as he turned to leave. She found it hard to believe that Michael had told Rockhurst to keep Ian away from her. The past few days she had been thinking that perhaps she was being childish. She had been in love with Michael for so long, and now she could have everything she had always wanted, but then he goes and does something like that to make her blood boil. And then there was the secrecy surrounding his whereabouts and why he had disappeared the past few days. Even Hawk had no idea as to where he had gone. It definitely was a mystery she had every intention of solving. He had told her that he would be back in time for the ball tonight, and she had a few questions for him when she saw him.

The Duke and Duchess of Hawksford's Ball

The ball could not have been a bigger success unless the King and Queen themselves attended. Of course, with the king out of touch with reality, that was unlikely to happen, but regardless, the ton would be talking about Persephone's achievement for weeks. As expected, the ballroom glittered with candlelight and everything was enchanting. While the skeptics of the ton may have doubted Persephone's abilities, tonight she had proved to everyone that she was worthy of her new position. Of course, her brother lovingly stood by his wife's side as they greeted their guests and it was obvious to everyone in attendance that the duke was thoroughly in love with his duchess.

Catherine's dance card had filled up quickly and as the current young lord continued to twirl her around the room, she took the opportunity to scan the crowd once again for Michael. He had yet to arrive, and she was beginning to think that perhaps he would not arrive back in London in time to attend.

"You look very lovely tonight, my lady."

The young man's voice brought her back to the present. She smiled but for the life of her, she could not remember his name. "Thank you, my lord."

He beamed and pulled her closer. "I will be the envy of my friends you know."

She wrinkled her brow at the strange comment. "Your friends?"

"Yes, we all wanted to dance with you, but I'm the only one that had the nerve to ask."

She tried not to roll her eyes at the ridiculous statement. He was young and obviously didn't have much experience with ladies. She gave him a sweet smile but did not respond to the comment. When the dance was over, he led her to the side of the ballroom where some of the other young ladies were standing.

She looked around the room again but still no sign of Michael.

"Stop fretting, I'm sure he will be here shortly," Lord Rockhurst said as he came to stand beside her.

She looked up at him cocking her head to the side slightly. "Where is your charge? Did McDonough somehow manage to escape? Or do you have him locked away somewhere?"

He did have the good grace to look ashamed. "He told you?"

She raised an eyebrow. "Yes, he told me. Now you tell me where Michael has been for the past three days."

He held up his hands in mock surrender. "I honestly have no idea. He didn't tell me anything. All I know is that he is back in London."

She looked at him in surprise. "He is back?"

"Yes, he got back early this morning." He looked over her shoulder. "Can I escort you somewhere? I seem to have drawn the attention of a group of unmarried ladies, one of which I recognize as being on my father's approved list of brides."

Catherine waved him off. "Please make your escape while you can, I will be fine." She opened her dance card. "Lord Penworthy is my next dance partner, and I'm sure he will be here soon to collect me."

He nodded toward her then stealthily moved away and disappeared into the crowd. She waited off to the side rising up on her tiptoes to see if she could see Michael over the heads of the crowd.

"I couldn't help but overhear your conversation, Lady Catherine."

Catherine turned sharply at the feminine voice coming from behind her to see a lady wearing heavy makeup and a strong perfume. Her gown was bright red silk and very revealing and Catherine wondered why she had never seen before.

The lady must have recognized the look of confusion on her face. "I don't believe we have met before, Lady Catherine. I'm Lady Jane Rutherford, I have known Lord Rockhurst, Leicester, and your brother for many years."

Catherine eyed the lady warily. "I don't remember my brother mentioning you, Lady Rutherford."

The lady smiled, but it wasn't a happy smile. "I don't imagine he would, dear."

At her words Catherine felt uneasy. "Yes, well it was good to meet you, if you will excuse me."

"I thought you might be interested to know where Leicester has been the past few days."

This made Catherine stop dead in her tracks. "How do you know where he has been?"

The lady flipped open her fan. "It's not a secret that he has housed a mistress outside of town. Doesn't it make sense that he has been spending time with her?"

Catherine narrowed his eyes. "If his best friend does not know his whereabouts, then why would you?"

Lady Rutherford laughed. "You are so young, dear. You have yet to realize that men often do not tell the truth. Why would they share such inappropriate matters with such a young unmarried lady? I'm sure they are all aware of his whereabouts."

Catherine got a sickening feeling in the pit of her stomach. "Why are you telling me this?"

The other lady snapped her fan closed. "It has been rumored that Leicester has lost his head over you, Lady Catherine. And when I heard your conversation with Lord Rockhurst I felt it my duty to share what I know." She backed a few steps away. "If you don't believe me, ask Rockhurst or your brother. It is common knowledge that he has a mistress kept at one of his country estates."

Catherine felt as if she would be sick. How could she have allowed herself to be played for a fool again? She stumbled as she moved away. She had to find Rockhurst, her brother would still be greeting his guests and would not like her asking questions about mistresses. Her mind blocked out the noise of the music and the people laughing and talking as she blindly moved through the crowd towards the gaming room where she saw Rockhurst standing to the side watching a game of hazard being played. When he saw her face, he moved toward her.

"I need to ask you something."

He walked with her away from everyone. "What is it?"

"Does Michael have a mistress that he keeps on one of his other estates?"

He frowned. "Who has told you such nonsense?"

"So, it isn't true?"

He hesitated. "You shouldn't be talking about such things, Catherine. Gentlemen do not discuss such things as mistresses with ladies. Hawk will have my hide if he finds out."

She took a deep breath. "Can you tell me if what I asked is the truth?"

He shifted his feet. "Catherine, what Michael may have done in the past should have no bearing on the present. He does not have a mistress at this time."

"But he has in the past kept a mistress on one of his estates?"

"You are asking questions about things ladies should not be concerned with."

She grew angry. "Well, I am concerned! Do you know where he has been? Is it possible that he could have been with a mistress?"

Rockhurst shook his head in denial. "It is not my place to tell you where he has been even if I did know. But I can tell you confidently that he has not been with another woman. Now tell me who has put such nonsense in your head."

"Lady Jane Rutherford, she said she is good friends with you."

Rockhurst narrowed his eyes. "Lady Rutherford is not a friend of mine nor does she have any intimate knowledge of Leicester. She is trying to start trouble and seems to be succeeding. She is not someone you should be associated with and I am surprised she is even allowed in this house. She must have arrived as the guest of someone because I know Hawk would never have sent her an invitation."

Catherine shook her head and looked around the room. She felt a bit dizzy. "I need to get some air."

Rockhurst grabbed her arm. "I'll go with you."

"No," she replied rather sharply. "I need to be alone for a few minutes to think. There are so many unanswered questions."

"Catherine, I'm sure Michael has his reasons for not informing us of his actions over the past few days. As his friend I trust him and you should as well."

She looked over her shoulder at him. "Should I?"

She turned to make her way back to the ballroom. She glanced over to see Persephone dancing a waltz with Hawk. Most everyone had turned their attention to the dance floor and she moved slowly toward the terrace doors. The ballroom was warm and the fresh air would do her some good. She would be careful not to stay out too long. Thankfully the terrace was empty and she made her way down the stairs to the gardens. There was a rose arbor with a bench where she could sit away from everyone and have some time to herself. The air was cool and refreshing.

Once she reached the arbor she sat on the bench and looked out over the gardens. This had always been her mother's favorite spot to think and just be alone. She could still hear the music from the ballroom floating on the breeze. While it was nice to be alone for even a few minutes, she knew it was not wise to stay outside for long.

Just as she was thinking of going back inside to join the others, a voice came out of the darkness.

"What could have possibly driven you outside away from the ball, Catherine?"

She turned her head to see Michael moving through the darkness toward her. "So, it's true, you have returned to town. How was your trip?"

He moved to stand before her. "Uneventful. What are you doing out here alone?"

She looked away from him. "I came outside to get some fresh air."

"Allow me to escort you back inside." He reached for her hand, but she pulled it away.

She stood and moved a step away from him. He looked devilishly handsome in his evening attire. Perfectly fitted trousers with a coat cut just for him. His white shirt and intricately folded cravat shown bright in the darkness. His lean muscular body and chiseled facial features had made women swoon since he came into his majority. He was sin embodied and if she didn't stay out of arm's length, he could easily make her forget her irritation with him.

She took a deep breath. "I'm curious, where have you really been the past few days."

He took a step toward her, and she could see his eyes narrow marginally in the darkness. "I told you I had some business on one of my estates."

"What sort of business?"

He crossed his arms over his chest. "Business that is my own. I'm not used to having my motives questioned. Tell me what this is all about, Catherine."

She raised her chin a notch higher. "Were you with your mistress?"

He dropped his arms and looked at her curiously. "My mistress?" His lips turned up on the corners. "Are you jealous, Catherine?"

"Jealous?! Don't be ridiculous."

"If you are not jealous, then why may I ask are you questioning me about a mistress?" She put her hands on her hips and he chuckled at the outraged expression on her face. "I do not have a mistress, darling. Now whatever made you ask such a question."

"There was a lady at the ball who told me you were visiting your mistress at your estate outside of town."

His smile faded. "What lady told you such lies?"

"Lady Jane Rutherford."

He moved closer to her. "Jane Rutherford is neither a lady by title nor character. What the devil is she doing here and why was she filling your head with such nonsense?"

She shrugged her shoulders. "I don't know. I have never met her before. Rockhurst said she was not a friend of yours as she claimed."

He placed his hands on her upper arms. "No, she is not nor ever will be a friend of mine." He leaned over and pressed a kiss to her cheek. "You look beautiful tonight, Catherine."

She felt her skin shiver at his touch, but she still wanted answers. "It is quite a mystery as to your whereabouts. Won't you tell me?"

He removed his hands from her arms. "It is nothing that concerns you, Catherine."

With that she spun on her heels and headed back toward the house. She knew he would catch up to her, but she was determined to know why he was being so secretive about the last few days. She did believe him about not having a mistress, but there was something going on and she was determined to discover what it was.

He grabbed her arm and spun her around. "Catherine, I will tell you in time when it is safe to do so. You must trust me."

"I must trust you? Like you trust me I suppose."

He didn't release her but asked, "What the hell are you talking about now, Catherine?"

She narrowed her eyes. "Do you deny having Lord Rockhurst keep Ian occupied while you were out of town to keep him away from me?"

He pulled her into his chest. "How do you know that?"

"Hah! So, you don't deny it then?"

"No, I don't deny it." He leaned down and captured her mouth in a searing kiss. "And I will not apologize for it."

"Let me go," she said breathlessly as she pushed against his chest.

He leaned closer. "Do you really think I would leave you alone in London with that Scotsman sniffing around your skirts? And it has nothing to do with trusting you, love but everything to do with protecting what is mine."

"I do not belong to you, your grace," she hissed through clenched teeth.

He leaned over and pressed soft kisses down her neck. "You have always belonged to me, Catherine. You were made for me and you know it."

He released her, and she took one step backward away from him. "If that is the case then why will you not share with me the reason you left London? And don't say it was to protect me or my reputation because you were not concerned with protecting my reputation when you were undressing me in my room a few nights ago."

They both heard the shocked gasps and slowly turned to see a small group had gathered and heard their exchange including her brother, Persephone, as well as two of the ton's dowagers, one of which was a notorious gossip. Catherine's mouth fell open as Michael moved to stand beside her.

Catherine didn't know what to say. The anger on her brother's face made her want to shrink away. The two older ladies were whispering behind their fans and Persephone was still in wide-eyed shock. It was her brother who eventually took charge of the situation as was his way.

He turned to the two older ladies. "I trust ladies that you will not mention the engagement of my sister to the Duke of Leicester. We were to announce it tonight, but Leicester has been out of town making arrangements and we were not sure he would be back in time. He also wanted his mother to be present and she was unable to make it to London."

Lady Longwood put a hand over her heart. "Your grace, we are delighted to hear such wonderful news and of course we would never think of breathing a word of the engagement to anyone."

Hawk smiled and bowed politely. "You have my thanks. Persephone, why don't you escort the ladies back to the ball? There will be another time to show them the gardens."

Persephone managed to shake herself back to reality. "Of course. Ladies have you met my cousin, Ian McDonough, Duke of Sunbridge? He is visiting from Scotland for the season. He arrived a few minutes ago and I know he would love to meet two lovely ladies such as yourselves."

Catherine heard the older ladies giggle. "I have heard he is quite magnificent in his kilt. Will he be wearing it tonight, I wonder?"

Once the ladies were out of sight Hawk turned back to Catherine and Michael, his face red with anger. Catherine moved to step toward him, but Michael grabbed her arm to keep her beside him.

"Hawk, I, . . ."

Her brother held up his hand. "You will go to your room, Catherine and remain there until I send for you."

Michael stepped forward. "Do not berate her for this, Hawk. It was my doing, not hers and I was planning on speaking with you later tonight and offering for her hand."

"She is my damn sister, Michael!"

"Yes, and she is going to be my wife," Michael said taking a menacing step forward.

Her brother clenched his hands into fists. "I will expect you in my office tomorrow with an agreement drawn up by your solicitors."

Catherine watched the exchange between the two of them. "Do you really think all of this is necessary?"

Her brother rounded on her. "Necessary! You just announced to two of the biggest gossips in the ton that you allowed him to undress you in your bedchamber. Even if you didn't want to marry him, no one would have you now. You are damaged goods."

"That is enough!" Michael said as he moved to stand between her and her brother. "She may be your sister, but she will be my duchess and I will not let anyone, including you, speak to her in that tone."

Catherine hated this. Michael and Hawk had been friends ever since she could remember. They were inseparable growing up and now they were at each other's throats because of her. "I'm sure this can all be resolved tomorrow when we have cooler heads. If we stay outside much longer, we will attract more attention and none of us want that."

She watched as her brother took a deep breath. "I will join Persephone before other guests begin to grow suspicious. Catherine, go to your room. I will send for you later. Michael, I'm sure you have arrangements to make."

Michael nodded and Hawk turned to walk back toward the house. Once they were alone, he turned to her. "I will escort you back inside and then take my leave." He squeezed her hand. "Hawk will not stay angry, Catherine."

She blindly allowed him to lead her back toward the house, but she didn't know what to say. When she was a little girl, she dreamed about the day she would marry, but she never imagined things happening like this. Michael and Hawk discussed it as if she were not even there. Did she truly have no say in the matter?

"You don't have to walk me inside."

Michael turned her to face him. "Catherine, I'm sorry things happened this way, but I am not sorry you will be my wife."

She turned to face him but only nodded as she really didn't know what to say. She pasted a smile on her face and moved along the side of the ballroom hoping to make it upstairs to her chambers without drawing too much attention.

Ian came up to her with a concerned look on his face. "I just spoke with Persephone. Are you alright?" She looked up at him and felt her knees buckle. His arm wrapped around her waist holding her upright as he ushered her quickly through the doors and out of the ballroom.

Michael watched from the terrace doors. When he saw Catherine begin to sway and McDonough wrap his arms around her to hold her upright, he made a move forward but was stopped when Rockhurst reached out and grabbed his arm. "Steady, there has been enough trouble tonight. No need in making a bigger scene than has already occurred."

"You already heard?"

Rockhurst nodded. "I saw Hawk when he came back inside and from the look on his face, I put two and two together."

Michael continued to watch Catherine being led away. "Let me go, McDonough needs to take his hands off of her."

"One thing I found out about McDonough while I was entrusted with keeping watch over him while you were away, is that he is not interested in Catherine any more than she is interested in him."

Michael turned to stare at him. "Then why is he always hovering about her?"

Rockhurst chuckled. "They are merely friends, and I suppose he felt you deserved it after the wild goose chase you sent him on the second day he was in town."

Michael still did not like the Scot and this newfound revelation did not make him feel any better about the man's arms being wrapped around his soon-to-be wife's waist. "I have things that need to be taken care of tonight."

"By all means, I will leave with you. I'm more than a little interested in what happened out in the gardens, and I would rather hear it firsthand than through the gossip mill."

Michael was not in the mood for companionship, but he was interested in what Rockhurst had just revealed about the Scottish duke. This was a messy business, but the sooner it was taken care of and all of it behind them the better. Besides the thought of having Catherine all to himself was more than a little appealing.

Chapter Twelve

When Catherine ran into Ian at the ball everything that had happened seemed to crash down on her at once, and she felt her knees give way. Thankfully he was there to catch her and hold her upright without anyone noticing her distress. He helped her to the bottom of the stairs and after assuring him that she would be alright, she made her way up to her room. The ball continued downstairs for hours, and she did not expect Hawk to send for her until the morning. She had gotten undressed with her maid's help and slipped into her nightgown. She paced the room, tried to read, and sat by the fire, but she was much too nervous to sleep.

She was not the first lady to be married by special license. Hawk and Persephone were married quickly by special license, although it was for Persephone's protection, not because she had announced to the world that a man had been in her bedchamber. Her Aunt Louisa had always warned her about her mouth and her willingness to say things without thinking. Now she would pay for her discretion. Perhaps if she could convince Hawk there was another way to avoid scandal this could all be avoided. She kept going over everything in her mind, but she could not come up with anything.

Two years ago, she would have thought all her dreams were coming true, but she was older and wiser now. Michael had secrets and she wasn't sure if she would ever know what those secrets were. She wasn't so naïve that she didn't know that most wives didn't know everything about their husbands. Wives were supposed to be silent and not ask questions. Their sole purpose was to beget heirs, but she didn't want to live like that. It was not in her nature to be submissive and meek. How could she be married to a man that kept her in the dark about his whereabouts? She also knew about his wild past, and while she was aware that most men kept mistresses before they married, even her brother, she was not the type of woman that could share her husband with another. If he decided to keep other women, she wasn't sure she could deal with that.

It was nearly dawn when she decided to give up trying to sleep and get dressed. She was certain that Hawk would send for her before breakfast and she wanted to be ready. Her stomach seemed to be tied in knots and she felt a little nauseous. She sat in the window seat and watched as the sun came up and the streets of Mayfair came alive with activity. When there was a soft knock at the door, she nearly jumped out of her skin. She turned as Persephone peeked her head into her room.

"Did you sleep at all last night?"

Catherine stood up and moved toward her. "No, I'm afraid I have made a mess I can't get out of this time. Is Hawk still very angry with me?"

Persephone moved to place a loose curl behind her ear. "I'm afraid so, dear. I tried to talk with him, but he wouldn't listen to anything I had to say either. He sent me to come get you. He expects you in ten minutes."

Catherine frowned. "Why do I feel as if I am being summoned to the tower?"

Her friend took her hand. "I will go with you."

Catherine nodded. "Thank you. I need a friend with me right now."

Persephone gave her a sad smile. "You know Ian came to me last night and was so upset over what happened. He wanted me to tell you that if Leicester's proposal does not meet with your approval, he is more than willing to make an offer himself."

Catherine wiped away an errant tear as it slid down her cheek. "That is very kind of him, but I could never ask him to suffer himself on the sacrificial altar of matrimony for my benefit. Although, I suppose I should consider all my options."

Persephone nodded and looked at her with such sympathy that it made Catherine want to cry again.

"Let's not keep Hawk waiting. I would hate to end up with my head on the block for missing my deadline."

Catherine followed Persephone down the stairs to her brother's study. The house was still quiet as it was so early. She took a deep breath readying herself for the set down she was about to receive. Her hands shook slightly as she made her way to the settee.

Hawk was standing in front of his desk with his arms crossed and a fierce look on his face. Persephone came to sit beside her and reached over to hold her hand.

"I suppose you realize the shame you have brought upon this family."

Catherine lowered her eyes. "I am sorry, Hawk. I should have been more careful with my words, but I know there has to be some way to remedy the situation."

Her brother's voice was harsh. "Careful with your words?! It sounds to me like you should have been more careful with your virtue!"

Catherine sucked in her breath but held her tongue. She hated being forced to endure a lecture for something that would not be a problem had she been born male.

"Luckily the two ladies that overheard you will think twice about spreading rumors since my influence holds much weight within the ton. But there will be consequences as you very well know."

"If there is no chance for scandal, why do there have to be consequences?"

"Don't start, Catherine! Today, Leicester will be here with a contract from his solicitors and he will ask for your hand. You will accept."

With as much bravery as she could muster, she raised her chin a notch. "I will not!"

Both she and Persephone jumped as her brother slammed his fist on his desk knocking several items to the floor. "Damn it, Catherine! You will accept! I will have no arguments from you on this matter. I will not have my sister looked upon as soiled goods. If you will not marry Leicester no one of any significance will have you. Do you want to be relegated to the wife of a poor country squire or worse forced to sell yourself as a member of the demi monde?"

Catherine felt her eyes filling with tears. Her brother had never spoken to her so harshly before and that he thought so little of her hurt her heart. She stood slowly with Persephone at her side and tried to keep her voice from shaking. "I will have you know my virtue, as you like to refer to it, is intact. Is that all?"

"I will send for you when Leicester arrives."

She nodded her head and let go of Persephone's hand as she left the study to return to her room. She would not allow herself to cry until she was safe behind closed doors and alone.

Once the doors closed, Hawk put a hand up to his forehead trying to ward off the headache that was sure to come. "Oh darling, I will be glad when this whole mess is over. Hopefully we will have a son and will not have this worry ever again," he said as he walked toward his wife and reached out to her.

Persephone rounded on him. "Don't you dare touch me!"

He was taken aback by his normally sweet wife's tone. "What?"

She poked a finger into his chest. "I will remind you that your sister did not do anything that we did not do ourselves before you married me! Is that what you think of me? Am I some piece of soiled goods only fit to lie beneath any man to have his babies or would I have been a better whore?"

His face paled at her words, but she was not finished. "You have behaved like a beast last night and this morning and treated your own sister with contempt. I didn't say too much last night hoping you would calm down, but the way you talked to Catherine just now was beyond anything I could have imagined."

"I did what anyone responsible for a young girl would do in this situation! She should count herself lucky. At least she is in love with Michael, she could have been saddled with someone she detested. And I will not be chastised by you." He realized his mistake the moment the words left his mouth. "Persephone, darling, I don't want to fight with you."

She held up her hand. "Until you start acting like the man I married, I will not be speaking to you. I will have my things moved to the duchess's rooms. And just so you are aware, Ian McDonough has also offered for Catherine as well, and I believe she will consider his offer. So perhaps she will not be relegated to be just any man's whore as you suggested." She turned quickly on her heels slamming the door on her way out.

Michael had his solicitors working through the night on a marriage settlement. Once he met with Hawk and talked to Catherine today, he would apply for a special license. He was not worried about being granted one, money could buy almost anything even in the church. His relationship with Hawk was a concern though. They had been friends for what seemed like forever. He hoped this incident did not cause a rift between them that could not be breached.

As he approached the front door at Hawksford House, the door was opened for him and he was shown into the study where he found Hawk waiting.

"Good morning, Hawk."

His friend was sitting in a chair staring into the fire. "I have already spoken with Catherine. I feel confident she will accept your suit."

"I never meant for this to happen. I spoke the truth last night when I said I was already going to ask for her hand. The fact that we were heard during an unpleasant conversation does not change that fact."

Hawk turned and motioned for him to sit in the chair opposite his. "You were in my house, Michael. In my sister's bedroom."

"Yes, I probably should have thought that through a bit more. Rockhurst told me congratulations are in order. How is Persephone feeling?"

His friend reached over and refilled his glass of brandy. "She isn't talking to me right now. If she truly intends to carry out her threat, she is moving out of my bedchamber as we speak."

"What the devil? What happened to cause her to do that?"

Hawk gave him a frown. "This whole mess is what happened. I summoned Catherine this morning and said some things I probably should not have said or at least Persephone thinks I should not have said them."

Michael leaned forward. "What exactly did you say?"

"It's no use repeating it. I was furious and made some rash accusations regarding Catherine's character as well as her morals."

Michael stood up quickly ready to challenge his long-time friend. "I told you not to take this out on her. If you want someone to blame, here I am!"

Hawk didn't move from his seat but causally looked up at this friend's angry face. "It does you credit to defend my sister so staunchly."

"She is to be my duchess, what kind of a man would I be if I allowed her to be treated thus?"

Hawk nodded. "Sit and have a drink. I have something else to tell you that I'm sure will not improve your mood."

Michael refused the drink that was offered and took a seat.

"You are not the only gentleman that has offered for Catherine."

Michael narrowed his eyes as uneasiness began to set in. "What are you talking about? Who else has offered for her?"

"Last night when Catherine returned to the ball, McDonough saw her distressed and escorted her."

"If you are about to tell me that the bastard took her to her room, I will have to kill him."

Hawk closed his eyes and shook his head in irritation. "Please don't interrupt, you know how I hate that. He escorted her to the foot of the stairs, apparently, she almost swooned. Can you believe that? Catherine has never been the type of woman to swoon. I don't understand it."

"Damn it, Hawk?"

Hawk grinned just a bit obviously deriving some pleasure from his torture. "When he found out what happened in the garden and saw how upset Catherine was, he approached Persephone and told her that he intended to offer for her as well. He seems to think that perhaps she isn't as thrilled to be your duchess as you believe."

"Bloody hell! Does Catherine know about this?"

His friend chuckled. "Oh yes, Persephone told her and from my understanding she is considering his offer."

Michael stood from his seat. "That's not going to happen. Where is Catherine?"

"She is in her room."

Michael turned and headed for the door, but Hawk's voice stopped him. "I think there has been enough of you sneaking into my sister's bedchamber. I will have her brought down to you and give you a few minutes of privacy." Before he left the room, he turned to Michael and said with a grin, "If it makes you feel any better, I am hoping she chooses you."

Michael did not find the remark amusing and began pacing the room while he waited on Catherine to make an appearance. Waiting had never been something he enjoyed. Impatience was not new to him. Being a duke, he was seldom kept waiting for anything, but Catherine seemed to be in no hurry to meet with him. Could she truly be considering McDonough's proposal? Rockhurst had led him to believe the man was not a threat, but it seems as if his friend had been wrong on that account. He was just about to give up and go retrieve her himself when the door to the study quietly opened, and Catherine walked slowly towards him. She looked beautiful as usual, but the skin under her eyes was dark and her eyes which were normally bright seemed dull and lifeless. Her face was pale and she looked so very tired. He wanted to lift her into his arms and reassure her that everything was going to be alright, to take away all her worries.

She gave him a small, tired smile. "I'm sorry to keep you waiting, Michael."

He moved toward her and reached out to touch her cheek. "Did you sleep at all last night, darling?"

She shook her head. "No, none at all." She moved to stand before the fire. "I have made a mess of everything, haven't I?"

He couldn't stand this defeated demeanor. He was used to her spitting fire and flaunting the rules, this was not his Catherine. "You haven't done anything of the sort, Catherine."

She turned around to face him. "Yes, I have. Hawk and Persephone are fighting because of me. She moved out of his bedchamber this morning. I have brought shame upon the family name and scandal if word of our indiscretion gets out."

"It won't, Catherine. I have made certain of that."

She tilted her head slightly to the side wondering what he meant by that statement but was too tired to ask questions. "Ian has offered to sacrifice his freedom and marry me."

He moved quickly and wrapped his arms around her. "Hawk told me as much, but he can't have you, Catherine. You will be my wife, my duchess."

She sighed as she pushed against his chest trying to put some distance between them. "Why do you want me now, Michael? I chased after you relentlessly when I was younger and you showed no interest at all, and we all know what was said last year. What has changed to make you desire to have me as your wife now?"

"Catherine, you were so young. You must remember I am ten years older than you." He cupped her face in his hands. "I was not the man I am now. When you returned to London, defiant, so full of life, and more beautiful than ever, I couldn't resist. But the day you refused for me to escort you to the British Museum, and then I saw you marching up those steps alone, that was when I knew you were destined to be mine." He stepped closer and bent down to kiss her. "And if you think for one bloody minute that I will allow another man to have you, you are sorely mistaken." He kissed her again, this time with more passion as he pulled her closer into his body.

Catherine melted into him reveling in the feel of his strong arms about her and the way his lips took possession of hers. While she still had her doubts, especially about the secrets he was keeping from everyone, including her, but of this she was certain. She wanted Michael as much now as she did last year when he broke her heart.

He pulled his lips away from hers just a fraction of an inch. "What of McDonough?"

She opened her eyes. "Ian?"

"Yes, damn it?"

"I sent him a note this morning thanking him for his offer but knowing he did not want to marry me any more than I did him, I refused him. He is a good friend, but we never had anything other than friendship."

He kissed her again this time lifting her up on her toes. "It has driven me to the brink of insanity thinking that you might choose him over me." He wrapped his arms about her waist and kissed the tip of her nose. "You know that I would never have allowed him to have you."

"Hawk will not allow me to stay here much longer, so if there is something you would like to ask me, you had better do so before he returns. I am only allowed out of my prison for a short amount of time."

He frowned. "I will speak with him about his treatment of you before I leave."

"Good heavens don't do that. I certainly don't want to cause animosity between the two of you. I'm sure I will survive being locked in my room. If he decides to have me put on the rack, I will send word."

He chuckled, glad to see some life coming back into her. "Are you agreeing to be my duchess? Once you say yes, there will be no turning back."

She nodded her head. "I suppose it would be prudent to do so. I would much rather be called the Duchess of Leicester than the whore of Hawksford."

His expression darkened. "Is that what Hawk said to you?"

"No, not in so many words."

He tilted her chin up so he could look into her eyes. "Catherine as my wife I will protect you from all things. No one will dare utter a harsh word about you, or they will face my wrath."

She smiled feeling some of the weight being lifted off her shoulders. "Careful, you are beginning to sound like one of those storybook heroes you used to make fun of me for reading about."

Hawk knocked loudly on the door before entering and she quickly stepped out of Michael's arms. "Is there cause for celebration?"

Michael didn't like being disturbed. There was more he wanted to say, and if he had his choice, she would leave with him now. "Catherine has agreed to become my wife. I will seek a special license and if it is alright with her, I would like to be married as soon as possible."

Catherine looked over at him quickly and he said, "I would take you today if I could, but seeing as Hawk will insist on you remaining here until after the ceremony, I must respect his wishes. But as soon as I acquire the license, I will be back for you."

Her brother cleared his throat loudly from the doorway. "You don't have to sound so medieval, Michael. A week from today will do nicely. You can be married here in the parlor and we will have a small wedding breakfast following the ceremony. Catherine, why don't you go upstairs and speak with Persephone? I'm sure she will be thrilled with the news and will want to make plans right away."

She nodded to her brother and quietly left the two friends alone.

"I'm glad it all worked out for the best," Hawk said as he closed the door behind her.

Michael stepped closer to his friend. "Did you call her a whore?"

Hawk looked down and shifted his feet. "No, but I wasn't kind. Hence the reason my wife is not speaking with me still."

"I have known you for years, Hawk and loved you like a brother, but you will apologize to Catherine."

"I don't need you to tell me that, Michael. I feel horrible. Not only do I need to make amends with Catherine, but I am fairly certain a good deal of groveling and very expensive jewelry will be required to get my wife to join me back in my bed." He moved to stand behind his desk. "I suppose you would like to talk about a marriage settlement, as you know Catherine comes with an impressive dowry."

"It will be hers to do with as she pleases, or put aside for our children, I have no need of her money."

Hawk nodded. "I know that, but it is customary to mention. I assume you wish to make arrangements immediately so I will not keep you. I will however say that I am happy for the both of you, and I wish you all the luck in the world. She is always going to be a handful and I am thankful her care and safety will now fall to you." He poured them both a drink and handed his friend a glass. "May neither of us ever have daughters."

Michael smiled and raised his glass. "Heaven help us if we do."

Chapter Thirteen

Catherine took another look at herself in the mirror. It had been a week since the ball and potential scandal that could have resulted if she had not agreed to marry Michael. He had no trouble acquiring a special license for the wedding, less than three days, but even though he had tried to convince her brother to allow the wedding to take place sooner, Hawk had stuck to his guns and insisted they wait till the end of the week.

She had only seen Michael once in that time. Persephone kept her busy buying dresses and a new trousseau. When she did finally get to see him, Hawk made sure she was properly chaperoned. Ian had visited her once as well. The relief on his face was almost comical when she once again thanked him for his proposal but insisted that she wouldn't dream of forcing a marriage on him that neither of them wanted. He was a good friend and hopefully would continue to be once Michael got over his jealousy. Ian had let her know that he and Lord Rockhurst had been spending a great deal of time together, and he was thinking of staying in London for an extended period of time before returning to Scotland. She could only imagine the happiness that would evoke in the ladies of the ton.

Hawk had come to her a few days after she accepted Michael's proposal and apologized for how he had spoken to her. She wasn't sure if it was because Persephone had refused to share a bed with him until he did so, or if it was because Michael had insisted, he apologize. Either way, she readily accepted. She loved her brother and knew he had just been frustrated with the situation. Things after that had gone back to normal in the household. Persephone had moved back into the duke's bedchamber, and the staff was no longer on edge.

She looked around her room knowing she would never again sleep in her bed. It was an odd feeling. She had longed for this and now that the time was upon her, she was a little scared. Hawksford House and Hawk's Hill in Kent had always been home to her. When her father and mother were alive, she had never known anything but love and contentment. When they passed and her brother assumed his role as duke, she still knew that there was always a place for her. Now all her things were packed away and she would be leaving. She would be mistress over Leicester House in London and Leicester Hall, the duke's family seat also in Kent. She felt an intense sense of panic beginning to settle over her. She wasn't ready for this. She felt herself struggling to breathe. She couldn't suck in enough air. Her heart was beating faster as she stood from her seat and moved toward the window knocking over the chair in the process.

She tugged on the window trying to open it, but it wouldn't budge. She hit the panes with her hands and was almost ready to hurl something through the glass when Persephone came inside and hurried over to her.

"My God, Catherine, what's the matter?"

Catherine clutched her throat. "I can't breathe! I need to leave, I need air."

Her friend looked at her maid with concern. "Go downstairs and inform his grace that we will be a few minutes longer."

The maid bobbed a quick curtsy then hurried out the door closing it behind her.

Persephone grabbed her hand and led her over to the bed. "Here sit." She began fanning her face. "Take small steady breaths, love. It's going to pass."

Catherine's eyes were wide with fear. "I can't do this, Persephone."

Her friend looked at her curiously. "Get married?"

Catherine closed her eyes and tried to concentrate on breathing. "I don't think I can."

Persephone took her by her shoulders. "I would have never taken you of all people as a coward." Catherine opened her eyes and she continued. "When we were ambushed by Comte Domingo and I was kidnapped, did you not stand toe to toe with our assailants while a gun was pointed to your head?"

"This is different." Her voice sounded small to her own ears.

"Different? Did you also not take a severe beating trying to protect me? And when I was scared out of my wits about marrying your brother and becoming the Duchess of Hawksford, was it not you that told me I was being silly and could handle anything that came my way?"

There was a loud knock on the door. Persephone turned her irritation to whoever was disturbing them. "Yes?"

Hawk opened the door and looked at both of them with concern. "Your maid said you would be a while and from the concerned look on her face I thought I had better make certain you had not escaped through a window." His attempt at humor was not appreciated. "Rockhurst is practically restraining Leicester. If you don't come down soon, I'm afraid he will come to retrieve you himself."

Persephone waved him off. "We will be down momentarily. She is just having a bout of nerves."

His face instantly turned scarlet. "Oh nerves, well I will leave you to handle that then darling." He nearly stumbled over himself trying to leave the room.

Her friend rolled her eyes. "Goodness, he thinks you are nervous about the wedding night. That should keep them away for a bit longer."

Catherine could feel that her breathing was more controlled. "I'm sorry, everything seemed to come crashing down on me at once. This has always been home to me and after today it will be no longer."

Persephone wrapped her arms around her. "Darling, this will always be your home and you will always be welcome here."

Catherine took another deep calming breath. "It's not just that. All those years of fantasizing about marrying Michael and now faced with the daunting prospect of being the Duchess of Leicester has me feeling more than a little anxious."

Her friend laughed. "Catherine, if I can be a duchess, you must know that you can be also. You were literally born for it, the daughter of a duke and sister of a duke. This is what you were made for, dear. I'm certain you will be a glorious duchess."

Catherine lowered her head. "I also have other concerns. Michael has secrets. He has never told me where he was those days when he left London. He hasn't told anyone and I feel as if he might be involved in something sinister."

"Sinister? Michael? Catherine, you are letting your imagination run away with you. There are no dragons to slay. I'm sure it is nothing more than business." She patted her hand. "You are the bravest, strongest, and most headstrong woman I know. I am surprised you are feeling this vulnerable."

Catherine's lips turned up into a small sad smile. "I'm sorry. After talking with you I feel rather silly. It's a good thing the window wouldn't open, or I might have attempted to shimmy down the tree and escape." She gave her another hug. "I guess we should go downstairs and get this done."

Persephone laughed. "I said something similar on my wedding day to Aunt Louisa, I can't remember what her response was but it was something like, you are getting married not getting a tooth pulled. Are you alright now?"

Catherine nodded. "I will be fine, thank you."

Together they walked down the stairs. Hawk was waiting for them on the bottom landing, and Persephone went ahead leaving them alone for a minute.

Catherine took her brother's hand when he extended it to her. "You look so much like our mother, Catherine."

She lowered her eyes and smiled hoping to keep the tears that threatened to spill down her cheeks at bay. "I hope I make her proud, goodness knows I gave her many moments of anxiety growing up."

He laughed and tucked her hand on his sleeve. "You always made both her and father proud." He leaned over and placed a brief kiss on her cheek. "I've always been proud of you too, Catherine. Michael is a good man and if anyone is capable of handling you, it would be him."

He led her through the doors of the drawing room. It was lit with candles and Persephone had seen that it was decorated with fresh flowers. The bishop was standing at the front of the room beside Michael. Lord Rockhurst as well as Ian McDonough were in attendance. Her lady's maid was standing towards the back sniffling into a handkerchief and a few of the other servants she had grown up with were present as well. She had hoped her Aunt Louisa would make it to the wedding, but neither she nor Michael's mother were able to attend. Even though it was a small family affair she felt a sense of alarm as everyone watched her move forward.

When she reached the front of the room, Michael took her hand in his as the bishop began the ceremony. She repeated the words required of her as the room seemed to grow smaller. When Michael placed a ring upon her finger and the bishop pronounced them husband and wife, she felt her breathing increase. Then Michael turned her to face him and gave her a quick wink and a smile before he lowered his lips to hers and kissed her. In that instant, she knew it was right.

Congratulations swirled around them before she had time to react to his kiss. Persephone hugged them both and Lord Rockhurst shook hands with Michael before raising her hand to his lips for a kiss. "Congratulations, duchess."

She smiled, but it was odd being referred as such. The wedding breakfast seemed to go by quickly and before she knew it Michael was telling her it was time for them to make their departure. She gave Persephone a lingering hug and her brother as well. Then she took Michael's hand as he led her out to his carriage. He assisted her inside and then took the seat opposite her. She waved out the window as the horses started toward Leicester House. They would not be traveling very far. It was only a few blocks away. She turned to see Michael staring at her.

"What is it?" she asked turning her head to the side.

He reached out and took her hand in his. "You are just so very beautiful, and I can't believe that you are now mine." He pulled her across the carriage to settle on his lap. "All mine, Catherine, my duchess, my wife." He softly kissed her lips as he let his fingers trail along her arms. "When your maid came downstairs to tell us that you would be longer than expected, I feared you had changed your mind."

She chuckled softly. "I just had a moment of panic and since the window would not open, here I still am."

He leaned back to study her face. He lightly touched her cheek. "Darling what on earth would make you panic?"

"Leaving Hawksford House, becoming a duchess, getting married, it seemed to all hit me at once."

He wrapped his arms about her waist to hold her closer. "Sweetheart, we are only going to be a few blocks from Hawksford House, and I can't think of anyone who would make a better duchess."

"It was just nerves."

He leaned closer wanting her right then. "It has been killing me waiting a week for you. I have never wanted anything so badly. Were you upset that we did not have a large ceremony?"

"No, I do wish Aunt Louisa could have been there and what of your mother? Will she not be upset that we wed without her in attendance?"

He placed a kiss to the side of her neck. "My mother will just be happy to see me wed. She was beginning to give up any hope, and I know your Aunt Louisa would have been here if she was able."

She gave him a faint smile. "Aunt Louisa is a free spirit. I'm sure she will show up when we least expect it and no, I am not upset about a large ceremony."

"You are a lot like your Aunt Louisa. You are so strong and confident." He kissed her again. "And passionate about what you feel is right and who you love."

His hands crept up her waist to her breast, but the carriage began to slow, and he sighed heavily as he placed her back on the seat across from him. "The household staff will be assembled to greet you. Finn, my butler, will give you a brief tour of the house and introduce the staff. Bucephalus was moved to the stables this morning. When you are settled, I'm sure you will want to go see to him."

She nodded and looked out the window as the house came into view. She knew Leicester House but had only been there a handful of times as a child when her family had been invited to dinner or a morning brunch. The staff was assembled out front and livered footmen were waiting to assist them as the carriage came to a stop. When the door was opened, he stepped out and then reached to help her.

Finn came forward and bowed deeply at the waist. "Your grace, we would like to welcome you home to Leicester House."

She gave him a bright smile, and Michael watched as she reached out and took the old man's hand. "Thank you so much, Finn. I hope that I will not be a bother. I will need your assistance as I adjust."

The older man blushed. "Allow me to introduce you to the staff, your grace."

Michael followed behind them as Catherine continued to charm the rest of the household staff. It was safe to say that they were all pleased with their new duchess. Mrs. Gibbons came forward and curtsied. "Allow me to show you to the duchess's chambers."

Michael continued to follow behind them. He leaned closer so Catherine could hear. "The rooms may be yours, but I have no intention of you sleeping in them."

Catherine turned to give him a cheeky smile then hurried to catch up with Mrs. Gibbons. The duchess's chambers were every bit as big as the ones at Hawksford House. There was a large bed with a lovely white lace coverlet near the middle of the room. A fireplace was on one wall and two large sets of windows stretched nearly to the ceiling. It was a beautiful room. There was a sitting room as well as a dressing room attached. Michael nodded to Mrs. Gibbons who quickly left them alone shutting the door behind them. He took her hand and led her through a set of communicating doors into the duke's chambers.

He moved behind her and wrapped his arms about her waist. "This is my bedchamber and where you will be sleeping as well."

Catherine turned in his arms. "Everyone is so nice and Leicester House is magnificent."

"You have won over their hearts for certain." He kissed her sweetly on both cheeks. "Should we postpone the remainder of the tour? I have been longing to get you all to myself since you agreed to be my wife."

Catherine shivered at the look of desire in his eyes. "You don't think it will upset them?"

He began walking her backward toward the bed. "I don't give a damn if they are upset or not." He tumbled her back onto the bed just as a loud knock sounded from his door.

He buried his nose in the crook of her neck before rising on his elbows. "Go away!"

"Excuse me, your grace but there is a messenger downstairs, and he insists on seeing you right away. He says it is most urgent," Finn announced nervously through the door.

He practically growled as he moved from the bed. "Do not move from this room. I will be right back."

Catherine grinned when she heard a few curses escape from him as he headed through the door. While he was gone, she thought she would take a minute to explore the room and perhaps get more acquainted with her rooms.

Michael had never been so frustrated. He had waited all week to have Catherine all to himself and now when he was just moments from finally bedding his wife someone had managed to disturb them. All he knew was it had better be important, or the messenger would pay for his disturbance with a bloody nose.

Finn was nervously waiting for him at the foot of the stairs. "I have shown the man into your study."

Michael gave him an annoyed look then marched forward nearly slamming the doors open. Standing on the other side of the room was a man he had not seen before. He moved closer to get a better look. "Who the hell are you and what do you want?"

The man looked unperturbed by his anger. "My name is Walter Meeks, your grace. I have been sent here by Mr. Thomas Harrison."

Michael was no less upset. "Harrison, I met with Harrison last week. What does he want now?"

"There has been an unforeseen situation that has occurred and I'm afraid that he has asked that you join him at his office immediately. It is a matter of national security."

Michael moved closer hoping to intimidate the much smaller man. "Mr. Meeks, I am not sure that you or Mr. Harrison are aware, but I have just been married this morning. And you must know that I have no desire to leave my new bride."

The man did not flinch. "We are aware of your recent nuptials and offer our felicitations. It does not change the fact that your presence is required."

"Well, whatever it is will have to wait."

Mr. Meeks did not move from where he stood. "We are at war, your grace, and the fate of the British Empire is at stake every single day. If you will forgive me, Napoleon does not give a damn about whether or not you have had the time to bed your new wife."

Michael moved swiftly grabbing the man by the collar. "You will not speak of my wife!"

Mr. Meeks was not easily intimidated. "If you will release me, your grace, and allow me to continue."

Michael reluctantly let him go. "Continue."

Mr. Meeks adjusted his collar. "A note arrived this morning stating that your man that you had asked to keep an eye on things at your estate has disappeared. We are unsure of his safety. The note also eludes that more is at stake than the simple smuggling of goods and liquor. Mr. Harrison and his superiors would like to speak with you further on the matter. They are waiting for you now. I am to escort you."

Michael moved away from him. "I must go speak to my wife. Give me a few minutes and I will go with you."

"Your grace, as you well know this is a matter of national security and no one must know why I am here. Your wife's safety might be at risk as well."

Michael did not like where this was going, but he nodded his understanding before storming out of the room and upstairs to find Catherine. How was he going to explain having to leave her? She was already suspicious about why he left London over a week ago. She was not going to be pleased to hear that he was leaving tonight. How could he let her know of the importance without telling her the truth? The thing he was certain of is that this would not go well.

He slowly opened the door to his room and felt his cock stiffen at the sight before him. Catherine had taken the pins from her hair and the lush brown curls cascaded down her back. She was sitting in a chair by the fire. Her dress was pulled up and she was slowly rolling her stocking down her leg. He couldn't pull his eyes away from her exposed flesh. He swallowed as he moved further into the room. If she was not a maiden, he would make Meeks wait while he took her quickly. But this was Catherine, his wife, and she deserved more for her first time.

She gave him a small smile. "I hope you don't mind if I made myself more comfortable."

He closed his eyes for a second cursing Napoleon and damning his own government in his head. "Catherine, this is your home and of course you may do as you please."

She studied his face as he moved closer. "What's wrong?"

He took her hand and helped her to stand. "Something has come up unexpectantly, and I must leave for a few hours. I will return as soon as I can."

Catherine pushed out of his arms. "What's going on, Michael? Are you in some kind of trouble?"

He shook his head. "No, no, nothing like that. It is just something I need to take care of tonight."

She bent down and grabbed her slippers. "I'll go with you."

"No! You can stay here. Mrs. Gibbons can continue the tour of the house, and I will be back as soon as I can."

She narrowed her eyes and put her hands on her hips. "We were just married this morning, and you are leaving me. Does this have something to do with the reason you disappeared last week?"

He moved to place his hands on her shoulders, but she stepped out of his reach. "Catherine, I promise everything will be alright. I will return as soon as I can."

"Why can't you tell me?"

His frustration was growing. It was his wedding day, and instead of bedding his wife, he was having to argue with her. It wasn't her fault; he knew that, but the longer she kept him arguing the longer it would be before he could return. "I'm done discussing this, Catherine. You are my wife, and you will do as I say."

The moment the words left his mouth he knew he had made a mistake. Catherine was not the type of woman to take orders. She sucked in her breath in shock at what he said then recovered herself quickly. "I may be your wife but in name only, and I will remain your wife in name only. You want to keep secrets, do so. But do not expect me to give myself to you freely, your grace."

He grabbed her arm and pulled her back toward him when she tried to walk away. "You will share my bed, Catherine," he said through clenched teeth as he tightened his hold on her arm.

Catherine was not intimidated. "Not. . . willingly." She pulled free of his grasp and marched from his bedchamber to her own slamming the door behind her.

Michael clenched his hands into fists. "This isn't over, Catherine. When I return, we will settle this!" The only sound he received in return was the click of the lock on her door.

He walked over to where a set of glasses were sitting by a decanter of some of his best brandy. He took one of the glasses and threw it against the wall shattering glass along the floor. He marched out of his room slamming the door behind him. He was so angry he felt as if he could defeat the entire French army with his bare hands. Heaven help Thomas Harrison if this business could have waited until the morning.

Catherine heard the glass shatter against the wall. She leaned back against the door and let her body slide slowly to the floor. How could this day have gone so horribly wrong? She pulled her knees up to her chest and let her head fall to them. She had made a monumental mistake from which she would never be able to escape. She could seek an annulment she supposed, especially since the marriage had not been consummated. She felt the tears filling her eyes. An annulment would create a greater scandal than the scene in the gardens at Persephone's ball. Hawk would be furious, and it would have ramifications that affected the entire family. No, she could never do that to her family.

She felt her chest grow heavy and as strong as she tried to be, she couldn't stop the sobs from escaping her lips, or the tears from flowing freely down her cheeks. She lay there on the floor for what seemed like hours. There was no sound from the other room, so she got up and undressed put on one of her new nightgowns and climbed into bed. It had started to rain and she turned so she could see the droplets slide down her window. She blew out the candles that were lit and lay there in silence. Tomorrow, she would pull herself together and get on with her life but tonight, she would feel sorry for herself, and lament the wedding night that was not to be.

Office of the War Department

Michael had joined Mr. Meeks and together they had left Leicester House for Thomas Harrison's offices. Mr. Meeks remained quiet as they sat in the carriage for which Michael was thankful. He had no desire to converse with anyone right now. When the carriage finally came to a stop, he followed Meeks up the steps into the office. It was eerily quiet as his boots clicked across the marble floor.

Mr. Meeks stepped to the side and allowed him to enter Thomas's office first. Thomas was not alone. Three other men were sitting there, men he did not recognize. When he entered, they stood and bowed respectfully in deference to his rank.

Thomas moved from behind his desk and walked toward him offering his hand in greeting. "Your grace, we do apologize for taking you away from your home on such a monumental occasion. We offer our congratulations on your marriage."

Michael scowled as he eyed the other gentlemen in the room. "What is all this about? The message you sent me stated that my groom had gone missing, and I was needed here right away."

Thomas nervously looked around the room. "Your groom is missing, but we do not believe he has come to any harm." He moved to stand back behind his desk. "Things have gotten more complicated I'm afraid, and we need more of your help than we first expected."

Michael stepped closer his anger barely under control. "I did as you asked."

"We know that, and we are truly appreciative of your efforts. But as you know, this is a delicate matter."

"Where is my groom? I was assured what he was being asked to do was safe and now he is missing. I will not put my staff in danger."

Thomas held up his hands. "As I said before, we feel that your groom will come to no harm."

Michael raked his hand through his hair. "None of this is making sense! Why am I here?"

"You are here because I feel there is no one better suited for the task at hand. I need your help, and I trust you with my life," a deep voice said from the shadows.

Michael turned around swiftly at the familiar voice and watched in shock as his longtime friend Rockhurst moved out of the shadows into the light of the room. "Son of a bitch, what the hell are you doing here?"

His friend gave him a wicked grin. "I knew you would be furious, but there really was no better time. Have a seat and let me explain."

Michael watched his friend warily as he moved around to take a seat beside him. The other three men in the room stood and left leaving them alone with Thomas Harrison.

"Would you like a drink before we continue?" Harrison asked as he poured some brandy into a glass.

Michael accepted what was offered and drank the contents quickly. "I think you should start explaining things to me right now."

Rockhurst nodded and took the seat across from him. "I was approached over a year ago to do some work for the foreign affairs office, gather intelligence when needed, and gain the trust of individuals that might be useful or those that were under suspicion."

Michael narrowed his eyes. "You have been working for the crown?"

Rockhurst grinned. "You would be surprised the information one can gain in a bedroom, Michael. It wasn't always an unpleasant assignment."

"So, you knew why I had been asked to leave London then?"

Rockhurst looked over at Thomas before answering. "Yes, I knew."

"Explain to me what this has to do with me, and why it was so urgent that I had to leave my wife on our wedding day." Michael scowled at his friend. "Catherine is no longer speaking to me, by the way."

"She will come around."

Thomas saw the vein begin to bulge on Michael's neck and tried to explain further. "The man we suspect was a smuggler may be more than we first thought. You already knew that we suspected he was transporting information, but we aren't sure whose side he is on or who he is working with here in the foreign office."

Michael turned to listen further.

Thomas continued. "We are fairly certain he is gathering information on Napoleon and troop movements and relaying the information to his contact here. Possibly using smuggling as a cover. But there is no record of anyone in this office knowing anything about it. There is much we do not know. Is the information true? Who is he working with? We don't even know his name." Thomas glanced over at Rockhurst, and Michael got an uncomfortable feeling.

"What exactly do you know about the man?"

"The only thing we do know is that he has asked around about Catherine," Rockhurst said fully expecting the eruption that was about to take place.

Michael quickly stood from his seat. "Catherine!? How in the hell does this man know my wife!?"

Rockhurst stood as well and took a step toward his friend. "Calm down, Michael. All we know is that he must have met her in Brighton. He has made inquiries about her."

Michael began pacing the room. "Is she in danger?"

"No, we don't think she is in any danger at all. But we would like you to leave London and travel to Hart's Manor for a few days. Think of it as a wedding trip. We have already reached out to others working for us to make inquiries. We are trying to set up a meeting so we can determine if this man is friend or foe."

Michael's frown intensified. "If I go to Hart's Manor, Catherine could be at risk. I will not put her life in danger."

"Catherine would not be in danger. I would never ask you to risk her life, Michael. I simply need someone I can trust. You are English through and through and I would trust you with my life. I simply need someone to watch my back."

Thomas stood tall and proud clasping his hands behind his back. "We as a nation are at a dangerous point in history. Napoleon is treacherous, and the sovereignty of the crown is at stake. This is an opportunity for you to aid your country."

Michael glared at his friend. "What would you have me do, Rockhurst?"

"Take a wedding trip to Hart's Manor under the guise of checking on your estates. Spend time with your lovely bride. I will try to arrange a meeting with this man to discover his intentions, and when all is settled, I would like for you to attend with me to watch my back and if necessary, return to London with information. Catherine need never know anything about this other than it is a trip away from London."

Michael didn't like this at all. "Why could this not have waited?"

Thomas shrugged his shoulders. "I am leaving town first thing in the morning. I wanted to be assured of your cooperation. Lord Rockhurst has been invaluable in gathering information, and he was insistent that you are the only one he fully trusts."

"Catherine is not pleased with me at the moment, but I will try to plan for us to leave London within the week."

Rockhurst let out a small sigh of relief. "Thank you, Michael."

"If anything happens to Catherine you will answer to me."

Both Thomas and Rockhurst nodded in understanding as Michael grabbed his coat and headed for the door. Once they were alone again Rockhurst turned to Thomas. "You didn't tell him everything."

Thomas shook his head. "Do you really think he would have agreed to travel with his wife to Hart's Manor if I told him that I have every intention of using his wife as bait to draw out this mysterious smuggler or spy?"

Rockhurst stared at the closed door. "No, but if anything happens to her, I will have lost both of my closest friends, and you will have two very upset dukes after your head. There will not be a place in England safe for either of us."

Thomas nodded in agreement. "We will have to make certain nothing happens to her grace then."

Chapter Fourteen

———⟡———

It was very late when Michael returned to Leicester House. He climbed the stairs to his bedroom hoping that Catherine would be in his bed, but he had no such luck. He walked over to the connecting door to find it still locked. He was not in the mood for another argument, and he was certain she would already be asleep at this time of night, so he made his way over to the large chair before his fireplace. His valet must have come in to find the broken glass and cleaned everything up. He pulled off his cravat and tossed it aside as he pulled his shirt over his head. He looked over towards the bed. It was his wedding night and instead of holding his naked wife in his arms after thoroughly making love to her, he was sitting alone with a bottle of brandy wondering how in the hell he managed to get tangled up in all the lies and deceit of spying for the crown.

He poured himself another drink hoping the liquor would help him sleep. Rockhurst had been involved in this intrigue for over a year, and he never suspected him of anything other than a rake looking for his next bed partner. The thing that bothered him most was that tonight he had hurt Catherine and said things that would create a rift between them, and he had no idea how to make her understand without telling her the truth. The truth was the last thing she needed to hear. Catherine was the type of woman who would jump at the chance for an adventure and in doing so might get herself hurt. No, it was best to keep her in the dark about what was going on in order to keep her safe.

As the liquor burned down his throat, he felt his eyelids grow heavy. Tomorrow he would make things right between them. He had no intention of sleeping alone another night.

Catherine heard the door to Michael's room open and close. He had finally returned home. She rolled to her back looking at the ceiling. How could he keep secrets from her? She was sure Hawk didn't keep anything from Persephone. Perhaps she could do a little investigating on her own to discover what Michael was involved in and keeping from her. She lay awake until she saw the first rays of sunshine peeking over the horizon.

Since she wasn't sleeping anyway, she thought it would be the perfect time to go have Bucephalus saddled and take a ride through the park. This early, Rotten Row would be fairly empty and she could get in a good run. If she hurried, she could be out of the house and gone before Michael even got out of bed. Ha, making him wonder where she was and what secrets she was keeping would serve him right.

Once she was dressed in her riding habit, she quietly opened the door to her room not wanting to disturb the household and made her way downstairs and out to the stables. The grooms were surprised to see her but quickly got her horse saddled as she requested.

"Will his grace be joining you?" the head groom asked as he brought Bucephalus out for her.

"No, he has decided to sleep in this morning."

"Then I will have someone ride with you," he said as he motioned for another horse to be saddled and brought around.

Catherine waited patiently, and when the young groom who was to accompany her made his way around, she turned Bucephalus and headed off in the direction of the park. A good run was exactly what she needed today. The fresh cool crisp air would help her think and clear her head.

When she reached Rotten Row, she told her groom to stay put as she sank in her heels and urged Bucephalus into a gallop. She leaned down over his neck and gave him the reins. He was a magnificent animal, and it almost felt as if she were flying across the path. When she reached the end, he easily sailed over the hedges landing on the other side with ease. Catherine pulled him up and slowed him to a canter as she headed back to where her groom was waiting.

"You are an excellent rider, your grace," an all too familiar and much welcomed voice said.

She turned to see Lord Rockhurst headed toward her. "I have been riding since I was a little girl, but Bucephalus makes it look easy, does he not?" She leaned over and patted the horse's neck.

He laughed. "The experience of the rider can make even the worst horses look like champions."

She smiled softly. "What has you out so early this morning?"

"I was about to ask you the same thing. The night after your wedding I would think you would be sleeping later." He raised an eyebrow as he gave her a small, wicked grin.

Her smile turned to a frown. "I enjoy early morning rides."

"As do I, Catherine."

She appreciated that he didn't continue questioning her. She was not in the mood to discuss her situation with anyone at the moment. "Would you care to join me?"

He inclined his head. "I would be honored."

Catherine turned her horse and he maneuvered his alongside her. They rode in silence for a few minutes before Rockhurst said, "I remember the evening you raced Lord Brookhaven in Brighton, you were magnificent. If you had been mounted on Bucephalus at that time Brookhaven would still be trying to catch up with you."

Catherine genuinely laughed pleased with the compliment. "That was the race that got me sent back to London."

He nodded. "Yes, I know. In Brighton it seems as if everyone has more freedom."

She glanced over at him. "Yes, I enjoyed my time there, but I would have returned just as the rest of the beau monde to London for the season anyway."

"Ah the season, the dreaded time of year where unmarried ladies are set upon us bachelors like a pack of wolves. It is a most trying time for devoted bachelors like myself."

Catherine smiled at his description. "I assume you are still actively avoiding the marriage trap."

"You assume correctly, my dear, much to my father's dismay and anger. When the season is over, I will return to Brighton to seek more pleasurable pursuits." He looked over at her so he could study the reaction on her face as he asked, "While you were in Brighton, did you happen to meet anyone that stood out to you, Catherine? Someone who interested you or showed you particular attention."

She pulled her horse to a stop. "What a peculiar question." She turned her head to the side as if contemplating her answer. "I met several people and gentlemen while in Brighton but most were silly fools. Not one person caught my attention. Why do you ask?"

He shrugged his shoulders. "No reason, just curious how all those gentlemen let you slip through their fingers."

She rolled her eyes as a chuckle escaped her. "You are an expert flatterer, my lord."

His smile took on a wicked look. "Guilty, your grace."

She pulled her horse to a stop and put a finger to her lips to silence him. "Do you hear that? It sounds like a whimper."

He got down from his horse and moved to a clump of bushes where the sound was coming from. "Stay where you are, Catherine."

Catherine watched curiously as he pushed through the bushes and reemerged with a dirty scraggly clump of fur. "What is it?"

He held the creature away from him and wrinkled his nose. "I believe it is a dog, although I'm not sure why he smells so offensive."

She reached her arms out to take him. "He is so small. He must be lost."

"I don't think you want this mongrel touching you, Catherine. He is filthy and probably covered in vermin."

She reached down and took the little ball of dirt and fur anyway. "He just needs a bath. I will take him home and get him cleaned up and something to eat. He is probably starving."

Rockhurst wiped his hands against his pants. "You will need to throw away that riding habit if you let him ride all the way home with you. Besides, I'm not certain Michael will appreciate the mongrel being in his house."

He saw her eyes narrow. "It is my house too, my lord." She held the little dog up in the air so she could see his face. "I think I will call you Rupert."

Rockhurst mounted his horse. "Rupert is a fine name for him. He will probably grow up to look very regal."

Catherine bundled him up closer to her. "I don't know about regal, but Rupert is a good name for him." She reached down for the reins. "I'm afraid I will have to cut my ride short this morning, my lord."

"Yes, I understand. Rupert certainly needs your attention."

She turned her horse and headed back to Leicester House with her groom following close behind her. The sooner Rupert got a bath, the better.

Late morning

Michael awoke with a start. He turned his head slowly wincing at the pain in his neck. He had fallen asleep in his chair and slept at an odd angle. He reached up and massaged the back of his neck with his hand as he turned his head side to side trying to loosen up. He stood up and stretched then looking over at his empty bed remembered the reason he had slept alone. He walked over to the communicating door; it was still locked.

He knocked, "Catherine!"

He heard no movement from inside. Perhaps she had already gone down to breakfast. He quickly washed and dressed without the help of his valet. He brushed his hair back from his face noting the dark circles under his eyes. He huffed out a long slow breath. Hopefully Catherine would be in a better mood and willing to hear him out.

Otherwise, he was not sure how he would be able to convince her to travel with him to Harts Manor.

He made his way downstairs and found Finn who was waiting beside the dining room entrance. "Good morning, Finn. Is her grace at breakfast?"

"No, your grace. She left early this morning to ride in the park."

Michael noted that his long-time butler was nervous. "Did she go alone?"

"No, your grace. A groom accompanied her."

Michael was getting irritated at having to ask so many questions. "Please inform me the minute she returns."

"She has already returned, your grace."

Michael pinched the bridge of his nose for patience. "For heaven's sake, Finn, where is she?"

"I believe she is still out back giving Rupert a bath, your grace."

"Rupert? Who the hell is Rupert?"

"I told her not to bring it inside, your grace. But she would not listen."

"Yes, that much I do know, Finn. Never mind, I will go see this Rupert for myself." He marched through the house heading toward the stables. Once outside he heard splashing and laughter and followed it to find her on her knees beside a washtub scrubbing a black ball of fur. From the looks of how wet her riding habit was, it appeared the mongrel was none too pleased with the predicament he found himself in and was protesting quite vehemently.

"Now Rupert, if you don't be still, I will never get you clean enough to come inside the house. Finn will throw both of us into the streets if I can't get you smelling better." The little dog yapped at her comment and splashed water all over the bodice of her riding habit. "Rupert! You are being terribly naughty."

He watched with amusement as she continued to wrangle the little dog, at least he thought that's what it was, and ended up almost tumbling over into the basin herself. He strode forward and knelt beside her. "Would you like some help?"

His voice must have startled her and she loosened her hold on the little dog so he tried for a valiant escape. Water splashed up in her face and he reached out to grab hold of the pup and put him back in the water.

Catherine reached up and wiped her face with her sleeve. She must look a mess. Her hair had come out of its pins and wet ringlets hung down her face. Her habit was ruined and some of Rupert's odor had transferred to her. Michael was smiling and looking as handsome as ever. Rupert yapped loudly and broke the spell he seemed to have on her.

"I guess Finn told you about Rupert."

Michael nodded. "I came downstairs looking for you. He was very nervous about it. I came outside following the splashing and laughter to find you here."

Catherine leaned down and continued scrubbing the little dog. "Do you intend on making me get rid of him?"

He brushed a wet curl out of her eyes. "I love seeing you happy, Catherine, and if that dirty bit of fluff and fur makes you laugh, how can I ask you to get rid of him."

Her smile widened. "Thank you, Michael."

He looked back toward the dirty water basin. "Where did he come from?"

She lifted the dog from the water and wrapped him in a towel. "Lord Rockhurst and I found him while out riding this morning."

That got his attention. "Rockhurst went riding with you this morning?"

"Yes, we found him in some bushes in the park."

Michael rose to his feet. "Why the hell would Rockhurst be with you this morning?"

Catherine stared at him confused at why he would be upset. "We didn't plan on meeting there if that's what you are thinking. He just happened by when I was galloping Bucephalus down Rotten Row." She stood up clutching the now shivering dog close to her chest. "Are you questioning my character? I would have you know that I have known Rockhurst for almost as long as I have known you. He is a family friend."

He took a step closer. "I just find it odd that he just happened to be riding the same time as you."

Catherine sucked in a breath. "You are questioning my character! How dare you!"

Michael moved to take her arms, but she stepped out of his reach. "Catherine, I didn't come here to argue with you. I am living in torment. That is the only excuse I have for my behavior. All I want is to hold you in my arms and make you mine." He took another step forward reaching out to touch her cheek. "Have mercy on me, Catherine." Even to his own ears his voice sounded raspy with desire and pain. "Come to bed with me now, Catherine. Let me show you how good it will be between us."

She raised her face to his and was just about to give in when Finn came around the corner.

"Excuse me, your graces. But there is a messenger waiting in the corridor."

"Tell him to go away!" Michael said never taking his eyes from hers.

Catherine took a step backward. "More secrets," she said softly. "Go ahead, you don't want to keep them waiting." With that she turned and headed back toward the house. Just when they were about to heal the chasm between them, something else happens that makes her move farther away. She climbed the steps to the duchess's rooms and asked her maid to prepare a bath. Rupert might be smelling and feeling better, but she certainly wasn't.

Michael cursed under his breath as he watched her walk away. He turned and walked into his study where Finn stood waiting holding a note. He dismissed him and closed the door to the study so he could be alone. The note was from Rockhurst requesting him to come to his house at his earliest convenience. It seems like some new information had been received about the mysterious man they were looking for, and he wanted to share the information with him.

Michael needed to make arrangements with his secretary to leave for Harts Manor by the end of the week. There was much to do, but the only thing he wanted, was to be with his wife and make things right between them. She would not take the news of him leaving again tonight well at all, and he couldn't blame her. He wasn't happy about it either. King and country be damned. He was tempted to just tell her everything and tell Harrison to find someone else to do his spying for him. If it were not for the fact that Rockhurst had asked him specifically, he would do just that. But if his friend was hurt or killed because he wasn't there to watch his back, he would never forgive himself.

Catherine stepped into the steaming water and eased down into the large copper tub. Rupert was sleeping peacefully by the window and had finally stopped yapping. She took the pins from her hair and dunked herself below the surface of the water to wet her hair. When she reemerged, she wiped the water from her face and eyes to find Michael leaning against the door staring at her.

"My goodness, you were quiet. I didn't hear you come in." She crossed her arms over her chest and pulled her knees up.

He continued to watch her as the water dripped down her skin. Her hair was wet and hung down her back. He stayed where he was not trusting himself to move any closer. "You were under the water when I came in. I had feared you were trying to drown yourself."

"I'm afraid that whatever was so smelly on Rupert rubbed off on me. I will probably have to soak an hour or more to smell human again." She reached over and took a bottle of scented oil and poured a few drops into the water.

He knew he should leave her to her bath, but he couldn't pull his eyes away. She took some soap and began rubbing it between her hands.

"I see Rupert finally stopped making all that racket."

She looked over to where the dog was sleeping by the window. "Yes, thank goodness. I got some ham from cook and fed him. He has a full belly now and should sleep for a while." She began rubbing the soap over her arms. "Was there something you needed?"

He needed to lift her out of the tub and carry her to his bed where he could lick the water from her soft skin. "I just wanted to let you know that I would be out for a bit."

She shrugged her shoulders and the action caused the tops of her breasts to float above the water for a brief glimpse. He swallowed and closed his eyes willing his cock not to stir at the sight.

She splashed some water over her arms. "I thought you might be leaving since you received a message." She began washing her hair and the motion of her breasts moving in the water made him groan. Was she deliberately trying to torture him? He watched for a minute longer. Then she disappeared back under the water to rinse. When she rose again, he did see her nipples breach the water's surface and she stretched out one long slender leg to begin washing. "Have a good evening, Michael. I will try to keep Rupert quiet so you are not disturbed tonight."

He nodded. She was trying to torture him. Giving him just glimpses of her glorious naked body while letting him know she had no intention of allowing him access to it. He must be in hell, for how could he take much more of this? He turned and left her room closing the door quietly behind him. Hopefully Rockhurst would be in the mood to spar with him because he certainly needed someone on which to take out his frustrations.

Catherine sank down further into the hot water. Michael receiving these mysterious messages was strange, to say the least, and she thought it was unusual for Rockhurst to question her about her time in Brighton She was hoping Michael would give in and tell her what was going on especially with her denying him access to her bed, but that didn't seem to be working either. Perhaps she should do a little investigating herself to discover what secrets her husband was hiding from her.

Chapter Fifteen

Catherine didn't know where else to look. After getting dressed after her bath, she had looked around Michael's bedchamber and found nothing of interest. Rupert had awoken from his nap and required attention, so she took him outside to the garden for a bit then left him in the care of her maid while she snuck into Michael's study. She rifled through the papers on his desk and his ledgers but didn't find anything other than accounts and business transactions. At one point she had to duck behind the desk when she heard footsteps that sounded like they were headed her way, but with a sigh of relief whoever it was just passed by the study. There was a locked drawer, but she didn't have a key and had no experience breaking into locked doors, so no luck there. Feeling defeated, she sat down in the chair behind his desk reaching the end of her search. If there was anything in the house that would give her the answers she was searching for, she didn't know where it could be. It was beginning to get late and cook would be serving dinner in a few hours. She wondered if Michael would be out late again tonight.

After carefully putting everything back the way she found it, she left the study and was walking up the stairs when the front door opened and Michael came through. She waited for him on the landing. When he reached her, she could see the bruise on his face and smelled the liquor on his breath. He obviously had been sparing and drinking with Rockhurst. The thought angered her even though she had given him no reason to want to stay home with her.

"I'm going to change before dinner." He moved past her barely sparing her a glance.

She quickly fell in step behind him with Rupert on her heels and followed him into his bedchamber. "You spent the entire day sparing and drinking?"

"Not the entire day, but a good portion of it." He whipped his shirt over his head, and she gasp at the large purple bruise on his side.

She moved forward and poured some water into the basin. "Why ever would you do something like this?" She took a cloth and wet it intending to clean up his bloody knuckles and wash the dried blood from his face. She reached up and carefully wiped his lip causing him to suck in air.

"We were blowing off steam."

She continued to wipe the blood from his knuckles. "What a silly way to blow off steam. You could seriously get hurt."

He stared into her face watching her as she cleaned up his injuries. When she finally raised her eyes to his he said, "I had to find some way to ease my frustrations. I am open to other suggestions." He let a single finger glide along her cheek.

Catherine felt her throat constrict. His eyes were dark with desire and she wanted nothing more than to give in to her own impulses. She quickly looked away and walked over to return the cloth to the water basin. He was naked to the waist, and her eyes once again scanned over the bruises on his torso. "Does it hurt?"

He watched her curiously. "What?"

She blushed and replied softly. "The bruises on your side."

He turned and looked at the purple spot just under his ribs. "No, just a little tender. Rockhurst tends to take it easy on me." He glanced down at Rupert as he sat patiently at her feet. "Rupert looks and smells much better."

She looked down at the little dog. "I'm afraid he has a long way to go before he earns the affection of Finn."

"Finn will come around eventually." He reached for the flaps on his breeches and paused as her eyes followed his movements. "You are welcome to stay."

Catherine shook her head. "I will leave you. I was just worried that you were hurt."

He moved closer to her and she backed up against the door. He took her hand and brought the tips of her fingers to his lips. "I am hurting, Catherine, but you could make the pain go away if you would stay with me." He braced his hands on the door on either side of her face trapping her between the exit and his body.

Catherine kept her gaze level with his throat not having the courage to look him in the eyes. She knew how close she was to capitulating. It would not take much effort on his part to make her forget everything and fall hopelessly into his arms.

"Look at me, Catherine," he said in a deep husky whisper.

She slowly lifted her face to his just as his lips claimed hers. He pulled her into his arms away from the door. "I need you, Catherine." She put her hands on his bare chest revealing in the warmth of his skin but stepped out of his arms when there was a knock on the door.

"Go away!" he yelled in frustration.

"There is a visitor for her grace, shall I send them away?" Finn answered nervously from the other side of the door.

"Yes," he replied at the same time she said, "No."

"I will be right there, Finn." She picked up Rupert. "I had better go see who is here."

He took her hand and held her. "Tell whoever it is to go to the devil."

She hesitated for a second wishing she could do just that. "Dinner will be ready in a couple of hours. Will you be here or did you have plans to go out?"

He released her hand and walked back over to the basin of water. "I will be here."

She sighed softly as she watched him turn his back to her but instead of commenting, she quietly left the room. This couldn't go on. She was beginning to doubt her ability to resist her handsome husband's charms nor did she think she wanted to any longer. She put Rupert back on the floor and hurried downstairs to see her guest.

When she got to the bottom landing, she gasped in surprise and ran the rest of the way to embrace the woman standing there. "Aunt Louisa! I didn't expect it to be you. When did you arrive in London and where will you be staying?"

"Gracious, child. So many questions."

Catherine chuckled. "I'm sorry, Aunt Louisa. I was just so surprised to see you. Does Persephone know you are in town?"

Her aunt began walking with her to the drawing room. "Not yet, dear. I thought I would stop off and see you first. Where is your handsome rapscallion of a husband?"

The older woman noticed the shadow fall on her face as her smile faded. "Michael is upstairs in his room."

Her aunt took a seat on the settee and patted the space beside her for her niece to sit. "I sense there is something wrong, Catherine." She leaned in a little closer and spoke softly. "Was the bedding not everything you expected? I thought with the experience Leicester has in that arena he would be most proficient."

Catherine blushed, surprised at her aunt's outspokenness. She looked away then asked, "Did you have a nice trip in from Brighton?"

Her aunt reached out and took her hand. "Catherine, what is wrong? Have you not bedded your husband?"

Catherine rolled her eyes wishing her aunt didn't see through her so well. "Is bedding really so important, aunt?"

Aunt Louisa put a hand over her heart. "Dear child, I don't know what could be more important than bedding one's husband. Especially as young and beautiful as you are with a husband, who let's be honest, can make a woman swoon with one look." The older lady flipped open her fan. "What has happened to cause you not to share his bed?"

Catherine looked over at her aunt. "I think he is keeping something from me. He left London a few days before our engagement and not one person knows why or where he went. Then on our wedding day he was called away for an urgent meeting and would not share

with me any of the details. I don't like him keeping secrets from me."
She crossed her arms over her chest much like a petulant child.

"So, as punishment you denied him access to your bed, am
I correct?"

"Yes."

Her aunt tsked. "What a foolish child you are, Catherine. First
off, a man's business is his own." When her niece made to interrupt
her, she held up her hand to silence her. "Secondly, denying him
access to your bed is a most certain way to drive him to another's bed.
Thirdly, has he given you reason not to trust him?"

She saw her niece's mind working. "Darling, I know you have
quite the imagination, do you not think that you are making more
of this than there is? Besides, there are better ways to find out what
you want to know than locking your bedroom door."

The older lady patted her hand. "I must be going now. I just
wanted to stop in and check on you, my dear. I will be at my town-
house should you need me." She leaned over and pressed a kiss to her
niece's cheek. "Don't be a fool, Catherine and don't tell Persephone
I am in town just yet. I may need a few days alone before I descend
on the rest of the family."

Catherine smiled glad to have her aunt back in London. She
showed her to the door then turned and looked down at Rupert. "Do
you think she is right?" The little dog stood and yapped wagging his
tail furiously.

"Finn, I think I will have dinner in my rooms tonight."

The butler nodded. "Yes, your grace. I will inform the duke
once he comes downstairs."

She lifted her skirts and hurried up the stairs. She had much to think about. Her aunt always had given the best advice.

Michael sat beside the fire in his bedchamber drinking more brandy. Since his marriage he had stayed in his cups. Today Rockhurst had beat him nearly senseless in their sparing match, and he had welcomed it. This whole business for the crown was not to his liking, and the fact that the mysterious man was now someone linked to Catherine had him on edge. He was even more surprised that Rockhurst was involved. He had never imagined him the kind that would put his life on the line for anything. His friend had always been a seeker of pleasure and not much else interested him. He supposed the rift between him and his father had something to do with it. Rockhurst was always looking for some way to rebel against the duke. He was certain if the Duke of Avanley knew his only son and heir were involved in anything so dangerous, he would have expressly forbidden it and possibly gone to the prince.

He felt as if Hawk should be made aware, but Rockhurst insisted the fewer people knew, the better. He took another sip of his brandy. After discovering that Catherine would not even be joining him for dinner, he had lost his appetite for food and instead decided to drink his supper. His ribs hurt and his knuckles throbbed but nothing like the frustration he felt every minute he thought of Catherine.

The candles had burned down low and the room was illuminated by the flames from the fire. He turned his head slightly at the sound of a door opening. He thought it might be his valet coming to ask if he needed assistance, he had not expected the vision moving slowly toward him. He blinked his eyes a few times wondering if he was hallucinating. He watched as Catherine moved to stand before him. The flames from the fire turned her gown transparent and he felt his cock tighten at the sight of the silhouette of her body. He watched as she reached up to pull the pins from her hair letting the chestnut curls cascade down her back. He remained still, afraid any movement would break the spell or would cause her to vanish. He swallowed as her hands reached for the ribbon of her robe as she untied it slowly letting it slide down her arms to the floor.

When she reached for the ribbon at the neck of her gown he asked in a hoarse whisper, "Are you real, or have I drunk myself into oblivion?"

Catherine paused in her efforts to seduce her husband. It hadn't worked. She had worried she would do something wrong. It wasn't like she had any experience. Now she felt more of a fool than ever. She bent down to retrieve her robe and took a step toward the door. She didn't know how she would ever be able to look Michael in the eyes again.

Suddenly his hand reached out and caught hers. "Don't leave, for the love of God, Catherine don't leave." His voice was husky and his eyes pleading. She dropped the robe back to the floor and turned to face him as he slowly stood from the chair in which he had been sitting.

He still held her hand but did not offer to touch her further. She reached up and gathered her courage as she untied the gown she was wearing. He watched her fingers and his breathing increased as she slid the sheer material over her shoulders then down to her waist baring her breasts.

She watched a muscle twitch in his cheek as he stared at her. It gave her an odd feeling of power. He tentatively reached up and touched her shoulders allowing his hands to move slowly over the skin on her arms. She looked up at him seeing a fire burning in his eyes and she stood on her tiptoes to kiss the corner of his lips where earlier she had wiped the blood clean. When her lips touched his, he wrapped his arms around her waist and lifted her off her feet as his lips claimed hers in a possessive and punishing kiss.

Catherine intertwined her hands behind his neck as he swooped her into his arms and carried her to the bed. He moved over her hovering just above her body. "You are so bloody perfect, Catherine. Please tell me you want this as much as I do." He stretched his hand out to hover over her skin but didn't touch her. "Because I don't know how much more I can take being so close to you, having you sleeping just beyond that door, and not making you mine. If you meant to punish me for my sins you have accomplished your mission. Please put me out of my misery, love."

Catherine saw his hand tremble as it hovered over her skin and heard the tremor in his voice. She reached up and placed a hand on his cheek. He closed his eyes and leaned into her touch. "I want to be yours, Michael, not just in name. I want to belong to you in both body and soul."

He whipped his shirt over his head and captured her lips with his. He felt as if he were ravenous and she was the only thing that could satisfy him. He took a deep breath reminding himself to take it slow. "You are so incredibly beautiful, Catherine." His hand trembled as he caressed her breasts. He pressed his lips against the side of her neck just behind her ear breathing in her scent.

Catherine shivered at his touch and reached out to run her hands along his back reveling in how his muscles tensed beneath her touch. Michael moved atop her allowing the tips of her breasts to lightly touch his chest before moving to the side so his hands could glide over her body. He took her breast in his mouth as his hand glided over her flat belly to the curls at the juncture of her thighs. His cock hardened as dipped a finger between her folds to find her wet for him. She sighed and sucked in her breath as he slowly slid a finger inside her.

His mouth moved lower down her belly flicking his tongue out over her navel as he continued lower. He grabbed her hips as they bucked upward when his tongue flicked over her core.

Catherine wound her hands through his hair as his mouth suckled and licked between her thighs. She felt as if she would die. "Michael," she said his name in a sexy seductive whimper.

He quickly stood from the bed and removed his trousers coming over her naked. She felt him press her legs further apart with his knee as he settled atop her. "Catherine, I can't wait another moment." He pressed his cock slowly into her entrance holding her still as she tried to move away from the invasion. "Hold on to me, love."

Catherine had gone from feeling intense pleasure to a moment of panic. Of course, she had been told a little about what happened between a man and woman, but she had not expected this. She tried to move further up on the bed, but he held her steady. She grabbed his shoulders and looked up at his face.

Michael recognized the look of panic and stopped moving forward. He hated that she would feel pain the first time. He should have taken more time to prepare her, but he had been too eager to have her. He leaned down and kissed her gently holding himself still allowing her body to adjust to his intrusion. When he felt her relax, he pressed forward till he reached the barrier of her maidenhead. He raised up on her elbows and lowered his forehead to hers trying to control himself.

"Catherine," he breathed her name in a husky whisper.

She looked up at him, and he didn't see fear in her eyes he saw trust and at that moment he knew he would do whatever it took for her to always trust him. He leaned forward and kissed her lips passionately as he thrust forward through her maidenhead. He swallowed her cry of pain and forced himself to remain still while her body adjusted to his intrusion and she relaxed again.

Catherine had not expected the intense stabbing pain when Michael entered her fully. She wanted to escape and was thankful when he stilled. He leaned down and kissed her cheeks and then the sensitive area of her neck.

"I'm sorry, Catherine."

She was still breathing heavily. "Neither Persephone nor Aunt Louisa told me about this. All they said was that the first time would be awkward and maybe a little uncomfortable."

He kissed her lightly on the lips again. "It will not hurt ever again, only the first time."

She managed to give him a small smile. "Well, that's a good thing because if it felt like that every time, I am not certain you would ever get me in your bed again."

He chuckled and pulled out of her slowly before coming back again. "I will endeavor to make it a most pleasant experience, my beautiful duchess because I most definitely want you in my bed again." He saw a look of pleasure cross her face as he slowly moved in and out of her body. "If I ever let you leave my bed at all."

She wrapped her arms around his neck and pulled his lips down to hers. "Right now, I'm not sure if I ever want to leave." He kissed her fiercely as his thrusts became wilder and more rapid. He heard her moan and felt her body convulse around him just as he reached his climax and released himself inside her.

He rolled off then turned to the side pulling her body into his. He pressed soft kisses to her shoulder and neck as he tried to get his breathing under control. "You are now mine, Catherine in every conceivable way."

She closed her eyes as she felt his lips on her skin. "I have always been yours, Michael."

The lights from the candles burned down lower as they lay intertwined in bed. Michael held her close feeling as if nothing could destroy their happiness now. She was his wife, his duchess, and he would do whatever it took to keep her safe and happy. There was a feeling of contentment he had never felt before. She was his everything.

Catherine opened her eyes and blinked slowly to adjust to the light being let into the room. She and Michael had made love two more times through the night and as he promised each time was more pleasant than the last. She stretched her arms out to find the bed empty. She sat up letting the covers slip down to her waist as she brushed her wild tangled mass of hair from her face. Michael was standing at the foot of the bed watching her with hungry eyes.

"I brought you some breakfast, sweet pastries, and a cup of chocolate. I'm not certain the pastries are as good as Hawk's chef makes, but they should be a close second."

Catherine sat up further in bed and pulled the sheet up to cover herself. She smiled when he frowned at her movement. "A cup of chocolate does sound delicious. Aren't you having anything?"

He sat the tray down beside the bed. "I am starving, but I have something a little different in mind."

Catherine blushed knowing full well his meaning then popped a small bite-sized pastry into her mouth.

Michael grinned as she licked the frosting from her fingers. "I have had a bath prepared for you in my dressing room. Once you have finished breakfast, I'm sure you will find it relaxing to soak in some warm water."

Catherine sipped her chocolate. "Where will you be?"

He gave her that wicked grin she loved so much. "I intend on enjoying the view while you do so."

She tried to stifle a giggle. "You are so wicked, your grace."

"You don't know the half of it, my duchess." He watched her thinking her the most glorious woman he had ever seen. "I have given the staff instructions that no one is to be admitted, even the prince himself will be denied entry if he decided to visit today. We will not be disturbed. The only way someone could possibly enter the house is if they scaled to the roof and scurried down one of the chimneys or through an open window."

Her laughter rippled through the air. "Let's hope no one is that desperate."

"I will see if your bath is ready, love. Finish your breakfast and when you are done come into the dressing room."

Catherine nodded then popped one more pastry into her mouth. She took one more sip of chocolate and then threw back the covers. She was surprised at how tender she was. She grabbed her robe and slowly made her way to the dressing room.

Michael was putting a few drops of something in her water. She moved over to the tub and let her fingers skim the surface. "It's perfect, but you don't have to stay. I'm sure you have other things to do."

She clutched her robe tighter around her. He moved closer and slowly lifted the robe from her body. She did see him frown when he noticed the small amount of blood between her thighs.

"I'm sorry, darling.," he said as he wrapped his arms around her. "Are you very sore?"

She shrugged her shoulders. "A little, but I'm sure I will be fine."

He pushed her hair away from her forehead. "I wasn't certain. I've never bedded a virgin before." He kissed her quickly. "You are my first."

She raised an eyebrow. "And last."

He lifted her into his arms and slowly lowered her into the water not caring that the sleeves of his shirt were getting soaked. "My only." He took a cloth and dipped his hands beneath the surface of the water and began to cleanse her body.

Catherine marveled at how gentle he was with her. She touched his cheek then pulled his head down to hers. She kissed him. "I love you, Michael."

He was taken aback by her words. He had never expected love in his marriage. It was unusual to find that emotion in any of the marriages of the ton. Hawk and Persephone had found love, and he thought it a rare gift his friend had received. Now as he looked down at his wife, he knew that he had been a fool for refusing her advances so many times in the past. She was a treasure and she was his. He leaned down and kissed her deeply feeling so many emotions coursing through him.

He took her face in his hands. "I love you, Catherine. Everything about you, your smile, your laugh, your spirit for adventure, your vivid imagination, the way you manage to find trouble, your body, your lips, your eyes. My God, Catherine, I have been a fool for so long. I love you." He kissed her again when he saw the shocked expression on her face. Never again would his wife ever doubt his love for her.

Chapter Sixteen

The Next Day

Catherine gave her husband a sleepy smile when he woke her the next morning with a sweet kiss. She snuggled closer against him loving the way her body seemed to mold perfectly against his. She heard him sigh heavily as he wrapped his arms around her.

"Finn will be sending breakfast up to the room soon." He pressed another kiss to her bare shoulder as his hand slid under the sheets to glide over her hip. "While I would love to remain in bed for the remainder of the day, I do have some arrangements to make for us."

She rolled onto her back. "Arrangements?"

His hand moved up to cup her breast. "Yes, I thought we might leave London for a while. We could retire early to Leicester and perhaps make a stop along the way to Hart's Manor along the coast."

"Leave London during the height of the season?"

He leaned down and kissed her lips as he moved to position himself above her. "I have no desire to share you with the rest of London. I want you all to myself." He nudged her legs further apart and pushed slowly inside of her. "All I want to do is make love to my wife and there are several places on our estate in Leicester where I will do just that." To reiterate his point, he thrust harder causing her to gasp and arch her back to take him in fully.

Catherine clutched his shoulders feeling her body tighten around his. She leaned up to capture his lips and was surprised when he flipped her so that she was on top of him. She sat up and looked at him questionably. Michael put his hands on either side of her hips and urged her to rise slowly before bringing her down again on his cock. He repeated the action, but it did not take long for Catherine to figure out how to move. She leaned back as she rocked her hips causing Michael to gasp in pleasure as he squeezed her breasts. Catherine felt the tension building inside her as the tempo of her movements increased, Michael swiftly reversed their positions again so she was on her back. He lifted her legs higher as his thrusts became faster, harder, and deeper. Her body trembled and tightened as they both found release together. Michael collapsed on top of her and lay still for a moment before rolling to his back, taking her with him so she lay across his chest. They both remained silent, as he continued to caress her skin as they recovered.

Catherine lay still listening to his heartbeat, before rising up and asking, "When would we be leaving?"

He brushed her hair away from her face. "Tomorrow. We can leave early and hopefully reach Hart's Manor tomorrow night. We will travel by carriage with a few outriders. In order for us to make better time, your maid and my valet will travel later."

"If I am to leave tomorrow, I should get out of bed and start making arrangements of my own. I will send Persephone and Hawk a note letting them know our plans so she will not worry when I disappear."

She moved to roll off him taking the sheet with her. He watched her as she slipped her thin robe over her naked body. He sat up hoping this business would be over soon. There was something not sitting right about the whole thing, but he hadn't figured it out yet. He grabbed his shirt and slipped it over his head.

"The servants will have prepared baths for both of us. When I return later today, we will have dinner and I will tell you about Hart's Manor." He walked over to where she sat brushing out her hair and kissed the top of her head.

She looked up at him. "You are leaving?"

He quickly looked away. "Yes, I do have some matters to attend to before we leave."

Catherine didn't question him further but thought it odd and wondered why he suddenly looked guilty. "Yes, well I'm sure you have much to do, as do I. She rose from her seat. I think I will see if my bath is prepared."

He nodded and watched her go. Keeping her safe was his top priority throughout this. He needed to find out what had happened to his groom and discover the identity of the smuggler turned spy so he could turn all this information over to Rockhurst. Then he was taking his wife to the safety of Leicester where they could put all of this behind them. If he was careful, she would never know about any of this. As the thought crossed his mind a feeling of dread went through him. He turned to look toward the closed door, where his wife would now be soaking in a warm tub. Perhaps it would be safer for her if he left her in London. No, she would never agree to that, and now after he had her in his bed the thought of her getting angry enough to deny him access to her was unthinkable. Besides the fact that she could get into just as much trouble alone in London as she could with him. He was just going to have to keep his eye on her.

Catherine had joined her husband downstairs as he prepared to go out for the day. Finn helped him into his greatcoat, and he leaned over to kiss her cheek. "I will return soon, Catherine."

"I will begin getting my things ready."

He smiled. "If you leave the house be sure to take a footman with you."

She gave him a small grin. "I still wear a knife strapped to my thigh."

He took her by her arms. "Please don't remind me. I would prefer however that my wife not be required to lift her skirts to retrieve a weapon." He kissed her forehead. "Consider me an overprotective husband if you will, but do not go out alone." He left quickly taking his hat from Finn as he walked out the door.

Catherine looked down at Rupert who was chewing on the hem of her dress. "Well Rupert, what are we to do now?" She was about to turn and go back up the stairs when she heard the front door being opened and Persephone's voice thanking Finn as she entered.

Catherine came forward. "Persephone, your timing could not be more perfect."

Her friend smiled. "It's good to see you too. I thought it would be alright if I visited you this morning. I saw Michael leaving as my carriage arrived. He said you could use some company today as he would be out."

Catherine grinned. "I assume your carriage is still waiting outside."

"Yes," her friend said as she looked down in horror at the mangled bit of fur nipping at her slippers. "My goodness, Catherine. What is this thing?"

Catherine picked up the raggedy bit of fur and teeth. "This is Rupert. He is a dog I found in the park while out riding."

Persephone wrinkled her nose. "He doesn't look like any dog I have ever seen before."

Catherine rolled her eyes. "Come along, we don't have time to waste talking here. I will explain once we are in the carriage."

She grabbed her cloak and went outside with Persephone following behind her. They were assisted into the Hawksford carriage and once inside Persephone asked. "Where are we going?"

Catherine leaned out the window and told the driver to follow Leicester's carriage but try not to get too close. Once back inside the carriage's window, she glanced at her friend who wore a shocked expression on her face. "We are following my husband."

Persephone sighed shaking her head slowly. "Oh Catherine, what the devil are you up to now?"

Catherine sat Rupert on the seat beside her. "Michael is up to something, Persephone. I just know it, and I am determined to find out what it is."

"This is ridiculous! What makes you think he is up to something?"

Catherine told her about their fight on the day of their marriage and about how she had forbidden him from sharing her bed. She also told her about how he had suggested they go to Hart's Manor and how he kept getting secret messages. When she was finished her friend looked doubtful.

"You do realize that as a duke Michael has many responsibilities and estates to run, not to mention his participation in the House of Lords. You are being very fantastical, Catherine."

Catherine crossed her arms over her chest. "I searched his rooms and his study and haven't found anything. I must follow him to see if he is meeting anyone."

Persephone was horrified. "You searched his office and study? If he finds out he will be furious, Catherine. You had no right to do such a thing."

"You are absolutely no fun since you have gotten married, Persephone. Have you no sense of adventure?"

She saw her friend's eyes narrow and knew she had said the wrong thing. "I'm sorry, Persephone."

Her friend frowned. "I have had enough adventure to last me a lifetime, as have you, Catherine."

Catherine knew she was referring to her abduction and torture she had endured at the hands of Comte Domingo. The incident was the very reason Catherine kept a blade attached to her leg. She never wanted to feel that helpless again. "You are right of course, but what harm could come from following him this morning? If nothing suspicious comes from our little outing, I will forget the whole thing and be a dutiful wife for the remainder of my days."

Persephone rolled her eyes. "You will never be a dutiful wife, Catherine, but I don't think it will hurt to follow him as long as we stay in the carriage so we aren't seen. I would hate for Michael to discover us and think I condoned this behavior."

"You sound very much like an old dowager, Persephone, but thank you for coming with me. I told Michael I would not leave the house alone."

Persephone glanced over at the ball of fur and teeth chewing on Catherine's cloak. "I can't believe Michael allows you to keep that thing in the house."

Catherine frowned as she pulled her cloak from Rupert's sharp little teeth. "He is still learning his manners, but he will be fine."

"He is so tiny. He looks more like a rat than a dog."

Catherine rubbed Rupert's head as the little dog tried to latch onto her fingers. "Don't hurt his feelings."

Persephone looked out the window. "It looks like Michael's carriage is turning right up ahead. It's the street that leads to the House of Lords and other political offices. I told you he wasn't up to anything nefarious."

Catherine sat quietly not wanting to argue further with her friend and sister-in-law. When the carriage finally came to a stop, she leaned out the window and asked the driver. "What building is he going into?"

"I believe it is the foreign affairs or the war office, your grace."

Catherine put her head back inside the carriage window and looked at Persephone. "Why would he be at the foreign affairs office?"

Persephone pointed out the other side of the carriage. "He is meeting Rockhurst it looks like."

Catherine strained to look around her friend. "Rockhurst, hmm, interesting."

Persephone laughed. "Oh Catherine, how is that interesting? They have been friends for many years."

Catherine frowned. "Stay here with Rupert, I'll be right back."

She heard Persephone protest but had already left the carriage making her way through the crowds of people mingling along the sidewalks of the government buildings. She saw an older well-dressed man standing on the steps of one of the buildings smoking a cheroot. "Excuse me, sir could you tell me what offices are housed in the building there?"

He eyed her curiously. "Those offices would hold no interest for a lady such as yourself I am certain."

Catherine grew frustrated afraid he would not tell her anything simply because she was a woman. "I'm sorry I bothered you. You looked as if you were a man that would know about such things. So powerful and interesting."

She saw the man's chest puff out and knew she was making progress. "Perhaps I can inquire of someone else."

The man cleared his throat loudly. "My dear, those are the foreign affairs offices as well as the war department. They hold many secrets within those walls."

"Secrets?"

He leaned closer and she cringed at the yellow teeth crooked smile he gave her. "Spies, dear child. Espionage and intrigue abide within those walls and a good thing too with Bonaparte on a rampage."

Catherine had not expected that response. "Thank you, sir."

She quickly turned and headed back to the carriage. Once she climbed inside, she looked at Persephone who was holding Rupert well away from her face. "Nothing, you say? Well, I think Michael is a spy."

Persephone handed Rupert back to her and flipped open her fan nervously. "You can't be serious?"

"I am most serious. It all makes sense now. His disappearance from London before your ball and the reason not one person knew where he had gone or why. Did you not think that odd that Hawk had no idea? They have been friends their entire lives and up until recently they were inseparable." She saw her friend begin to question things in her mind so she continued, "And the message on our wedding day, our wedding day, Persephone. Who leaves their new bride on their wedding day after receiving a mysterious note? He was out very late that night. And now meeting Rockhurst here, I bet he is a spy too."

Persephone closed her eyes and leaned her head back against the cushions. "I suppose you are going to tell me Hawk is a part of this as well."

She shook her head. "I have seen nothing to indicate he is involved."

"Catherine, don't go off on some wild tangent, talk to your husband and find out the truth."

Catherine huffed in disgust. "You just don't understand do you, Persephone? A spy isn't going to confess to being a spy just because his wife asks him." Her eyes widened. "You don't think he would kill me for discovering his identity, do you?"

Persephone rolled her eyes. "Really Catherine?"

Her friend did not seem to hear her. "What if he is in some kind of trouble or has a dangerous mission he must embark on?"

Persephone laughed. "I do love your imagination, my dear. Trust me, you are making too much of this and if Michael discovers that you have been snooping through his personal papers and following him not to mention accusing him of espionage, he will be very angry indeed, as will your brother." She reached across the carriage and took her friend's hands in hers. "Let this go, Catherine and be happy that you married the man you have loved for years. Don't be foolish."

Catherine sank back down onto the carriage seat and rapped on the top for the driver to return them home. "I suppose you are right. We are leaving tomorrow by the way."

"Leaving London before the end of the season?"

Catherine nodded her head. "Yes, Michael wants to attend to something at his estate Hart's Manor beside the coast in Kent before we journey to Leicester."

"I didn't know Michael had an estate along the coast."

Catherine scratched Rupert behind the ear. "I didn't know either. He has never mentioned it before in all the years I have known him." She continued to stare out the window. "Please don't mention any of this to Hawk. He will certainly tell Michael, and I feel foolish enough already."

Persephone didn't like the look on her friend's face. "I will not say a word. Will you write to me while in the country?"

Catherine gave her a sad smile. "Of course, I will."

When the carriage arrived back at Leicester House, Catherine hopped down with Rupert in her arms. "Thank you for humoring me today, Persephone."

Persephone frowned, "Catherine, I don't like to see you this way. Are you sure you are alright?"

"I am fine, Persephone, but I do have a lot to do if we are to leave at first light tomorrow." She shut the carriage door and hurried up the stairs. She knew Persephone thought her suspicions ridiculous, but in her heart, she was certain there was more to it. When Michael returned, she would have to be careful not to let on that she was trying to unravel the mystery surrounding him.

Michael made his way up the steps of the old building with his friend Rockhurst at his side. They didn't speak until they reached Thomas Harrison's office, and the door was closed firmly behind them.

Michael looked over at his friend. "My wife and I will be leaving tomorrow for Hart's Manor. Has there been any word as to the whereabouts of my groom or any other news I should know before I put my wife in danger?"

Rockhurst moved forward pouring the three of them a glass of brandy. "One of my informants believes he may have joined up with the smugglers. Of course, nothing has been confirmed." He walked over and handed Michael the glass. "We still do not know the identity of the man we are seeking nor do we know exactly whose side he is on. Is he loyal to the Crown or to the French? Or he could be loyal only to himself and the coin he gets for sharing information and selling prohibited goods."

Michael sipped the brandy noting it was not the best quality. "So, while I am at Hart's Manor, what exactly am I to do?"

Mr. Harrison moved from behind his desk. "It has been made known that you will be in residence. Simply keep your eyes open. The man is very clever. He has yet to make an appearance other than in Brighton this last year. We are hoping to get a message to him and arrange a meeting with Rockhurst. If he feels comfortable enough to attend the meeting, we will be able to determine if he is on our side. If so, he could be a great asset, if not, he will have to be dealt with."

Michael swirled the liquor in his glass. "Brighton must be where he saw Catherine. Let's assume he has heard of our marriage, an announcement was in the Times, would that put her in danger?"

Rockhurst moved toward the window. "He only asked about her, Michael it is not as if he made advances or has posed a danger to her. I'm sure Catherine will be safe."

Michael stood from his seat. "What makes you think he will tell you the truth? I am not comfortable with this, Charles. I feel as if you aren't telling me something."

His friend turned back to face him. "I need you to accompany me to the meeting if it can be arranged."

Michael nodded. "I will be there, but what makes you certain this man will come alone or not have some trick up his sleeve? I would hate to make Catherine a widow."

Rockhurst gave him a dangerous grin. "What makes you think we will be alone or that I don't have some sort of plan or diversion? Trust me, Michael. I know what I'm doing."

"Very well. At least tell me everything you do know so I can feel more prepared."

Mr. Harrison took a seat and opened up a file. "I suppose I should start at the beginning."

Rockhurst nodded toward Harrison and they shared a secret look. He would tell Michael everything he could, but he would leave out anything to do with Catherine. Rockhurst drank the remainder of his drink. He felt horrible for deceiving his friend. The man they were searching for had done quite a bit more than simply ask after Catherine. He had seen her in Brighton and from what Rockhurst could determine, the man had been quite smitten with her. Luckily, Hawk had heard about the race with Brookhaven and summoned her back to London. Rockhurst had been in Brighton to keep an eye on her and was relieved when she returned to the safety of her family.

Harrison had made it known that she would be arriving with her husband at Hart's Manor hoping the man would make the mistake of trying to see her. They were using her as bait to draw out the man, and if Michael knew that he would never agree to it. If things went badly, he could quite possibly lose his friendship over this.

Rockhurst sat back and listened as Harrison went over everything they knew about the man. Sometimes he wondered if king and country were worth the risks. He had known Catherine since she was a young girl. He had spent holidays with her family and her brother and her husband were the two best friends he had in the world, closer than any family he had. Now in order to stop Bonaparte and his threat against the country, he was putting everything he cared for at risk. He would have to make certain Catherine was kept safe even if it meant sacrificing his own life.

Chapter Seventeen

Catherine had never been fond of traveling in a carriage and she was learning that traveling with a puppy that wanted to chew on everything his mouth would fit around was even more of a challenge. Rupert had finally decided to take a nap and she sighed with relief since Michael had already threatened to have the little mutt ride up front with the driver. She had closed her eyes and drifted off to sleep herself for a few minutes before the carriage hit a bumpy spot in the road and rattled her awake. She blinked a few times then noticed Michael watching her in the seat across from her.

"I thought you were reading?" she asked as she rubbed her eyes.

He smiled and reached over to pull her onto his lap. "I was for a few minutes then I was distracted watching you sleep. You looked so peaceful."

She snuggled closer in his arms. "We left so early and I thought I should take advantage of Rupert sleeping to get some peace."

His arms tightened around her. "He is a vicious little creature. Thank goodness he is so small. As it is, I'm afraid we will arrive at

Hart's Manor with our clothes and shoes in tatters if he wakes and starts gnawing on us again."

Catherine giggled. "I am sorry. He does have sharp teeth."

Michael lifted her and placed her so she sat astride him. "Since we do have a reprieve from Rupert, might I suggest we use our time more wisely or at least in a more pleasurable way." He began loosening the buttons at the back of her dress until he could push her bodice down exposing her breasts. He breathed in deeply before lowering his head to suck her breast into his mouth nipping her nipple with his teeth.

Catherine's head lolled backward as she gripped his shoulders. She loved the way his touch caused her body to shudder. Everywhere his fingers touched almost burned with pleasure. She pulled his head up to kiss his lips. "Persephone once told me something, if you don't mind, I would like to see if it is true."

He grinned and quirked his eyebrow questioning. "Should I be scared?"

"I don't think so." She began loosening the knot of his cravat before moving to the buttons of his shirt. She pressed a kiss to the pulse at the base of his throat as her fingers slipped inside his shirt to caress his chest. She moved slowly from his lap to kneel before him pressing kisses down his chest to his waist. When she reached for the flaps of his britches, he grabbed her hand.

"Catherine?"

She looked up with a devilish grin of her own. "Do you not trust me, your grace?" She noted that his breathing increased as she went back to work. Once his cock sprang free, she reached out tentatively with her fingers marveling at how he jumped slightly at her touch. She watched his face as she wrapped her fingers around him. He closed his eyes and his head rolled to the side. Persephone had told her that when she tried this the first time it had been shocking how much power she had felt over her husband. She leaned forward and let her tongue flick out over his member, startled by the sound her response elicited from her husband. She continued letting her tongue slide along his length as her teeth gently nipped the tip.

"Bloody hell, Catherine!" he called out in a breathless moan.

She stopped. "Am I not doing this correctly?"

He gripped her shoulders. "Yes, good god, yes."

She smiled at his words and took him fully into her mouth. He gripped the seat and cried out as she closed her lips around him. Then suddenly she felt him lift her into the air to settle on his lap once more.

"You are killing me, Catherine," he said breathlessly as he frantically pushed at her skirts moving them out of his way, then once free of that encumberment he lifted her slightly positioning his cock at her entrance before sliding her body down over him.

Catherine gasped as he lifted her again this time bringing her down with more force. She began to move with him riding his cock as he buried his face between her breasts clinging to her. Catherine cried out loudly as she felt her body begin to convulse as he thrust upward again releasing himself inside her. She collapsed against him needing his arms around her for support. Her knees felt like jelly and his breathing was still ragged. Both had a fine sheen of perspiration on their bodies.

Michael lifted her again so he could cradle her in his arms. He kissed the top of her head. "My darling, you are such a wonder."

Catherine chuckled. "We should probably make ourselves more presentable. Shouldn't we be stopping to change horses soon?"

He still held her tight. "We have an hour or so to go before we stop. I have no desire to release you from my arms right now, love."

Catherine looked up and smiled seeing the intense look of love he had in his eyes. She snuggled closer thinking perhaps leaving London would be a good thing. Maybe Persephone was right and she was letting her imagination run away with her. After all, she had always been prone to fanciful thoughts and dreams. She would simply enjoy being with her husband and think nothing more of her fears of spies and secrets.

Two Days Later

Catherine sat outside in the garden of Hart's Manor enjoying the fresh sea air. While she could not see the coast from the estate, it was close enough to smell the salt air. The first day had been spent mostly introducing her to the staff and showing her around the house. It was not nearly as large as the house in London and certainly not as palatial as Hawks Hill, but it was a lovely home, nonetheless. The gardens were impeccable and the staff, though small, were all very friendly and welcoming.

Michael had explained how his great grandfather had won the estate years ago at the turn of a hand of cards and that he seldom ever visited. She hoped that would change now that they were married. She had a feeling Hart's Manor would hold a special place in her heart after this visit. She pulled the shawl closer around her shoulders as a stiff breeze blew over her. Rupert never strayed far from her side, and she laughed as he hopped across the grass chasing a bug.

"He seems to like being outside in the garden."

She looked over her shoulder to see Michael walking toward her. "Yes, he has been quite busy this morning chasing everything that moves."

He bent down and placed a lingering kiss on her lips. "Why don't you leave Rupert with one of the grooms in the stable, and the two of us will take a ride around the estate? Bucephalus is giving the grooms a rough time, and a good run will probably do him some good."

She perked up at the thought. "I'm so glad you thought to bring him with us. Perhaps you can take me to see the coast. I can smell the salty air from here. It can't be too far."

He helped her rise from the chair in which she had been seated. "We shall see, my love. I have heard the coast can be a bit dangerous with thieves and brigands about. I would not want to take any chances with your safety."

She gave him a quick kiss on the cheek. "I'm sure it will be alright. I'll go change into my riding habit and join you out in the stables shortly."

He watched as she ran back toward the house. He of course had no intention of taking her by the sea until he knew more about these smugglers and where they were operating. So far, he had not gathered any details that could be useful, and Rockhurst had not yet contacted him regarding the meeting with the group's leader.

But as this was a part of his wedding trip with his beautiful new bride, he would take advantage of the day and do something he knew she loved. There were some old ruins on the estate somewhere and if he could find them, he would take her there. It had been many years since he had spent any amount of time here, and he was looking forward to seeing everything again with his wife.

He bent down and picked up Rupert who had started chewing on his boot and headed toward the stables. "Come along, Rupert."

Michael pulled back on the reins of his horse and watched as Catherine sailed past him on Bucephalus. Catherine had always been a good rider, but up until recently, he had not known exactly how proficient she truly was. She slowed her horse down and turned back to him. Her hair had come from its pins and was blowing wildly around her face. She was laughing and the sight made his heart skip a beat. He rode over to her and leaned over to kiss her.

"You let me win," she said as she reached down to stroke her horse's neck.

Michael shrugged his shoulders and grinned. "You would have won anyway; I saw no need in fighting the inevitable."

She laughed and urged her horse into a walk as they continued their tour of the estate. It was a very nice piece of property even if much smaller than most country estates owned by the nobility. It was surrounded by green meadows and if you continued riding, you would eventually reach the coastline and if you crossed the English Channel from there Calais in France.

"Dover must not be very far from here. Are you sure we can't ride to the coast?"

Michael sighed, "I know of a place where we can ride to and see the coast safely from the cliffs, but I would prefer not to go down to the beaches."

She laughed softly as she looked over at him. "For someone that has always been considered one of the most dangerous rakes in London you certainly are being overly cautious."

He reached over and took her hand in his before bringing it up to his lips. "That was before I had you. I'm very protective of what is mine, Catherine. I will not take any chances with your safety, my love." He gave her a wink and nudged his horse forward into a slow canter knowing she would follow closely behind him.

Catherine followed her husband, happy that she had been able to convince him to take her further away from the estate. They rode for about an hour, and Catherine stopped her horse so she could hear the waves. Michael stopped his horse and dismounted to walk back over to her.

"Come, let me help you dismount."

Catherine leaned over and slipped into his arms as he slowly dragged her body down his until she stood before him. He wrapped his arms around her waist and held her closely.

"I have been assisted in dismounting before, but never anything like this," she said as she stood on her tiptoes to press a kiss against his lips.

He raised an eyebrow. "My darling, if anyone attempted to hold you as I am now, they would not live long enough to do it a second time." He reached around and let both hands grab her firm buttocks as he lifted her off her feet.

Catherine giggled and he sat her back on the ground and took her hand to lead her to the edge of the cliff. "Don't get too close the edges are crumbling in places."

Catherine pushed her hair back and lifted her face into the cool ocean breeze. "It's so beautiful, isn't it?"

Michael watched her as the wind whipped around her. "Yes, indeed."

Catherine glanced over at him. "I wonder if you could swim here?"

"It would be much too cold, my love not to mention the currents can be very swift. There is a lake in Leicester where we can swim during the summer."

Catherine turned to him. "Do you remember the time you had to jump in the lake at Hawks Hill and rescue me?"

He took her hand. "Yes, I was so angry at you. I ruined a new pair of boots pulling you from the water. You were thirteen or fourteen years old; I think. I remember ranting at Hawk for you not being watched properly by your governess."

Catherine smiled at the memory. "You hated me then."

"I never hated you, Catherine. I was a young man in my earlier twenties and you were so very young."

Catherine nodded then looked away quickly. "I know we have been over this before. I know all about your feelings on that matter."

He turned her to face him. "Catherine, I was a fool that day and the fact that I hurt you so profoundly with my ill-spoken words torments me still, but I promise you, my love, I will spend the rest of my days making it up to you. You will never have to doubt my desire or my love for you." He moved to kiss her just as a clap of thunder sounded in the distance. He looked out and saw the clouds beginning to darken. "We should head back toward the house. From the looks of the clouds, we may not make it back before the rain."

Catherine hurried back to Bucephalus and Michael helped her to mount before mounting his own horse. Together they headed back toward the house. They were about an hour away when the first droplets of rain began to fall. By the time they got in sight of the house, the rain was falling in earnest.

Michael pulled his horse to a stop. "There is a carriage out front." He reached over and grabbed the reins of Catherine's horse. "I wasn't expecting anyone. Stay behind me until I know it is safe."

Catherine eyed him curiously. "Safe?"

He urged his horse forward slowly and pulled his pistol from under his coat. Catherine moved closer to him.

"Michael, what's wrong?"

"Probably nothing, but I want to make certain."

They rode closer and Catherine shielded her eyes from the rain. "That looks like Hawk's carriage."

Michael looked over at her. "It has the Hawksford Crest. What is your brother doing here?"

Catherine did not wait to answer fearing something must have happened to Persephone. She urged her horse into a gallop, and once she reached the house a footman came forward to take her horse. She slid to the ground and raced up the steps with Michael not far behind her. Once inside she breathed a sigh of relief when she saw her brother and Persephone standing in the entryway.

"My goodness, Catherine. You are soaked through the skin." Persephone said rushing forward. "Michael, what on earth possessed the two of you to be out in weather like this?"

Catherine turned to see Michael dripping wet just behind her. He took off his overcoat and handed it to the butler "It wasn't raining when we left, Persephone." He turned to Hawk. "What brings you to Hart's Manor."

Her brother looked toward his wife. "Why don't the two of you go upstairs and get into some dry clothes? Persephone and I will wait in the drawing room. Your housekeeper was preparing us something to eat and drink while we await dinner." He stretched his hand out toward his wife, and Persephone automatically moved toward him.

Michael walked over to Catherine and urged her up the stairs. "We should get changed before we drip water all over the house."

Catherine gripped her skirts and hurried up the stairs to their bedroom. Once inside she turned to Michael. "Can you help me with the buttons of my riding habit?"

He came forward and made quick work of her buttons before whipping his wet shirt over his head. When he turned around, he saw Catherine standing there with her wet chemise clinging to her body. She moved to the basin and grabbed some linens to dry her hair.

"How long do you think we have before your brother and Persephone come looking for us?"

Catherine looked up to see her completely naked husband stalking toward her. In one swift swoop, he had her wet chemise tossed to the floor. He gripped her buttocks and lifted her so that she straddled his waist before he roughly tossed her on the bed. Catherine gasped as he pushed her legs apart further and entered her in one swift forceful motion. He hooked his arm behind her knee and lifted her leg further to push deeper inside her. Catherine arched her back and gripped his shoulders as he continued to roughly pound into her body. It did not take long for them both to find their release. When Michael rolled to the side, he covered his eyes with his arm.

"I'm sorry, Catherine. I should have been gentler with you. But I have wanted to be inside of you all day and when I saw you standing there with that wet chemise clinging to every curve and those perfect rose-colored nipples peeking through, I lost all control of myself."

Catherine was still breathing heavily and her body ached a bit at the rough intrusion. She lowered her legs and moved to face her husband. When she moved her hand over his chest, he took it and brought her palm to his lips.

She snuggled against him draping one leg over his and then asked softly, "Is it wrong of me to say that I liked it?"

He pulled her so that she lay on top him. "Would it be wrong of me to go downstairs and bodily throw your brother out of the house and bar the doors?"

Catherine laughed. "I'm not sure Persephone would be as easy to manage." She slowly and seductively slid down his body letting her nipples glide over his skin till she moved between his legs. She flicked her tongue out over his cock before standing. "We should at least dress and see what brought them all the way here."

He groaned thinking of so many things he would rather do to his wife. "If we must, but once I have you alone my sweet seductive duchess, I am going to make you pay for this interruption."

She gave him a wink as she moved to her dressing room. "I look forward to it, your grace."

"What exactly prompted your visit to Hart's Manor?" Michael asked as he poured his friend a drink of port after their dinner.

"Persephone expressed a desire to leave London and head to the country earlier than we had planned."

Michael leaned back against his desk. "Hart's Manor is not on the way to your estate."

Hawk gave his friend a sly look. "No, it isn't, but Persephone was determined that she check on Catherine. It seems that Catherine must have said some things the last time they saw each other that caused her to worry about her." He took a sip of his port. "I know you have not been married long, but I assure you that when Persephone wants something she can be most convincing. Needless to say, if it is in my power for her to have her wishes come to fruition, I will see that they do."

Michael was no longer listening wondering if he had missed something. "Catherine has seemed very happy. I'm not sure why she would be worried."

Hawk waved his hand dismissively. "They are very close so maybe Catherine told her something to which you are unaware." He saw his friend's frown grow. "Persephone is also expecting a child. She has been very sensitive lately."

This seemed to make Michael relax. "How long will the two of you stay?"

Hawk put down his drink. "If Persephone is not opposed to it, I would like to leave the day after tomorrow. I'm sure you can tolerate my presence for that long."

Both gentlemen rose to their feet when Catherine and Persephone came inside the room. Persephone moved to stand beside her husband as Catherine moved toward where Michael was standing. "I was just showing Persephone the house."

"It is very lovely, Michael. I look forward to seeing Leicester Park once you return there."

He smiled at Persephone as he reached over and pulled Catherine closer to his side. "I'm hoping to take Catherine there very soon. Hart's Manor will be a temporary stop on our tour."

Catherine grinned up at him, and her brother cleared his throat loudly. "Well, it is getting late and I'm sure Persephone would like to retire early."

Persephone walked over and gave Catherine a kiss on the cheek and whispered in her ear. "I'm so glad you are feeling better, my dear." Then placed her hand on her husband's arm as they left the room to head upstairs to the chambers that had been prepared for them.

Once they were alone Catherine looked over at her husband. "It's so good to see Persephone happy and feeling better again."

Michael moved closer to her and took both of her hands in his. "Persephone was worried about you. That's why they are here." He slowly stroked the top of her hands with his thumb. "Are you happy, Catherine? Hawk seemed to think that you had confided in Persephone."

Catherine stared at him. "I am very happy, Michael." She looked down to where her hands were held in his. "I was afraid there were secrets between us, things that might possibly come to light and shatter what we have now. But I was just being silly." She kissed his cheek. "It is getting late and if I remember correctly there seems to be some kind of retribution planned for me this evening." She gave him a saucy wink as she headed out the door.

Michael smiled, but inside he knew he was keeping secrets from her. Secrets that were necessary to keep her safe. He only hoped she never became wise to them or he would lose her trust and he didn't want to lose anything that concerned Catherine.

The next morning Michael was having breakfast alone waiting for the others when a note arrived for him.

> *Meet me in the village at the tavern today at half past noon. The meeting has been arranged. It seems we have new developments. I know Hawk arrived yesterday; he is welcome to come along.*
>
> *Rockhurst*

Michael pushed his plate aside as his friend and now brother-in-law came into the room. Hawk walked over and fixed a plate of sausages and eggs from the sideboard. Then moved to take a seat beside him.

"Persephone is sleeping in this morning. She still feels ill at times." He took a bite of his breakfast before continuing. "Do you want to tell me what the hell is going on, Michael? Why are you here at Hart's Manor?"

Michael looked up at his friend wishing he could tell him everything. "I needed to check on the estate."

Hawk sipped his coffee. "That's what we have solicitors and estate managers for, Michael."

He decided to turn the conversation elsewhere. "I have to go into the village today to meet Rockhurst. Would you like to join me?"

Hawk stopped his fork in midair. "Rockhurst is in the village? How odd? Now I know something is wrong."

Michael grinned and took a sip of his tea. He could see his friend's mind begin to turn trying to figure out what was happening and why he had not been included. "We are to meet him at the tavern in town. Perhaps you can ask him why he is here."

Hawk nonchalantly continued his breakfast. "I intend to. Something is going on and I will find out what that is."

Catherine came into the room at that moment and both he and Hawk rose to their feet. She walked over and gave her brother a quick kiss on the cheek then walked to the sideboard and took a pastry and some jelly.

Michael moved to pull her chair out for her and kissed her cheek. "Hawk and I will be going into the village this afternoon. We should not be too long."

She spread some of the jelly on her pastry. "I think I will take Persephone on a tour of the estate. We might take a ride."

"Don't go too far."

Just then Rupert came running into the dining room barking.

Hawk jumped as the little dog nipped at this boot. "Good god, Leicester. What the hell is that?"

Catherine jumped from her seat and scooped up the ferocious ball of fur. "Rupert, stop it at once."

Hawk gave his friend a questioning look. "You allow her to keep that mongrel in the house."

Michael frowned. "Didn't you just tell me how convincing your wife could be when she wanted something?"

"Touché."

Catherine popped the last bit of pastry into her mouth. "I will leave you to enjoy your day. Rupert needs to go outside for a bit, and

I need to check on Persephone." She looked over at Michael. "We will see you at dinner tonight. I had cook prepare lamb."

Michael watched as she left the room. He fought the urge to go after her. Never in his life had he ever been so drawn to a woman. She occupied his every thought, and he didn't like being apart from her. He looked over to see his friend watching him with a smile.

"It doesn't get any better, you know."

Michael nodded then returned to his seat. "Would you like to go out to the stables before we head into the village?"

Hawk finished his coffee. "If we can have something stiff to drink once we come back inside."

Chapter Eighteen

<hr/>

"It really is a beautiful estate, Catherine. How far are we from the coast?" Persephone said as she rode beside her friend enjoying the fresh air.

Catherine shielded her eyes. "We aren't very far from Dover, but Michael took me to a place where we can see the coast from the cliff. He said it wouldn't be safe to go to the shore."

Persephone looked over at her. "Whyever not?"

Catherine shrugged her shoulders. "He thinks there might be bandits or smugglers around. I think he is being ridiculous. Let's see if we can find a path that leads down to the beach."

Persephone shook her head warily. "I'm not certain that's a good idea, especially if Michael said it could be dangerous."

Catherine rolled her eyes. "If it was up to Michael and Hawk, we would never leave the house without them. We used to do all sorts of things we weren't supposed to do Persephone. Let's have at least one more adventure."

Persephone giggled. "You are right of course. Besides I don't see what it could hurt."

They continued riding toward the spot where Michael had taken her the day before. When they reached the spot, Catherine began looking for a path to the beach. "I don't see anything here perhaps we should go down a bit further."

Persephone followed her. "We should have brought a groom with us, Catherine."

"We don't have very many servants here at Hart's Manor, and the ones we do have would have only slowed us down. We will be fine."

Catherine continued farther down until she did spot a path that led to the beach. "It looks like we can go down here, but it is a bit steep. We should probably dismount and lead the horses down."

Persephone dismounted and followed Catherine down the path. It was steep but wide enough for them to safely descend to the sands below. Once they reached the bottom Catherine stopped still holding the reins of Bucephalus in her hands. "It's beautiful isn't it."

Persephone came forward. "Yes, it is. Shall we ride along the beach?"

Catherine mounted her horse and smiled. "I think that is a lovely idea. Maybe once I tell Michael it was perfectly safe, he will agree to come with me next time."

They rode further down the beach through the surf talking and laughing not realizing they had gone much farther than they had intended. Persephone noticed something in the distance and turned to Catherine. "I think we should turn back."

Catherine saw that there were four men on horses headed toward them. "Yes, I think we should."

They turned their horses around and started back in the direction they had come. "Are they following us?" Persephone asked as Catherine turned her head around to see if the men were still there.

"They are behind us, but they haven't picked up speed. I will feel better though once we put more distance between us." She urged her horse into a faster canter and Persephone followed.

Catherine was beginning to get nervous. She started looking for the path, but they were still too far away. She looked over at Persephone and noticed the look of anxiety on her face. There was a bend up ahead, and she was certain the path that would lead to the top of the cliff was nearby. But as they rounded the corner, they pulled their horses to a stop when three more men on horseback came forward and blocked their way.

A large burly man came forward and took the reins of her horse. "Look what we have here. You are a bit far from London aren't ye little girl."

Catherine pulled herself up and lifted her chin higher into the air. "Let go of my horse and let us pass." Persephone remained quiet behind her.

The man moved his horse closer to her. "I'm afraid I can't do that, missy. You be coming with us."

Catherine took her riding crop and slapped the man across the face with it. "You will let me go at once!" She went to strike the man again this time connecting with his shoulder. The other men started laughing as she thrashed the man holding her horse before he finally managed to take hold of her arm and began wrestling the crop from her hand. In the fight, Catherine was pulled from her horse and the man tumbled off his horse landing on top of her.

She was still for a minute having the wind knocked out of her lungs. She struggled to breathe or cry out but no air would come. Finally, she managed to scream and kick the man between his legs as he continued struggling with her.

"Get the hell off of me!" She yelled and scratched as the man grabbed her arms. She heard Persephone scream and then suddenly the man was lifted off her and tossed to the side as if he was no more than a sack of flour.

She scrambled to get her feet underneath her and shielded her eyes to see her rescuer. There standing before her was a man dressed as elegantly as any lord in London. He held out his hand to assist her in rising.

"My apologies, duchess." He helped her to stand. Catherine looked over quickly to see Persephone still seated upon her mount but looking quite faint.

"Thank you for your assistance. My friend and I will be going now." She moved back toward her horse, but the man reached out and grabbed her arm stopping her from moving forward.

"I'm afraid I can't let you do that, duchess." He gave her a sly smile. "At least not yet."

Catherine looked back toward Persephone seeing the fear on her face. She knew she was thinking about her kidnapping, and the fear of going through that again showed clearly. Catherine moved over to her reached up and took her hand. "Everything's going to be alright, Persephone."

The man followed her to stand near Persephone's horse. "I have no intention of hurting either one of you." He looked up at Persephone. "You are the Duchess of Hawksford, correct?"

Persephone nodded her face still pale and her voice shaky. "Do I know you, sir?"

The man bowed at the waist. "No, your grace, I have never had the pleasure." He turned back to Catherine. "I have however had the pleasure of seeing you, Lady Gray. I suppose I should call you, your grace now since your marriage to the Duke of Leicester."

Catherine narrowed her eyes. "You know me?"

"We were never introduced, but I did see you earlier this year in Brighton."

Catherine felt a little more at ease. "If you know us and our husbands, why will you not allow us to leave?"

The man's lips turned up in a half smile. "I can explain everything a little later." He motioned for her horse. "If you will allow me to escort you to our camp, we can discuss things, and perhaps I can offer the two of you refreshment." He didn't bother to wait for an answer, but simply took Catherine by the arm and led her back to her horse where he lifted her back into her saddle then swiftly mounted behind her.

Catherine gasped when he wrapped his arms around her taking the reins from her hands. "This is entirely unnecessary not to mention improper. I can ride perfectly well without your help."

He leaned closer to her ear. "I have seen you ride, your grace. Don't think I'm fool enough to turn you loose on a horse."

Catherine scooted as far as she could from her captor and bit her tongue as they began moving toward his camp. She wished Persephone was not with her. She was afraid and Catherine didn't know what to say to ease her mind. The group of men continued until they reached a cave that went into the cliffs above. It was a large cave and they rode the horses into it.

Once inside the man dismounted, then lifted Catherine to her feet before going to assist Persephone. "If you ladies will follow me, I will have some wine and perhaps some bread and cheese for you. After you have eaten, I will try to explain who I am and why I brought you here."

Catherine reached over and took Persephone's hand in hers and squeezed it gently. They followed the man until he reached a place deep in the cave where there were crates and places for them to sit. He offered them a place on a large crate. The cave was well lit with lots of candles and lanterns and Catherine took a minute to look around at the contents inside. There were crates of wine and boxes upon boxes of silks and satins. She looked over at him as he watched her carefully.

"You are a smuggler, aren't you?"

He grinned as he handed her a glass of wine. "You are very astute."

Catherine took a sip of the wine and scooted closer to Persephone. "Why are we here and who are you?"

He took a seat across from them. "My name is Camden Davenport, your grace. And I have the dubious honor of being the bastard son of the Duke of Stafford." He glanced over at Persephone and said gently, "I assure you, your grace, that you will come to no harm while you are here." He gave her a small smile, and Catherine hoped it would ease her mind and she would relax a bit.

Persephone finally found her voice, "You know our husbands, my lord?"

He nodded. "Yes, I suppose you can say that. While I have never met them personally, I make it my business to know who the most powerful people in London are, and you can just call me Camden there is no reason to my lord me."

Catherine narrowed her eyes. "You do look familiar. You said you saw me in Brighton."

His smile widened. "I did indeed and was instantly intrigued although I never got an introduction. I also saw your ride with Lord Brookhaven. It was at that moment that I became captivated. I had every intention of finding you after the ride and making my introductions. You have enchanted me." His smile faded and he sighed heavily. "Alas, my work took me away from Brighton that night and when I returned, I learned that you had left for London." He took a sip of his wine. "I will never forgive Bonaparte for that. For while I was attending to matters in protection of the crown, the Duke of Leicester swept in and claimed you for his own."

Catherine's eyes widened. "Protection of the crown? I don't know what you mean."

Camden stood and spread his arms wide. "Look around and you see goods smuggled from France. I consider that payment for other things I am proficient at doing, most of which I rarely speak of."

Catherine watched him, her mind turning. "None of this makes sense. Why did you bring us here and why are you telling us all of this?"

He sat back down. "I transport more than wine and silk across the channel, your grace, I also bring information that is useful to our troops and those in power. Bonaparte is a threat to the British Empire and while I may not have held a commission in the British army, I am doing my part to stop him. Your husband is right now meeting with Lord Rockhurst at a tavern in the village. Rockhurst had been trying to ascertain my identity for quite a while now. He enlisted the help of your husband. Right about now they should be getting word of my identity as well as the fact that they are being called off by more important political members that sponsor my efforts. They are in fact discovering that we are on the same side."

Both Catherine and Persephone were shocked. "Michael is involved in this?"

He nodded. "Rockhurst convinced him to bring you to Hart's Manor hoping that my infatuation with you would draw me out. You see I have been making inquiries about you. Rockhurst and his contact in the foreign affairs office felt that if I found out you were here, I would make an attempt to see you. Once I made that mistake, they could capture me and find out who I truly work for and my identity."

Persephone gasp and gripped Catherine's hand. Catherine felt her breathing increase. "Michael brought me here as bait for a trap to catch you?"

"In a way, yes, but my benefactor is the head of the foreign office and has since called off all further investigations into my actions. What I do is too important for amateurs to interfere with."

Catherine stood and paced before him. "Michael kept all this from me." She said the words to herself, but Persephone heard her and got up to comfort her.

"I'm sure Michael has his reasons for doing this, Catherine."

Catherine felt her anger rising. "Yes, he did." She felt her chest heaving. "Was everything done to help Rockhurst? Is that why he married me? Has all of this been a farce?"

Persephone took her by the shoulders and shook her slightly. "No, Catherine. He married you because he loves you, not because of this. Not because of Rockhurst and whatever craziness he is involved in."

Catherine pulled away and marched up to her captor. "Why am I here? You have yet to answer that question."

He bowed before her. "You are here by chance, your grace. I had no intention of bringing you here or involving you in any of these dealings. But when I saw you on the beach, I couldn't help myself. It's a mistake I am sure to pay for eventually. The meeting your husband and Lord Rockhurst are at now was arranged by me. I thought it would be wise to meet the men who had been seeking me out. Unfortunately, I am unable to meet with them as I have received word that I must leave for Dover immediately, another mission for the crown."

Catherine was more than a little curious. "A mission?"

His smile took on a wicked gleam as if he could read her mind. "Yes, I have to ride to Dover tonight to meet a Monsieur Lavigne. He holds some information that will be most useful to Wellington and those in command. While Lavigne has always been trustworthy in the past, it would have been nice to have Rockhurst or Leicester to accompany me. It's always a good idea to have someone watch my back and it would have given us an opportunity to become more acquainted. After all they have been trying to find out my identity for a while now. I will have one of my men go with me instead and upon my return I will hand deliver the information to Rockhurst and he can take it to London."

Catherine was silent for a minute as she looked Camden in the eyes. "I'll go. I can be an extra set of eyes and bring the information to Rockhurst."

Camden's smile grew wider. "That would not be wise, your grace. Dover is about a two maybe three-hour ride from here, and we would be out very late together. Besides, if you are watching my back, who is watching yours, duchess?"

Catherine frowned. "How dangerous do you feel this to be?"

He shrugged his shoulders. "I am not overly worried, but there are always dangers in this type of business. It would be best if you returned home with your friend. This business is not meant for ladies."

Catherine put her hands on her hips. "My husband wasn't too worried when he brought me here as bait to draw you out, and at the time, he didn't know you were on the same side!"

"It's a little bit different, your grace."

"I would wager that I can ride better than any man you have here, so I will not slow you down. I will stay out of your way, and I am not afraid. Trust me, I am not one of those weak-minded females that will swoon or cry at the first sign of trouble."

The man's smile widened as his eyes sparkled with amusement. "I never expected you to be, duchess. We would have been so good together. But if you are recognized alone with me, it will tarnish your reputation. I respect you enough not to wish for you to come to any harm."

"I will not be recognized and we will not be gone very long. Besides, it will teach my husband a lesson. If it is alright for him to get involved in something dangerous, it should be for me as well. I want to do this."

Persephone instantly shot back to her feet. "Oh no, Catherine! You can't do this! It is entirely too dangerous and Michael will be furious."

Catherine ignored her friend. "Tell me more. When would we leave and who are we meeting? Should I carry a weapon?"

"We would leave shortly so we could arrive in Dover just after dark. We will meet Monsieur Lavigne and get the documents. Once we have what we came for, we will turn back for here. You would be home before midnight if everything goes as expected, or shortly thereafter, but like I said, there are always dangers and unexpected things could delay us."

Persephone moved to stand in front of her friend. "Absolutely not! This is asinine." She turned back to Catherine. "If word gets out that you did this, Catherine you will be ruined not to mention you could get hurt."

The man moved forward. "I would never put you in danger, your grace. I think your friend may be right. There are other ways to make your husband see the error of his ways without putting yourself in danger."

Catherine moved past Persephone. "I need to do this."

She then turned back to Davenport. "You need to understand something first, while my husband may be a manipulating devil, I still have no intention of dishonoring him or our marriage vows. I simply want to go on one last adventure and teach him a lesson for deceiving me."

He moved forward and took her hand in his before raising it to his lips. "I never thought you would, your grace. And I would never force my intentions upon you or any woman for that matter. You have my word that I will not touch you."

Persephone looked back and forth between this man and her friend. "Catherine don't do this. Michael may not forgive you."

Catherine turned sharply. "Forgive me? Did you not hear that he brought me here as bait for a trap?" She let go of Persephone's hand and faced Camden Davenport. "Will you take me with you?

And see that Persephone is returned home safely? I have to know she will be safe."

Camden nodded. "If you are certain you wish to do this, but you must know that this may cause problems between you and your husband. He will not be happy."

Catherine's eyes fell. "There are already problems between us. I just didn't know it until now."

Persephone came forward grabbing her hands. "I will go with you, Catherine. You can't go alone with this man. We don't even know if he is telling the truth."

Catherine smiled and gave her friend a quick hug. "You can't do that. Remember you are expecting a baby, and I would never forgive myself if something happened to you. I will have enough to worry about with Michael wanting to throttle me, I don't need Hawk wanting my head as well." She laughed hoping to put Persephone's mind to rest.

"I can assure you that I speak the truth, duchess. Lady Catherine will come to no harm by my hands, and you will be safely escorted back to Leicester's lands where you can make it back safely. I will send my most trusted friend to guide you." Camden said causing both ladies to turn in his direction.

Catherine nodded. "It's only for a few hours. I will be home by midnight, and Michael will find out that I am not to be manipulated again. One last adventure, Persephone. When we were little girls and used to hide in the cave waiting for the knight to come to slay the dragon that had captured us, well it looks like I'll have to slay my own dragon. And it's my chance to do something important, retrieving documents for Wellington no less."

Persephone sank back down on the crate and placed her head in her hands knowing she had lost the battle. "I'm not sure how many more *last* adventures I can stand."

Michael and Hawk sat at a table in a dark corner of the tavern in the village waiting on Rockhurst to arrive.

"I have to say that all of this is most perplexing. It would be nice if you would let me know what the hell is going on with the two of you," Hawk said just as they were joined at the table by Lord Rockhurst.

"I didn't let you know because I didn't want to have to listen to you chastise me about the dangers involved," Rockhurst said as he took a seat at the table beside his friends.

Michael narrowed his eyes. "Where is this man we are to meet?"

Rockhurst reached over and poured himself a drink. "I received a note from Harrison this morning. He will be here soon and explain everything."

"Thomas Harrison?" Hawk asked as he crossed his arms over his chest. "Didn't he attend Eton with us?"

"Yes, he is the one that has orchestrated the whole thing."

Hawk looked around the room. "Harrison couldn't find any-where nicer to meet? The liquor is horrible." He swiped his finger through the dust on the table. "And the cleanliness is questionable."

Rockhurst laughed deeply. "When you are dealing with the types of people we are doing business with, you don't meet them in a ballroom."

Just then another gentleman entered the room dusting off his coat and boots at the door before walking over to their table. "Gentlemen," he said before bowing slightly and taking a seat alongside them.

Rockhurst nodded then said, "Harrison, I believe you know the Duke of Hawksford."

Thomas bowed his head as Hawk nodded. "Your grace, I was not expecting to have you join us."

"I was not expecting to be here. I would however like to know what these two have gotten mixed up in," he said before giving each of his two friends a pointed look.

Thomas looked at Rockhurst. "Several months ago, I asked Lord Rockhurst to help me locate the identity of a man we believed to be a smuggler or a spy. Rockhurst has been garnering information over the past year or so for us in his usual way."

Hawk glared at his friend. "Usual way?"

Rockhurst smiled. "You would be surprised what one will uncover in the bedrooms of the ton."

Hawk shook his head and grinned. "And Leicester?"

Thomas looked over to where Michael sat frowning. "Leicester was brought in a few weeks ago. The man for which we had been searching for has been running goods out of France from a cove on Leicester's estate, Hart's Manor. I asked him to see if he could garner any information about the goings on from his servants. I had men stationed here but other matters called them away. Leicester had a groom he trusted, and he asked the man to keep his ears open in the village for any additional information. The man disappeared shortly afterward."

"My God! The two of you have entangled yourselves into something dangerous," Hawk said downing the rest of his drink.

"As it turns out, I have received word that the man we are seeking is not what we had first thought." Both Rockhurst and Leicester leaned forward to listen as Thomas continued. "I received a note from my superiors and the entire search for the man is being called off. His name is Camden Davenport and he is the bastard son of the Duke of Stafford. He takes orders directly from William Wickham who oversees all matters in this area. We are to cease our efforts in searching for him. He has been instrumental in bringing information from France to our offices and to my understanding he has also served in more capacities as well, but no one other than Wickham knew of his existence. When we were getting close to unraveling his smuggling operation, I was told to cease at once and leave the man to his own devices. Apparently, smuggling is a minor crime compared to the good he does for the crown and they are willing to overlook it."

Leicester leaned back in his seat. "So, there is no further need of my assistance in this matter?"

Thomas shook his head. "No, there is no need for you to be involved any longer. Your groom however has been located. He works for Davenport now as a member of his crew. He felt he could do more good for England serving Davenport. Being from the military he still has a strong desire to serve our country."

Hawk pushed his glass aside wanting no more of the foul liquor. "Since we are here, and it seems the danger has passed, I would be curious to know how Rockhurst became involved in this shady business as well as you Leicester. You brought my sister to Hart's Manor after all, knowing it was where this infamous smuggler had his operations."

Harrison cleared his throat and looked uncomfortable. "There is a reason behind that as well. It seems that Davenport saw Lady Catherine in Brighton and developed an interest in her."

Michael narrowed his eyes. "What kind of an interest?"

"He tried to seek an introduction but was called away for reasons I am not aware. After she left Brighton for London, he continued to make inquiries about her. We had the idea that if she came here, he might come out of hiding to seek her out. Once he did so, we could capture him. Of course, that was all before we discovered he is working for the British."

Michael's frown intensified. "You were using my wife to draw out a suspected spy?! You are a bastard, Harrison."

"I am that, your grace, but for whatever it is worth, I am thankful that was not necessary," Harrison said blatantly as he stared into his half-empty glass.

"So, tell me exactly what you contribute to this, Rockhurst?" Hawk asked.

Rockhurst grinned. "I suppose we have some time, but I warn you none of this information is to go beyond this table. I wouldn't want all the lovely ladies I had in my bed over the years to discover they were there for any purpose other than seduction."

Chapter Nineteen

Catherine stood beside Bucephalus waiting for Camden Davenport. Persephone had spent the last hour trying to convince her that she shouldn't go with him or to at least let her go with her. But Catherine had not changed her mind. Camden had also tried to talk her out of it, but if Michael could get involved with spies and smugglers, then so could she. Besides, he brought her to Hart's Manor to draw out the smuggler. She was bait for a trap. Far be it from her to ruin his plans. Now she was even questioning if any of this was real. Did he marry her just to use her for this? Had everything been a lie? She rested her head against the horse's neck.

"Catherine, are you still certain you want to do this?" Persephone asked one last time as she came to stand behind her.

"Michael started this, and I have gone too far to back out now."

"This is reckless and unwise, but I'm not sure if I would do anything different were I in your shoes."

Catherine turned and gave her friend a hug. "We are quite a pair aren't we."

"Yes, we are."

Camden Davenport walked up to them. "Your grace, my friend Duncan will escort you back onto Leicester's estate. He will ride along with you until you have the house in sight."

Persephone nodded. "You will make sure she is safe."

"I will, your grace."

She moved closer to him and poked a finger in his chest. "If you do not, you will answer to me."

He bowed. "I understand. John Cavendish is my right-hand man, and he will be going with us. I know Lady Catherine has agreed to watch my back, but I would feel better if someone was watching hers. Once we obtain the documents, I will give them to her for her to deliver to Lord Rockhurst. He will make sure they fall into the right hands."

Catherine mounted her horse. "Please wait at least an hour or more before heading back, Persephone. If you get back to Hart's Manor too soon Michael and Hawk will just ride out to stop me."

"What do I tell him?"

Catherine turned her horse to face her. "Tell him his plan was successful, that Davenport has taken the bait. Tell Rockhurst that I will be arriving with the documents as soon as Davenport and I locate Monsieur Lavigne."

Davenport mounted his horse along with Mr. Cavendish and the three of them rode off in the direction of Dover.

Two Hours Later

Michael was anxious to get back to Hart's Manor. He was beyond happy to have all of this behind him so he could focus on his wedding trip with Catherine. Perhaps now that the danger had passed, he would tell her about his involvement. She would be intrigued.

Hawk rode up alongside him. "I'm glad all has worked out for the two of you." He looked over at Rockhurst who had joined them. "I can't believe you kept all of this from us for so long, Charles."

"It was necessary." He looked at Michael. "Thank you for allowing me to stay at Hart's Manor tonight. I'm afraid my skin would crawl if I had to stay in the village at the posting inn. If the rooms had been as dreadful as the food and liquor, I'm not certain I could have survived the night."

Michael chuckled. "It would serve you right for getting me involved in all this. Catherine said this morning that we would be having lamb. The cook here is not nearly as skilled as our cook in London, but she will prepare a much better meal than anything the inn could offer."

The three men rode in front of the house and a groom came forward to take their horses. Michael walked up the steps and the butler opened the door for them. He wore a concerned look on his face and Michael was instantly alarmed.

"What has happened?"

The servant looked at the three men and began wringing his hands. "The duchesses went riding this morning after you left for the village, and they have not returned."

Hawk narrowed his eyes. "It's just like them to do something like this. Did they take anyone with them?"

The man shook his head. "No, your grace. They said it would only slow them down."

Michael turned on his heels and started back out the door. "I will ride out and look for them."

Just as he said it one of the grooms shouted. "One of the duchesses is riding in now, your grace."

Both Michael and Hawk rushed outside as Persephone rode to the front of the house. Rockhurst moved to take her horse as Hawk helped her from the saddle.

Michael came forward. "Where is Catherine?"

Persephone looked anxiously at her husband. "It's a long story."

"Where is she?" Michael asked growing more agitated."

Persephone looked at him. "We ran into someone the three of you might know while we were out riding, Camden Davenport." Michael and Rockhurst exchanged concerned looks before she continued. "We had a nice conversation. He told us about the meeting the three of you had with Thomas Harrison today and about you thinking him a suspected spy for the French and how he couldn't meet with you because he had to go to Dover to retrieve some important documents that would be beneficial to Wellington."

"My God, he told you everything?" Hawk asked as he looked down into his wife's face.

"Yes, he told us all about how you came to be here, and that Harrison had convinced you to bring Catherine here hoping her presence would draw him out of hiding."

Michael raked a hand through his hair in agitation. "Where is Catherine?"

"She is with Davenport."

She turned and started walking to the house leaving the men stunned. They raced up the steps after her, and Michael grabbed her arm. "Did Davenport kidnap her?"

She jerked her arm from his grasp. "No, she went with him willingly...on his mission. She told me to tell you that your trap worked, that he had taken the bait." She turned to Rockhurst. "She said to tell you that she will be bringing the information to you once it has been retrieved from Monsieur Lavigne."

"Why did she go with him?" Hawk asked.

"I tried to talk her out of it. Davenport tried to talk her out of it as well, but you know once Catherine has her mind set to do something, how hard changing it can be." She turned to Michael. "She is hurt. You kept secrets from her and then to discover that the reason the two of you came here was to see if you could draw out a supposed smuggler by using her. She is questioning everything now."

Michael took Persephone's shoulders frantically. "I never brought her here for that. Harrison was the one who wanted to use her. I didn't know anything about it until today. My God, what she must think of me."

Persephone felt sorry for him as she saw the grief and fear in his eyes. "She is upset, Michael, and when she is upset, she thinks irrationally."

Hawk stepped forward. "We are going after her. No matter what her reason, this is inexcusable. She is impulsive and reckless with her reputation and her safety. She is a married woman and should have consulted her husband before going off on this ridiculous adventure."

Michael was angry too. "Why did Davenport agree to take her?"

"He didn't agree, but she insisted. He promised me he would keep her safe. I think he has an.... affection for her."

At her words, Michael's face paled. He had not thought of that, but now he was remembering Harrison talking about Davenport's interest in his wife, and the thought that she was with him now made him feel a rage that he had never felt before. When he got his hands on Davenport, he would wring his neck. "I'm going after her."

"She has been gone for over two hours. They have probably reached Dover by now and are on the way back." She walked over and placed a hand on his arm. "I know you are angry at her, but she is angry too. She feels like you only married her and brought her here for this reason. She feels betrayed, and this was her way of being defiant. I know she loves you Michael, she has for most of her life. She will calm down and realize how stupid this decision was, but Davenport said this was not a dangerous mission, and she would return unharmed."

"She is doing this to get back at me for not letting her know my business with Harrison and Rockhurst. When I find her, I may lock her in her room till she learns her lesson."

Persephone crossed her arms over her chest. "You still don't understand. She did this because you were not honest with her. You should have told her."

"I was trying to keep her safe!"

She angrily put her hands on her hips. "You certainly did a good job of that didn't you?"

"That is enough, Persephone," Hawk said pulling his wife away. "The fact that you are defending her is concerning. Go upstairs and rest. We will be back once we have her."

Persephone jerked her arm out of her husband's grasp. "You will not dictate to me, your grace. I will be in the drawing room waiting for her return." With her head raised high, she sailed past them.

Rockhurst who had remained quiet while Hawk and Michael talked with Persephone came forward. "We have fresh horses waiting. If we hurry, we should meet them on the main road in an hour or so."

Hawk and Michael followed him to the waiting horses. Michael felt his temper rising with each passing mile they rode. Catherine was behaving like a foolish girl, and it was time he set her straight on who was in charge.

Dover

Catherine nervously pulled the cape Davenport had given her before they left closer around her to fight the chill as well as to hide the way her body shivered, more from fright than the cool seaside air. She and Davenport along with Mr. Cavendish had arrived at the seaside village of Dover about twenty minutes ago.

Mr. Cavendish was waiting with their horses around the corner watching for anyone that might pose a threat to their safety while she followed Davenport around to the alley at the back of a seedy tavern. It was dark and there were no lights from the street or the buildings. She could hear the bawdy laughter and commotion coming from inside the tavern, and she stepped closer to Davenport. He reached behind him and took her hand.

"Are you alright, duchess?"

Catherine straightened her shoulders and removed her hand from his. "I am perfectly fine. Is this where we are to find Monsieur Lavigne?"

He pushed her further behind him as they moved deeper into the shadows. "Yes, he will be here shortly."

No sooner had the words left his mouth did a man materialize around the corner. Catherine tried to stand on her tiptoes to see around Davenport but with his height it was nearly impossible.

"Stay here," Davenport said, his voice low and husky as he took a few steps forward to meet the man.

Catherine watched as the man handed Davenport a packet of papers. No words were spoken between them. It was all very anticlimactic. Once Davenport had the packet, he watched until Monsieur Lavigne was out of sight and turned back to her.

"Mission complete, duchess."

He walked back over to her and handed the packet of papers to her. "Now, will you be able to deliver these to Lord Rockhurst?"

Catherine took the papers and tapped down the disappointment that her adventure was not very adventurous at all. She tucked the packet into the inside pocket of the cloak. "I will see that he gets the information as soon as we get back."

He nodded and gave her a small grin before reaching for her elbow to lead her back to where Mr. Cavendish was waiting with the horses.

Suddenly a man wearing a long black overcoat and black hat emerged from the shadows with a pistol pointed right at Davenport. "Ahh, your taste in partners has improved over the years, Monsieur Davenport."

He nodded toward Catherine, the pistol moving slightly with his gaze. "Toussaint will be disappointed that he is not here to see you meet your end."

Catherine heard the change in Davenport's voice when he replied to the man, he sounded more dangerous, feral almost. "Now what makes you think that you would be successful where so many others have failed."

Catherine could not see his face fully, but she had the distinct impression that he frowned at Davenport's arrogant words. His accent was definitely French and she knew immediately that he must be after the papers they had received from Lavigne. She automatically clutched her hand over her cloak in an effort to protect the important information inside.

The man looked toward Catherine. "It is always a shame to kill a beautiful lady." He sighed heavily and shook his head mournfully as if he was going to regret having to end her life. "Pricks my conscience."

Davenport pushed her behind him protectively. "You don't have a conscience. Did Toussaint send you? Is he too cowardly to face me himself?"

The man laughed, but it was not a pleasurable sound. "You think your reputation scares him? *Ange de la mort*, indeed. I expected this to be a challenge, you disappoint me." He looked over at Catherine. "Give me the papers, madam."

Catherine clutched Davenport's coat hoping her voice sounded braver than she was feeling at the moment. "No, you will have to take them. I will not give them over freely."

She heard Davenport whisper, "Good girl," and she felt a sense of pride at his praise.

The man before her pointed the pistol at them, she felt Davenport's body shift forward as he pushed her more completely behind him. She heard the loud report of the shot as well as the acrid smell of gunpowder assailing her nostrils. Then Davenport fell to his knees. She placed both hands over her mouth to stifle a silent scream that seemed to be lodged in her throat and knelt down beside him. His eyes were closed and blood was oozing out of the hole in his shoulder. She said a silent prayer that he wasn't dead.

"Now that we have that nasty business out of the way, I will ask you one more time to hand over the papers." He shrugged his shoulders as he moved closer. "Or if you prefer, I could search you for them. I could start by removing that lovely riding habit."

Catherine held Davenport's body against her as she slowly slid her hand up her skirt to retrieve the knife she had strapped to her thigh. If this man thought she would be easy prey, he had a surprise coming. She loosened the knife and gripped it in her hand under her skirts as he stalked forward. He was close now, and she could see his eyes flicker with lust as he reached out to touch her, but before she could make a move, Davenport sprang to his feet. There was a brief scuffle, and then she watched in horror as Davenport slit the man's throat from ear to ear. His blood spurted from the wound onto the front of her bodice. It had all happened so fast. She had thought he was dead, but he was so quick, and the way he killed seemed like second nature. Now the wound in his shoulder was beginning to take its toll on his body. He released the man he had just killed and his body fell on top of Catherine. She pushed the weight off her and moved to catch Davenport as he once again fell to his knees.

She searched his face. "My God, I thought you were dead." She frantically ripped open his shirt to examine his wound.

He grabbed her hand to stop her. "You didn't think that I would let him kill me so easily did you, duchess." He smiled and she felt a rush of relief go through her.

She looked up to see Mr. Cavendish running toward them. "There were two more of them stationed around the alley. I took care of them, boss." Mr. Cavendish stood before her. "Are you alright, duchess?" His face was pale and she saw he was holding a bloody knife at his side.

Catherine looked down at the blood covering her chest. She took a moment to survey the scene before her, a dead man lay at her feet, his eyes wide open as the blood continued to ooze from his throat. Another bleeding man was laying against her, a hole through his shoulder, and Mr. Cavendish looked as if he had not had an easy time with the other two men that were involved. She reached up again and felt the packet of papers under her cloak.

"Duchess?" Mr. Cavendish called out to her once again.

"I'm fine." She looked over to where Davenport was laying against her. She took his face in her hands as his eyes fluttered open.

"Davenport?"

Mr. Cavendish knelt beside them and pulled open Davenport's shirt. "He lifted him slightly ignoring the grunts of pain he elicited to see if the bullet had passed through. Thankfully it had.

"Bullet went through your shoulder, boss. You will live, but we must get you out of here."

Davenport grimaced. "Help me stand."

"No!"

Both men turned to stare at her. "You are hurt, and no matter how you want to make it appear, that it is a serious wound, I am not foolish." She turned to Mr. Cavendish. "Go bring the horses here. I will stay with Davenport. Together we will get him on his horse and get back to Hart's Manor. Once there we can send for a doctor." Both men continued to stare at her. She rolled her eyes in irritation. "Go!"

Mr. Cavendish jumped to attention and went to do her bidding. In the meantime, she reached down and tore a bit of fabric from her skirts and pressed it tightly over the wound on Davenport's shoulder. She looked down at Davenport who was staring up at her with a slight grin on his face.

"I have been on countless missions and encountered many dangerous men while working for the crown and this is the first time I have met with any serious injury." He reached over and took her hand and squeezed it gently. "But if I had to be shot, I'm glad that you were here to be my nurse." He snuggled his head against her. "You are much softer than Cavendish would have been."

Catherine couldn't help but grin at his comment. But the grin faded when he grimaced as a pain shot through him. "Where is Cavendish?" she replied irritably.

"I'm here, your grace." He moved closer and helped her to her feet while both of them pulled Davenport toward the horses. The blood loss was making him weaker, and it took both of them to put him on the horse.

Catherine mounted Bucephalus and reached over to grab Davenport's coat to hold him upright. "Let's hurry, he needs a doctor."

Mr. Cavendish rode ahead to make certain it was safe and motioned for her to follow. Catherine held tight to Davenport as Mr. Cavendish took the reins of his horse. As they rode out of town the events of the night replayed before her eyes, and it occurred to her how close she had come to death. It was a sobering thought.

Michael stared down the empty road. They had ridden for over an hour. It was dark and they were beginning to think they should return to Hart's Manor and wait for Catherine there. They could have taken a different route or ran into trouble. Michael was torn on what he should do. He couldn't return without her, each passing minute his fury was giving way to fear. What if Davenport had lied and taken her? He may never see her again. His chest tightened at the thought. He would get her back, he didn't care how long he had to look, or where he had to go. Catherine was his wife, and he wanted her back in his arms.

"Perhaps we should turn around. They might have passed us on a different road," Rockhurst suggested as he pulled his horse to a halt.

"I'm not going back without her," Michael said just as they heard a horse in the wooded area ahead of them.

"Shh, someone is ahead of us on the edge of the road hidden in the trees," Rockhurst said as all three pulled their pistols from their coats. "Come out, we know you are there!" he yelled in the direction of the rustling.

A lone man on a horse moved out from the cover. "Are you the Dukes of Leicester and Hawksford?"

Michael moved forward while the others kept their pistols trained on the man before them. "I am Leicester."

The man nodded then turned back to the trees. "It's them, you can come out now it's safe."

Michael kept his pistol ready as he watched the movement from the trees then put it away quickly when he saw Catherine and a man slumped over on another horse riding toward them. She had her arm outstretched holding the man upright so he didn't fall from his horse.

"Catherine!" He moved forward and then jumped down from his horse to go to her. He looked over at the man slumped over. "What happened?"

The man that had first come out to greet them dismounted and walked over to them. "There was a little trouble after we got the information from Monsieur Lavigne, Davenport has been shot. Ball went through his shoulder. He has lost a lot of blood and needs a doctor."

Michael walked over to where Catherine sat on her horse looking straight ahead with a vacant look. "Are you hurt, Catherine?"

She didn't bother to look in his direction. "I'm fine."

Cavendish leaned over to him. "She hasn't said too much since we left Dover. I can explain all that happened, but I think we should get both the duchess and Davenport to your residence as quickly as possible."

The anger Michael had been feeling seemed to evaporate as he stared into his wife's vacant eyes. "Catherine," he said softly touching her knee.

Hawk moved closer on his mount. "Here let me take her place holding up Davenport and she can ride with you." Hawk maneuvered his horse between hers and Davenport's. "Catherine, I'll hold him on his horse for you."

She didn't answer but turned to look at him when he pried her fingers from Davenport's arm. "It's alright Catherine. You can let go. I have him."

Michael reached up and took her by the waist and pulled her to the ground. The clouds moved past the moon at that time, and he could see that both the cloak she was wearing and the front of her riding habit were covered in blood. "My God, Catherine. Are you sure you are not hurt?"

"It's not my blood," she said softly as she moved away from him.

Catherine allowed Michael to lead her to his horse, and then Rockhurst assisted in helping her mount in front of him. Michael wrapped his arms around her waist and pulled her close. She let her head rest on his chest as he urged his horse forward.

They rode slowly back to the house, Michael kept Catherine firmly held to him. He kissed the top of her head and talked softly to her as they rode, but she never spoke. He supposed she was in shock which was unlike Catherine. She had been through a rough ordeal with Persephone's kidnapping and had come through without any long-term effects.

When they rode up to the house. He dismounted and then reached up to lift her to the ground. Persephone rushed out of the house and gasped when she saw the state of Catherine's attire. Catherine blinked a few times when Persephone took her hands in hers. "Catherine, are you alright?"

Catherine looked over her shoulder at Michael and then back to Persephone. "I am alright."

Hawk came up then. "Rockhurst has gone into the village for a doctor for Davenport." He looked at Catherine. "Davenport's man said he took a bullet to save Catherine's life, that he put himself between her and their assailant."

Michael looked at Catherine, but she made no comment. She moved past him and Persephone and began walking up the steps. They watched as she slowly reached the top step and then without any warning, crumbled to the ground in a heap.

Michael heard Persephone's soft scream as he rushed up the steps to gather Catherine into his arms and carry her up the stairs to their bed chamber. The room was well-lit and warm. He carried her over to the bed and laid her down on top of the coverlet.

Persephone ran in right behind him. "We need to get her out of those clothes and cleaned. I will take care of that."

"No, I'll see to her."

He took Persephone's arm and led her to the door then quietly closed and locked it behind him. He went back over to where Catherine lay. Her breathing was steady and he guessed that she fainted from exhaustion and shock. He quickly removed her clothes, stripping her bare then bathed her with the water in the basin. He had sat it by the fire so it would be warm. Once he had the dried blood and grime cleaned off her, he dressed her in her nightgown and pulled the covers over her. He sat by her bed watching her breathe, thankful she was back safe but concerned that she was in the state that she was in. He wanted to see her eyes open, he wanted to talk to her and tell her that he had not been a part of the plan to use her to draw out Davenport. He wanted to know if Davenport made advances toward her, and what the hell happened that brought her home covered in blood. More than anything he wanted to tell her he loved her, see her smile, and kiss her lips. He needed her. He needed her like he needed air. The thought was sobering. Never before had he felt the existence of another person was vital to his own life and happiness, but as he brushed the hair away from Catherine's face, he knew that he could not lose this woman.

There was a faint knock on the door. He went and unlocked the door to see a very worried Persephone. "The doctor is here seeing to Davenport; he will come to check on Catherine when he is done. Hawk and Rockhurst are waiting for you in the study with Mr. Cavendish." She reached out and touched his arm. "I will sit with her, Michael and if she wakes, I will come get you."

He took one last lingering look at the bed then nodded and went downstairs to join the others. When he went into the study, he saw Hawk pacing back and forth before the fire. Rockhurst was sitting in a chair in front of the desk while Cavendish leaned against the wall. When he entered everyone turned their attention to him.

"How is she?"

"She is sleeping."

Cavendish sighed. "She is the bravest woman I have ever had the privilege to know."

Michael turned a severe frown his way. "Tell me what happened."

Cavendish straightened. "Everything was going as planned. We met Lavigne and got the documents. Her grace stayed close behind. Davenport made certain she was safe. When he paid Lavigne, I was watching from a distance while stationed out front. Thinking everything had gone as expected, I left to get the horses. While I was gone a man came out of the shadows, a man we have had dealings with before. He had been sent to collect the papers by Sabine Toussaint, who is a French spy and a consummate killer with no conscience. He demanded the papers from the duchess." He looked up at Michael with admiration shining in his eyes. "You should have seen her. She defiantly refused him as if she had an army of ten thousand men behind her. He pointed the pistol at her and Davenport stepped in front to take the bullet. Once Davenport fell, the duchess knelt beside him. She had readied herself for a fight retrieving the small knife she had strapped to her leg, but Davenport doesn't die easy. When the man moved to touch her, he struck fast and lethally. After that, the duchess took charge."

Michael closed his eyes just now realizing how close he came to losing his wife tonight. Hawk handed him a glass of brandy and he drank it in one swallow. "Please continue."

"Her grace helped me push the man off her and helped me get Davenport to his horse. I didn't know a woman could be so strong and courageous. She never let out a whimper or cried, no hysterics. You would think she was used to seeing things like that all the time. She was all business, but once we got out of town and away from danger, she became quiet and withdrawn. I think the shock of what happened must have overtaken her. But she was determined to get the documents back to Rockhurst."

Michael looked up at the man not sure if he wanted to know the answer to the next question. "Did she and Davenport at any time, did he, . . ."

Cavendish frowned and narrowed his eyes. "I wouldn't finish that question if I were you, your grace. The duchess should not be dishonored in that way. She went with us of her own accord, and I must tell you that if she had not been there, I would have had a hell of a time getting Davenport and those papers out of Dover alone. I am thankful for her assistance and amazed at her bravery and determination." He placed his glass back down on the table. "The doctor should be finished patching up Davenport, and I think I will go see how he is feeling. As soon as he can travel, we will move to the inn in the village." He bowed at the waist and left the room.

Hawk and Rockhurst remained silent as Michael moved to stand by the fire. Rockhurst stood from his seat. "I'm going to talk to Davenport. I'm glad Catherine is home safe."

When Hawk and he were alone he finally said. "I'm in love with her Hawk and while I may have had a hand in some of this, I did not use her as part of some trap."

"I know that."

"I need to talk to her. I need to know she understands."

"Then go to her, be the first face she sees when she wakes up. She is your wife, remind her that she is yours."

Michael nodded as he sat his glass down to leave the room. On the way up the stairs, he met the doctor coming down. "How is my wife?"

"The duchess is very fit, just a little overtired. A good night's rest and a day or two of limited excitement should do the trick. She is awake but resting now."

Michael shook the man's hand. "Thank you for coming out so late. I hope you will keep this quiet."

The doctor nodded in understanding and headed to the door where a carriage awaited to take him back into the village.

Michael was relieved to hear that Catherine was awake and would be alright with some rest. He turned to head back up the stairs when he heard a commotion. It sounded like someone was tearing the room to pieces. He raced up the stairs toward the noise.

Chapter Twenty

W̱hen he reached the bedchamber, he threw the door open ready for a fight, but there was no intruder ransacking the room. Catherine was frantically tearing through everything. The covers were off the bed, she had looked through the drawers in the desk, and papers were strewn over the floor.

"Catherine?"

She turned sharply, "Where are my clothes? The clothes I had on?"

He came into the room surprised at the look of anxiety on her face. "They could not be salvaged, darling. I sent them with the maids to burn them."

Catherine felt her knees grow weak. "No!" She pushed him away and made for the door. He rushed forward and grabbed her holding her to him as fought to get free. "Let me go! I must get them before they are destroyed! I have gone through too much to lose them now."

He took hold of her shoulders and shook. "Catherine, stop! I have them, they are safe."

Her breathing was heavy, but she stopped fighting him. "Where are they?"

He took an envelope out of his coat pocket and handed it to her. "I found it hidden in your cloak when I undressed you."

Catherine took the envelope and held it close to her chest and walked over to the bed. "I was told to give this to Lord Rockhurst, it's important."

He slowly walked over to where she sat and stood before her. "I know, that's why I kept it for you. I thought you would want to give it to him yourself."

She gave him a small smile that quickly faded to a frown. "Thank you for that. I went to so much trouble to get it." She placed the envelope beside her on the bed and looked up at him. "I suppose you are very angry with me for going with Davenport. When I found out everything that had been going on the past few weeks and knowing you kept things from me, I was livid. Persephone warned me against acting when I was so angry, but I've never behaved as a proper lady should, Aunt Louisa always said I would be the death of her."

Michael didn't speak but let her continue. "You should have told me. If I was needed to be used to entice Davenport out of hiding, I would gladly have consented if you had asked." She sighed heavily and raised her chin a notch higher. "I am sorry that I have caused us additional problems, and I am sorry for being so impulsive, but not sorry that I was able to help Davenport and Mr. Cavendish. I have not read what's inside this envelope, but I am told it is important for England and will save many lives." She wiped a lone tear from her cheek and continued, "My actions if discovered will tarnish your family name, so I will understand if you want to be done with me." Her brow wrinkled. "Although I am not sure how it is to be done, but I want you to know that I will not fight your decision. I would just like to know my fate now as I am not one who likes for things to linger." She clasped her hands in front of her and looked up with a face made of stone as if she were waiting for Old Bailey to pronounce judgement against her.

Michael moved away from her to stand facing the fire and spoke in a firm voice that brooked no quarter. "So, you will abide by my decision and will not fight or argue with it. You will accept the fate I decide." He turned to face her. She was now standing as he imagined Joan of Arc stood in defiance to accept her judgment. "Very well, hear now your fate. Lady Catherine Shelbourne you are hereby sentenced to remain by my side for the remainder of your life. We will hold no secrets from each other as we travel through this world together. You will belong to me. No other man will ever kiss your lips or hold you in his arms. You are destined to be the mother of my children and my companion and lover throughout time. You are hereby condemned to love me as I love you for the remainder of our days. Are you still willing to accept my judgement?"

Catherine had been trying to remain strong. She knew what she had done would be every reason for Michael to cast her away, and she had prepared for that since leaving Dover. She had thought she was ready for anything, but when he made that declaration, she felt her body begin to tremble, and the tears she had been holding in began to readily drop from her eyes. He didn't move from where he stood until she nodded in agreement then before she could catch her breath, she was in his arms. He was holding her so tight that she thought he might crush her. He kissed the top of her head and then her cheeks before claiming her lips.

"My darling, how could you ever think I would want to cast you away, that I would be able to live without you? I was angry, so very angry that you would put yourself in danger, and I had every intention of castigating you for it, but when I saw your riding habit covered in blood and heard Mr. Cavendish's account of the events that took place in Dover, all my anger faded away, replaced with a relentless fear that I could have lost you and pride at the bravery you displayed. When I think that a pistol was pointed at you it terrifies me." He wrapped his arms around her. "And while I was furious at Davenport for taking you with him, I am now beholding to him for protecting you with his own life." His arms tightened around her. "Although it irritates me to know he is halfway in love with you."

Catherine felt a relief sweep over her body. "I am sorry, Michael."

"I am sorry too, my love, but I want you to know and understand I did not tell you everything because I felt I was keeping you safe. I feared if you had known you would have wanted to get involved, and I did not have any part in using you to lure Davenport out of hiding. If I had known the extent of the man's interest in you, I never would have brought you to Hart's Manor."

Catherine leaned into him reveling in how safe and happy she felt in his arms. "I should get this information to Rockhurst. It's critical he gets it."

"Rockhurst can wait. Right now, I want to get my wife into bed." He swept her into his arms and carried her back to the bed where he gently lay her down on the pillows. He quickly removed his clothes and climbed in beside her, but instead of making love to her like she thought he would, he simply pulled her closer against him and held her until her eyes grew heavy and she was asleep.

The Next Morning

Catherine had slept in later than usual and when she finally did wake up, Michael had made love to her fiercely as if he couldn't get enough of her. He loved her thoroughly, and it had taken a while before she was able to leave the bed, much less come downstairs. As a result, she had missed breakfast, and it was nearly noon.

She held the envelope that contained the information they had received from Monsieur Lavigne close to her chest as she made her way downstairs to find Lord Rockhurst. She found him waiting for her in the front drawing room. She had known him for most of her life. He and Hawk had been friends for many years and while he had always given off the impression of being a carefree libertine only concerned with women, whiskey, and anything that brought pleasure. It was strange knowing that he had been involved in something so serious and so dangerous. She never would have thought that about him. She guessed that was why he was so good at what he did, no one would suspect him of anything.

"Good afternoon, Catherine," he said when she entered the room without turning. He had sensed her presence.

Catherine moved forward to stand beside him as he stared out the window. "I have something for you. Davenport said you would know how important it was and who it needed to be given to." She reached over and handed him the envelope.

He took it from her but did not open it. He sighed heavily and looked very serious. He was always so flirtatious and cheeky; it was odd seeing him look so solemn. "Catherine, the information you brought back with you will save countless lives. You are a very brave woman and while I am proud of you, I would ask that you never put yourself in harm's way again."

She was surprised at the anguish she saw briefly on his face. "I will try not to, but you know me."

At her words, she saw his lips turn up into that familiar mischievous grin she so loved to see. "I most certainly do, but I also know your husband, and I think he is more than capable of keeping you occupied with more, . . . pleasurable endeavors."

She blushed at his words, and he took her hand and raised it to his lips. "I must be leaving now. My horse is ready to take me and this information to London. I will see that it gets in the right hands."

Catherine smiled. "Take care of yourself, Charles."

"Always, darling." And with that he turned to leave the room.

She had one more visit to make this morning. Michael had not been pleased when she told him that she wanted to see Davenport before he and Mr. Cavendish left for the village. She had wanted him to stay longer to recuperate, and Michael had not liked that idea one bit. However, Mr. Cavendish said that he had already obtained accommodations in the village, and if they could make use of their carriage, he would see that Davenport recovered there. Michael had not wanted her to see Davenport and certainly not alone, but she had insisted that she needed to thank him for saving her life. So, he reluctantly relented although he insisted that he wait outside the door. She went up the steps, and there Michael stood waiting outside the guest bedchamber they had put Davenport in last night.

"I'll be right here, Catherine. If that bastard touches you, call out, and I'll make sure he never does so again." He crossed his arms over his chest, and his frown was fierce.

She gave him a smile and stood on her tiptoes to kiss him on the cheek. "There will be no need for that."

The frown between his eyes did not go away. "I'll still wait right here."

Catherine opened the door and quietly came further into the room. Davenport was sitting up in bed. His shirt was off and his arm was in a sling with his shoulder bandaged where the ball had passed through. He was a little pale but otherwise looked very fit. She thought that he was a handsome man and wondered why she never noticed him in Brighton.

She walked closer to the bed. "You look much better than the last time I saw you."

He gave her a devasting smile. "And you look as beautiful as ever. Is there any situation where you would not be the loveliest lady in the room?"

She giggled. "I didn't come here for your flattery. I came to check on you and to thank you for saving my life."

He raised his hand in invitation for her to place her hand in his. She hesitated, but eventually, she moved closer to him and allowed him to hold her hand. He looked up at her. "You are a very remarkable woman, your grace. I knew it the first time I saw you, but the way you handled yourself in Dover was beyond my expectations. Instead of swooning and going into hysterics like most ladies would have done, you took control, and Cavendish has told me that if not for your help, he wasn't sure he would have been able to get both the documents and me out of Dover alone. I owe you my thanks." He looked wistful for a moment before he continued, "If I had more time in Brighton before you returned to London things might be different now. Leicester is a very lucky man. You and I would have made a great team although I have to admit, if you were mine, I would put this life aside because I would not want to see you in danger."

She felt a little uncomfortable at his words. "The man in Dover called you, *Ange De La Mort.*"

He sighed heavily. "Do you know what it means?"

She nodded. "It means Angel of Death, I speak French fluently. I'm just curious as to how you acquired such a nickname."

He released her hand and turned his face from hers. "At times there are things a man must do, they aren't pleasant, but necessary for the remainder of our country to continue with the things they enjoy so freely. When that peace is threatened, men like me are called upon to deal with those threats." He looked back to her. "That is all you need to know, duchess."

She nodded in understanding. "I believe you to be a very dangerous man."

"That I am, duchess, but you have no need to fear me."

At that she chuckled softly. "Oh, I am not afraid of you."

"But I am of you."

Her smile widened, but she didn't bother to continue along the line of this conversation. "Mr. Cavendish says you will be leaving shortly, are you sure you feel capable to do so?"

"I will be alright, your grace. Besides I think your husband would prefer me to not be under your roof any longer."

She didn't argue that with him. "Will I see you in London?"

He shook his head. "Probably not, but should you ever need my assistance in any way contact Rockhurst or Harrison at the foreign affairs office, and they will get word to me."

She nodded and took her hand from his. "Good luck to you, Mr. Davenport."

He gave her a sideways grin. "Perhaps in another world or another time you would be mine, Catherine. As it is, I shall be envious of Leicester for the remainder of my days."

She turned to leave the room, but as her hand reached the door-knob she said, "Never fear, the lady you seek is out there somewhere." She opened the door and was gone. When she walked outside Michael was waiting for her, his frown more pronounced.

"I don't want you to see that man again, Catherine. The only thing that is keeping me from not throwing him out of my house is the fact that he took a bullet for you. The audacity of what he said to you."

"You heard?"

"Yes, I heard. I can tell you one thing I don't care what he says or what time or world he is in, you are mine, Catherine Shelbourne."

She wrapped her arms around his waist. "I'm yours, Michael."

That seemed to placate him. He wrapped his arms around her. "We need to go downstairs. Hawk and Persephone are preparing to leave."

"Leave? Why are they leaving now?"

"Your brother wants to get started so they can reach Hawks Hill as soon as possible. He is anxious to see Persephone settled in the country."

Catherine sighed. "I will miss her."

"Come, let's go bid them farewell. I'm anxious for everyone to leave so I can finally have you all to myself again."

Catherine smirked knowing exactly what he had in mind. Together they walked hand in hand down the stairs to where her brother and his wife were waiting. Persephone rushed forward and embraced her. "Catherine, if you need us to stay longer, we certainly can. I don't see the reason behind us rushing off anyway."

Hawk put out his hand and took her arm and pulled her back to him. "We will be at Hawk's Hill in a few days. Of course, we look forward to a visit very soon after you have been settled at Leicester's estate."

"Will you be returning to London for the remainder of the season before retiring to the country?" Persephone asked giving her husband a small frown.

Catherine looked over at Michael. "I'm not certain what Michael has planned, but I will write to you and let you know."

Persephone gave her a quick peck on the cheek. "Take care of yourself, Catherine and try not to get into any trouble, no more adventures."

Catherine laughed. "No more adventures? I'm not sure I can make that promise."

Michael came up behind her wrapping his arms around her waist. "I think there are many more adventures ahead of you, my darling. Only this time we will have them together." He kissed just behind her ear before turning back to Hawk and Persephone. "Have a safe journey."

Hawk took Persephone by her arm and led her toward their waiting carriage. "Come along, darling. We have a long journey ahead of us, and I have a few things in mind that will help us pass the time." He let his hand casually drop to cup his wife's backside causing her to shriek before looking up at him with a wicked grin of her own.

Catherine waved to the disappearing carriage and then turned back to her husband. "How long will we stay here at Hart's Manor before we head to your family seat?"

He kissed her cheek as he held her in his arms. "I think I would like to stay a week or so, but I'm not so anxious to go to my country estate. I thought we would continue our wedding trip. Where would you like to go? Perhaps we could plan a trip to the continent or go to one of my other estates? We will do whatever your heart desires."

She stepped away from him and started to walk away. "I'm not sure, but there is a secluded arbor in the rose garden that could use our attention." She gave him a provocative look over her shoulder then hurried toward the gardens with Michael following close behind her.

Epilogue

Seven Months Later
Hawk's Hill

"Oh Persephone, he is so wonderful," Catherine said as she adjusted the blanket around her chubby but extremely handsome one-day old nephew.

Persephone was propped up on pillows watching her sister-in-law coo at her newborn son. "I think he looks just like his father."

Catherine laughed softly. "He is just a day old, Persephone. I'm not sure you can tell who he is going to look like this young." She leaned over and pressed a kiss to the baby's forehead. "I wrote to Aunt Louisa to tell her about his birth. I'm sure she will descend upon us all as soon as she gets the letter."

"I'm sure she will." She glanced over at her friend. "I am sorry that he doesn't have a cousin to grow up with."

She saw a wide smile spread across Catherine's face. "Perhaps one day. We shall see."

Persephone pushed herself up higher on her pillows. "Catherine, are you. . .?"

Catherine bounced the baby softly in her arms watching as his eyes drifted closed. "Do not say anything. I have not told Michael yet and after seeing Hawk's face yesterday while you were giving birth, I'm not sure he will take it well."

Persephone smiled. "Of course, he will." She reached out her arms and Catherine moved forward placing the baby in her arms. She grinned as his tiny hand wrapped around her fingers. "He will be besotted I'm sure of it."

The Duke of Hawksford sat in his study with both the Duke of Leicester and Lord Rockhurst drinking champagne and celebrating the birth of his son, the new Marquis of Treymore. It had been a terrifying experience for him when his wife went into labor. Fortunately, Leicester had been there with him. They had arrived one day ahead of the birth. His sister Catherine would not have missed it for anything. She was totally smitten with her new nephew, and Persephone had been thrilled to have her there.

But once his wife went into labor, he had been an absolute wreck. Seeing his wife in so much pain and hearing her screams as she brought their son into the world had nearly been his undoing. It had taken about nine hours, but eventually the little marquis made his entrance into the world. Thankfully both mother and son were healthy and doing well.

"I must say, Hawk, I can't remember a time when I have seen you this happy and content," Rockhurst said before taking another sip of the champagne.

His friend smiled. "I can't explain it. I never thought I could feel this way, but I must say it was a terrifying few hours knowing what Persephone was going through." He gave Leicester a pointed look. "When do you think you will be blessed with a new addition to your family, Leicester?"

"After hearing Persephone scream and the stress of watching you pace the floor for nearly ten hours, I'm not certain I want to risk it."

They turned toward the door when a footman knocked. "I have a letter here for Lord Rockhurst, your grace."

Hawk walked over and retrieved the letter from the footman before returning and handing it to his friend before retaking his seat.

Leicester became concerned when he saw a dark shadow cross his friend's features. "Is everything alright, Charles?"

Rockhurst stood and walked over to the fire where he promptly threw in the letter. "It's a summons from my father."

Is he beckoning you to London for another meeting or inter-rogation?" Hawk asked knowing how the Duke of Avanley always managed to put his son in a foul mood every time they saw each other.

Rockhurst swallowed the last of his champagne. "No, I am to return to Avandale for my wedding."

Both Hawk and Leicester sprang to their feet. "Married? Who on earth to?"

Rockhurst stared into the flames. "Bloody hell if I know. Apparently, the duke has decided that he is tired of waiting for me to be responsible for the duchy and has picked my bride for me. If I refuse, he will see that I am disinherited."

Leicester shook his head. "He can't do that. You are his only legitimate heir."

"He can't take the duchy away from me, but everything that is not entailed he can leave to someone else." He gave his friends a humorless smile. "And he has quite a few holdings."

"So, you are just going to agree to his demands?"

"I suppose I am. Greed can make a man agree to almost anything, and while I would love to tell my father to go to the devil, I am not quite willing to see the money go with him. Make no mistake though, I will have the last laugh." He took one more deep breath. "Please give Persephone my congratulations and explain to Catherine my sudden departure."

"You are leaving now? Why don't you give yourself some time to think? There has to be a way to circumvent this. I don't want to see you react in haste only to regret it later. There must be a way to get out of this mess," Leicester said as he moved toward his friend.

Rockhurst shook his head. "No, I'm sure the old bastard has thought of everything. I am to return to Avandale immediately and be married upon my arrival."

"Bloody hell, the man is barbaric," Hawk said as he studied his friend's reaction.

"Indeed. Enjoy your evening, gentlemen. I will see you in London once you return." With that he left the room to go pack his belongings and accept his fate.

Later that night

"I hate that Charles had to leave so abruptly. Do you think he will go through with his father's wishes?" Catherine asked as she brushed out her hair as she sat in the bedchamber with her husband.

Leicester moved to stand behind her. "I don't know. I have a feeling it is not going to go well for him." He moved his wife's hair to one side and leaned down to kiss her neck. He smiled when he saw her shiver.

She stood up and moved into his arms. "I'm glad we were here for the birth of the baby. Persephone and Hawk are over the moon happy."

He slowly slid one of the straps of her nightgown off her shoulder as he kissed the spot it had been. "As they should be. I'm happy for them both." He let his hands move further down her hips until he cupped her buttocks in his hands.

Catherine smiled when she heard the low guttural moan escape his throat. "Do you think you would be just as happy as Hawk?"

He slipped the other strap down her arm and kissed her bare shoulder. "When the time comes, I'm sure I will be. But I am in no hurry, my love."

Catherine stepped out of his arms and turned to face him. "Well, you have about six months to get used to the idea." Her smile was wide as she saw her husband stand before her looking as if she had grown two heads. "Michael, are you going to be alright?"

He crossed the space between them and pulled her back into his arms tightening his hold around her. "Are you certain?"

She laughed and leaned forward to kiss his cheek. "Very much so, although you shouldn't be surprised with the frequency in which you take me to your bed, or the carriage, the stables, the meadows around the estate, and that time at the lake." She paused as if pondering. "Am I forgetting anywhere?"

He lifted her in his arms. "How about your brother's estate, our home in London, the yacht we sailed on last month." He kissed her softly. "We have had quite the adventurous love life, duchess."

She leaned forward and nibbled on his neck causing a low growl to erupt from his throat. "This is just the beginning of our adventures, my duke. At the rate we are going when we have been married twenty years, we will be collaborating on a list of places we have not made love."

He carried her over to a table sitting along the wall and placed her on it so he could stand between her legs. "I do love an adventure."

Meanwhile down the hall the mood was much more somber, Charles Newberg, Marquis of Rockhurst sat alone in his room staring into the flames of the fire burning in the grate. He had spent the past five years holding his father off from the idea of marriage, now it seemed the old man had finally bested him. A slow cynical smile spread across his lips, he was not known as one of the Devils of Mayfair for nothing and he had a little scheme of his own in mind.

Thank you for reading Catherine and Michael's story in the book, *A Duke Always Has A Secret*. I hope you enjoyed the second installment in the, *A Duke Always* series. Be sure to check out Rockhurst's story in the next book in the series, *A Duke Always Breaks the Rules*, coming soon.

Rebecca Leigh